Her Leading Man

by

Laura Liller

The Price of Fame, Book 2

Her Leading Man

Cover Art by *The Wild Rose Press, Inc.*

The Wild Rose Press, Inc.
PO Box 708
Adams Basin, NY 14410-0708
Visit us at www.thewildrosepress.com

Publishing History
First Edition, 2024
Trade Paperback ISBN 978-1-5092-5221-3
Digital ISBN 978-1-5092-5222-0

The Price of Fame, Book 2
Published in the United States of America

Eric stepped into the foyer. He took her waist in his hands and drew her close. Jenna didn't make any attempt to escape the steely grasp. Spellbound, she was caught in the blue fire of his stare. He walked, obliging her to match his easy footfalls but backward. Their stride was like a tango, slow and graceful, their bodies fitted perfectly together as they glided along the floor. Their journey ended only when Jenna's shoulder blades came to rest against a wall.

The length of Eric's body made contact with hers at every plane. His chest, abdomen, and thighs pressed close as he held her tight against the cool plaster. Her heartbeat matched the pulse she could see beating at the hollow of his throat. She had never been more aware of the surging rise and fall of her own breasts.

He stroked her face with his thumb, starting at her temple and glancing from cheek to jaw. "Your boyfriend doesn't know how to kiss." Eric slipped his fingers through her hair and covered her mouth with his.

The slow and sensual mingling of lips and tongues seemed to last forever. His hands slid down her ribs and around her back, and he pulled her closer. Womanly softness molded easily against hard muscles. His mouth was warm—the taste and fragrance of him a sweet persuasion that roared into a fiery memory. Jenna put up no resistance and melted into him. When it ended, she could feel his heart pounding against her breasts.

"I'll never let another man kiss you again."

Praise for Laura Liller

"…This much-anticipated sequel to *His Hollywood Blonde* brings Jenna and Eric back together. The characters and settings are relatable and perfectly crafted. The blending of passion, suspense, and glamour will leave you wanting more…"

~ Maria Gil, author of *Witch's Moon* and *Back in Belmont.*

Dedication

To my husband Mike who is, and always will be, my leading man.

Chapter One

Cromline NY, 2011

Jenna Black sat frozen in her seat as spilled tea fanned toward the edges of her coffee table. She'd broken her favorite cup—English bone with a pattern of pale pink rosebuds and celadon colored leaves. Shards of china now lay scattered at her feet, but she made no attempt to clean the mess. She remained motionless and staring at the television as a reporter grated on about the latest bombshell to hit the world of entertainment. Actor Eric Laine's perfect marriage to Bree Davis Laine was ending.

Pictures of the striking, A-list couple flashed on the screen—each with the intensity of a slap. Squinting, Jenna watched in the same manner one would view the more grisly scenes in a horror movie. "Oh my God," she whispered as another picture, one too intimately familiar, stared back at her. For the first time since moving to Cromline four years ago, she had cause to worry. Grabbing her keys, she headed to her car, leaving a steady stream of amber liquid trickling onto the floor.

Less than ten minutes later, head tipped down, she stole into her local supermarket. Jenna, usually a bright offering of courtesy, brushed by people sharing the aisles. At the checkout counter she grabbed copies of *Trend, Celebrity Weekly,* and *The Inquisitor*, paid for everything, and rushed from the store.

Once home, she tore into the periodicals. The lead articles were all the same. Former entertainment manager Bree Davis had molded her handsome, young husband into a superstar. But Hollywood's most glamorous duo had called it "quits." Jenna dropped *The Inquisitor* into a box by her fireplace. She'd have to burn it before her eight-year-old daughter Janie returned home from her scout meeting.

Jenna rubbed her burning eyes and picked up *Trend.* If there was anywhere a more sensational accounting of Eric's life could be found, it would be there, in the same magazine that had ripped open her own throat a decade ago. Her fingers shook as she turned the pages.

Pictures of a younger Eric, the beautiful boy she had once loved, were in the magazine's centerfold. A wistful sigh spilled from her lips as her eyes coasted from glossy photo to glossy photo. She turned the page, and the easy task of breathing became a sudden struggle.

Photos of herself, taken when she'd been a wide-eyed popstar known as Angel, gleamed on the paper, next to them grainy images of Eric being led away in handcuffs by the police. Headlines like splashes of blood were on the pages.

Jenna tossed the magazines into the fireplace. She struck a match and watched the pages blacken and curl. The last image she saw before the mass erupted into flames was of Eric's friend Mark Chambers—the man who raped her and stole her life.

Chapter Two

Eric Laine connected wires to the back of the television he'd ordered from a local appliance store. He plugged and unplugged the cords, but nothing appeared on the screen except pixilated shadows.

"Shit." After waiting all day for the delivery, the damned thing didn't even work.

A week ago, he'd fled from his Pacific Palisades mansion to go to North Carolina and the acreage he'd purchased sight unseen. Anxious to get away from the West Coast, he paid list price for a ramshackle farmhouse surrounded by overgrown fields, barns on the verge of collapse, and a stable that sheltered a dozen swayback horses. The house was no better. Walls were covered in yellowed paper, and his spartan collection of furniture consisted of a dinged table, two chairs with shredded caning, and a sofa covered in a snaggle of ripped fabric. Since his top-of-the-line flat screen TV was bent on rejecting a signal, it fit right in.

"Shit," he cursed again. The college basketball finals were starting that night, and he had a date with a pizza and a six-pack. Static lifted just long enough for him to hear the latest spin on his divorce. "Great. That crap the satellite dish picks up."

The screen again turned to snow before the name of his latest dalliance was revealed. *I hope I had a good time with whoever she is.* Supermarket rags linked Eric to every one of his more recent costars. The papers also hinted about a torrid affair he was purportedly having with a twenty-year-old singer, a young blonde who resembled Angel, the first Mrs. Laine.

Not even close, he'd thought when he'd first seen the article. *Not even close*.

He grabbed his leather jacket from the newel post on the rickety banister and headed outside to adjust the dish.

Later, after an hour of fiddling, he came to the sad conclusion that a night of watching college hoops wasn't happening. It didn't matter. He hadn't run from California to watch TV. He'd come East to shelter himself deep within the hilly grid of pines to escape the press, his agent, and most especially, his wife Bree.

He loped to the stables and checked on the horses. As he walked along the wide planks of pine, they poked their huge heads from their stalls. He scratched ears and muzzles, and they nickered thank you as if they knew he'd saved them from the slaughterhouse. Eric had been raised by an unforgiving hand and felt sorry for the defenseless animals. He hired grooms to tend to the horses as if they were champion thoroughbreds.

He ambled back to the house and scanned the rising knolls. The property wasn't like any of the others he owned. No decorative shrubbery skirted the house, and no tall palms lined, rank and file, to guard the driveway. No high-tech lighting system illuminated an outdoor spa or tennis court—things Eric didn't give a shit about and didn't care to see anyway.

Before becoming famous, he'd been a carpenter and planned to renovate the old farmstead himself rather than throw money at an interior designer. Nothing would ease his troubled spirit better than hard work and feeling the weight of a hammer in his hand.

He hiked the property, and afterward, still in denim perfumed with hay and horse, he lay nestled in a hammock. As he gazed up at the stars, his heart thrummed easy and content for what felt like the first time in years. Banishing all thought from his mind, he stretched aching muscles, yawned, and drifted into a peaceful sleep under the open sky. He left his burdens, past and present, to slip quietly into darkness till morning.

****

Daylight and reality arrived all too early. Eric lifted his head and rolled his neck from side to side, but the rest of his body resisted giving up the comfort of the hammock. The sun rose from the eastern hills and a blending of birdsong announced its arrival. Dew coated grass dotted with dandelions blanketed the fields. He stretched and swung himself out of his makeshift bed and walked back to the house, kicking clods of dirt as he went. He had to fly to L.A. for a meeting with his lawyers.

With most of his comfortable clothes caked in mud and damp with sweat, he donned a suit and tie. A limousine transported him to the airport and back to the reality of his life as a celebrity. He hadn't missed it. He preferred the simplicity of his derelict farm. Jeans and scuffed boots reminded him of a time when his life had been complete.

****

News about Eric's divorce played in an unending loop. Maybe it didn't, but to Jenna it certainly seemed to. Tabloid television and magazines latched on to the story like a junkyard dog shaking its prey till the life bled from it. She knew all too well how that worked.

A fleeting thought of how life would have been if she hadn't fled Hollywood drifted through her mind. She dismissed it quickly. Dwelling on the money and fame she had given up led her to thoughts of the brief marriage she had forsaken and to the man who'd forgotten her as easily as her fans.

She stepped outside and picked up a pair of clay caked sneakers lying by the front door. After a hard rap against the porch railing, the red-brown dust fell to the ground. Eric sidled his way back into her thoughts. How was he dealing with the ups and downs of fame? How did he deal with living a life as unpredictable and temperamental as the weather? Why were he and Bree Davis splitting up?

Jenna reflected back on the last time she'd seen him. She'd been at the Metropolitan Opera with a date. They'd been sipping champagne at intermission when she felt as if the temperature in the lobby had dropped by degrees. Icy fingers teased the ridge of her spine and she'd turned. Eric, a few yards away, stood unmoving, his eyes a rapt and unblinking stare. She'd felt a sudden rush to go to him and confess a long-buried secret. But Bree sauntered over and coiled her arm around his. Eric's wife had been a vision of scarlet satin and shimmering diamonds, her hair twined into an elegant knot. She'd raised dark brows and looked directly at Jenna. Bree's ruby glossed lips were slanted into a virtuous smile, but the smug glint in her eyes said *he's mine now, I've won.*

Jenna shook loose the memory and tossed the sneakers to the ground. Leaning against the porch railing, she wondered, as she always did, if she'd made a mistake on another long-ago night—the night she'd boarded a private jet under the cover of darkness to flee Hollywood. Through the years, she'd led a transient life masked by omissions and lies. Her daughter knew nothing about the past or that Eric Laine was her father. She was too young to know about the cruel reality of fame. *Damn Eric, and his divorce.* And damn the press for slipping Jenna's stage name Angel into their stories.

If her secrets were revealed, her life would be turned wrong side out.

****

The next morning, despite the weight that threatened to unbalance the quiet life she'd established, Jenna was at her shop at the usual time. Her landlady Cheryl, a member of the town's auspicious Baldwin family, pattered over. Bracelets jingled on her wrists, and chains tinkled across the bodice of a pink tweed jacket. She carried a fussy little purse that also dangled from a chain. *The woman wore enough metal to compete in a joust.*

"You-hoo, I need to speak to you for a moment."

Jenna turned. *To you. Of course.* Cheryl, who reigned supreme over the royal court of Cromline never spoke *with* anyone. She spoke *at* people, the flighty timbre of her voice as weightless as her frivolous subject matter. As she neared, her voice dropped to a whisper. "I've had some complaints from the other tenants about the loitering in front of your store."

Jenna replied with a saccharine smile. "It isn't loitering. It's customer turnover. The last owner of this shop carried ugly scarves and brooches and went out of business in six months." With a sweep of her arm she pointed to her window display. "Now that I carry rhinestone tiaras and purple mascara…your rent is on time." She purposefully stretched her mouth into an even wider crescent. "Your daughter Tiffany is my best customer."

Cheryl simpered but her expression didn't disguise the prickly glint in her eyes. She turned as her brother-in-law strode over. Ash Baldwin possessed the relaxed attitude of a politician yards ahead in the exit polls. "Ladies." He gave Cheryl an obligatory nod and promptly turned his handsome grin and attention to Jenna. "I've scheduled a time for the electrician to come by and fix that fluorescent light that's been shorting out."

"What?" Cheryl's voice was an irritated objection. "According to the lease, Ms. Black is responsible for all interior—"

Ash folded his arms and pressed them tight against his broad chest. "Shouldn't you be opening up the real estate office? It's after nine."

Cheryl's cheeks blushed a schoolgirl pink. "Of course. I'll see you over there in a bit."

As she tottered away, Jenna slipped through the door of her shop with Ash ambling close behind. "She's actually right. I am responsible for routine maintenance."

He inched a bit closer and grinned. Though his eyes were a color caught between sky and ice, they expressed a dreamy luminosity when he smiled. "I can't have my favorite tenant doing business in the *dark*." The word dark was delivered in a silky pour of intimacy.

Jenna took a quick step behind the counter to put three feet of glass between them. Although Ash had the fair-haired, good looks of an NFL quarterback, he was still her landlord and encouraging his flirting might not be a good idea.

"I'll make a deal with you," he began. "Go to the Chamber of Commerce banquet with me. We can discuss what to do about that annoying broken light."

"Oh, I don't know. I don't want any special favors. You know what they say about business and pleasure."

His smile broadened, but his eyes dipped into a heavy-lidded invitation. "I do. Go to the dinner with me as a friend, and as a friend I'll change out that fixture." Giving her no chance to refuse, he turned, and with an easy, athletic gait strode from the shop and slipped into his classic convertible.

Chapter Three

Nick Lombardo was waiting at the arrival gate at Hollywood-Burbank Airport in Eric's luxury SUV. With its layers of iridescent, blue-black paint, the vehicle glittered as bright as the Mojave's night sky. Eric hated the damned truck. Bree had only bought it because SUVs were "the thing to have."

"If I knew you were going to be all dressed up, I would have picked you up in a limo, boss."

"This thing *is* a limo…one with four-wheel drive. And I'm not your boss."

The statement was true. Nick and Eric were friends who'd met years ago when Nick was head of Jenna's security team. Now, though the two men were business partners and owned a fleet of limousines, the gargantuan Brooklyn native still moonlighted as Eric's bodyguard.

"If you *were* my boss I'd quit," Nick teased. "You're one moody son of a bitch lately."

Eric threw his bag in the back and slumped in his seat. As the car rolled into traffic, he glared at his friend. He glared through the window at scrubby grass dotting the mountain vista beyond the freeway. He glared at the loose change lying in the car's pearly leather console. He glared at everything in his sightline.

Nick commented on his surly expression. "Looks like your vacation didn't improve your mood. I'll be steering clear. I know first-hand what you're like when you're pissed off at something."

Eric narrowed his eyes. "Not something…someone. And by the way, I've been trying to get rid of you for years, but you never take the hint. I'm starting to think you're gay for me."

Nick laughed. "Sorry, buddy. You're not really my type."

"That's too bad. You can at least cook."

Nick laughed again, and after a bumper-to-bumper grind on the Ventura Freeway, he dropped Eric off at Jack Morrissey's estate. The Hollywood icon, more father to Eric than his own had ever been, insisted he move into the guest cottage while he sorted out his divorce.

Eric slipped a set of keys from his pocket and stepped through the double doorway onto pristine *calacatta* marble. He shook his head. *Cottage.* The place had sixteen rooms. As he set his bag down, his cell chimed, and his lawyer gave him the news that the divorce negotiations were not going well.

It came as no surprise.

"Please don't run off to North Carolina again," the attorney begged.

Eric ended the call, stripped out of his clothes and took a shower. He swore he still smelled like horse hide. Jack's housekeeper brought him a tray of food worthy of a royal banquet, and after slapping a few slices of roast beef on a roll, he sent the rest back. Still on east coast time, he was asleep by eight.

****

Promptly at nine the next morning, Eric was shown to a conference room at his lawyer's office. He tapped his fingers on the glass table as he awaited the grand entrance of his *darling* wife. After the clock ticked thirty-five, fashionably late minutes, Bree glided into the room with her own lawyers in tow. Wrapped in body-hugging blue silk, she eased into a chair in the same genteel manner of a royal about to occupy a throne. A smile teased her lips, but Eric stared blankly though her. Wealth hadn't changed his wife. It only heightened both her attitude and ambition.

After setting a briefcase on the table, her attorney opened it with a resonant click. "I have motions to have an independent auditor investigate Mister Laine's interest in a company called Jewel Incorporated." The attorney shook his head in a slow pivot like a parent about to lecture a child. "Its value appears to be in the millions, yet it wasn't listed among your assets."

Bree's blue eyes glowed with satisfaction. Eric stared at the sapphire peeking from under feathery false lashes and jerked his head. *When the hell did her eyes become blue?* One more piece of plastic attached, inserted, or injected, anywhere in or on her body and she would melt in the sun. He pinched the bridge of his nose and sighed. *It shouldn't be this much trouble getting divorced from a blow-up doll.*

Her lawyer cleared his throat with a loud hack. "Excuse me, Mr. Laine, any explanation? You're listed as the chief executive officer of this company. Why wasn't it listed?"

"I don't own it." Eric pointed at his wife. "And she knows it."

The attorney, whose smug expression mirrored Bree's, leaned back in his chair and tapped his pen on the papers. "This company was founded almost nine years ago, by you, Mr. Laine. Investments are made by you, and checks are signed by you. Yet *you* want us to believe you don't own the company. The I.R.S. just loves digging into shell corporations."

Both of Eric's attorneys turned and looked wide eyed at him. Eric stood and splayed his hands on the glass table. He steeled angry eyes at Bree. "Jewel stands for Jenna Welles Laine. The assets belong to my ex-wife. After she left me, I took my name off the deed to the house we owned and some other property and set up a company in her name. Bree was my business manager back then. She knew all about it."

"Is this true, Mrs. Laine?" her lawyer asked.

Bree flashed a smile of victory, her teeth shining white as tundra snow. "Mmm, I can't say I remember that."

"You won't get away with this," Eric warned. "Every penny in that company is accounted for, and it all belongs to Jenna. I gave up any claim to it long before you and I were married."

Bree rose and placed her hands flat against the table to match his pose. "How can you be so ungrateful? Without me you'd still be living on tips or breaking your back swinging a hammer. After all I've done for you, how can you even consider giving money to the woman who left you?"

A fine line seemed to blur the boundaries between Bree's sorrow and anger. It was impossible for Eric to read her expression. He didn't doubt the sincerity of her heartache, but he knew she feared losing her place in the Hollywood hierarchy more than losing him. He also knew she fought dirty.

Her eyes narrowed to resolute slits. "If I have to play hard ball, I will. I'm not giving up on us. I'm not letting you go." With her lawyers following, she swept from the room.

Eric dropped back down into his chair and tugged at his necktie so it settled in a loose knot below his throat. "She's going to tie me up in court forever."

One attorney riffled through papers in folders, while the other slipped his tablet from its sleeve and turned it on. "I'm going to need the accountant's-copy of all the Jewel tax returns."

Like anteing a bet in a poker game, Eric flipped a thumb drive onto the table. "All of last year's financials, including Jewel, are on this, but it's complicated."

"Complicated?" one lawyer asked.

"Jenna left me. She ran away…disappeared actually. I've been investing the money from Jewel and sitting on the profits."

The two lawyers, sharks who received truckloads of money to bring about the final and conclusive end of Eric's union with Bree, raised their eyebrows. Both faces expressed the "dog ate my homework" cynicism of a teacher.

Frustrated, Eric shrugged. "C'mon, guys, you work for me. You're supposed to be on my side."

The attorneys looked at each other, then toward the window. They appeared to study the jagged hump of the L.A. skyline. They both drummed their fingers on the table, clearly stalling. The younger of the two eventually spoke. "Your wife has a valid point. The fact that your ex never received any dividends from Jewel makes it look like you've used her name to set up a dummy corporation to hide money." He turned to his partner. "You used to be a corporate suit. How do we fix this mess?"

The older attorney shook his head as he scanned the thumb drive's files on his tablet. He grumbled as if they had insulted his mother. "The logical thing would be to turn everything over to your first wife before Bree's lawyers get some judge to freeze the account."

Eric rubbed at his burning eyes, then pressed his fingers deep into the sockets. "I don't know where my first wife is. I hired a detective years ago, but every time he got close to finding her, she disappeared. It took me a few years before I could admit I was one of the reasons she was hiding from the world."

Slumping in his chair, he let his thoughts drift. The labor of forcing Jenna from his mind was futile. He was Sisyphus, rolling the boulder uphill only to be crushed by it again and again. "I never should have given up. I should have tried harder to find her."

"Well you'd better try hard now," both attorneys answered.

Chapter Four

"How was school today?" Jenna asked her daughter as they walked through the school parking lot.

"Okay. We had a substitute, so we didn't have to pay attention...or behave."

"Jane!"

In eight and a half short years, Jenna had grown to know why people slapped their foreheads with the palms of their hands. Her child was, she liked to think, bright and spirited, but sometimes a handful.

Cheryl Baldwin pattered over. "Jenna!" Her voice was a squeaky chime accompanied by the clip clop of high heels. "Are you taking Jane to gymnastics practice?"

"Yep. Can I drop Tiffany off for you?"

"If you would."

Tiffany Baldwin, a reed of a girl, barely nine, but with streaked hair and waxed eyebrows, simpered. It was the spoiled child's rendering of "thank you." She and Janie trotted off to the car.

"Where are my manners?" Cheryl introduced Jenna to a woman standing nearby. She was heavyset and wore oversized sunglasses. "Jenna Black, this is Anne Mills...Anne, Jenna."

The woman nodded a curt hello as vehicles cruised a slow journey through the parking lot. Teachers, with totes hanging from their shoulders, escaped to their own cars; and school maintenance men in lime-colored vests directed traffic.

"Anne used to live here in Cromline, but her husband got transferred. Luckily for us, they're back. I could always use another volunteer for the park's committee." Cheryl tipped her head toward Jenna. "I expect to see *you* at the next meeting also."

Jenna glanced at her watch. "Gotta run. I've got to get the kids over to the gym. Nice meeting you, Anne."

With an expression caught somewhere between curiosity and scrutiny, Anne Mills studied Jenna. "I'll see you again. I hear your store is the hot spot for all the girls in town."

"Oh." Cheryl began to fidget, and her bracelets jangled their usual melody. "I don't know if the store is right for Riley."

"Why wouldn't it be?" Anne turned her head toward her daughter who was sitting, still and quiet, in the front seat of a van. Folding her arms across her weighty bosom, Anne planted her feet an aggressive distance apart. Jenna half expected her to tell Cheryl to "*drop and give me twenty.*"

"Make no mistake. Riley likes the same things other girls her age enjoy." Head held high, Anne strode away and climbed into a vehicle the size of a small condo.

"Well…that was uncalled for," Cheryl said.

"Mmm." Jenna replied with a cool grin. "You should probably watch what you say."

She boarded her car and pulled away, curious about the exchange between the two women. Few of Cromline's ladies dared to risk being on the bad side of Cheryl Baldwin, but Anne Mills didn't seem to care. Cheryl had obviously said something politely offensive, and Anne politely told her where to go. Her tone matched Cheryl's, imperious syllable for imperious syllable. *Good for her.* Maybe there was finally another woman in town, beside Jenna herself, not pining for the chance to attend Cheryl's exhausting luncheons. The importance the town's women attached to being part of Cromline's lofty circle reminded Jenna of high school.

High school. A shiver scuttled along her arms.

Anne Mills' voice and mannerisms sparked a distant memory that sped forward like a time-lapse photograph. *Shit.* The little barrel-shaped woman was Annabelle Walker from Pinehill. The bitchy leader of The Snotty Six, and the meanest girl in Jenna's class.

****

Sleep eluded Jenna that night. The nastiest girl to ever strut the streets of her hometown was living in Cromline. *Why here? Why now?*

Tabloid television shows continued to flash Jenna's picture on the screen, resurrecting the story of the fallen starlet Angel. The presence of Annabelle Walker almost guaranteed any privacy Jenna enjoyed in Cromline would be nothing but a memory.

Had Annabelle followed Angel's career? *Will she give up my secrets?* Of course she would. Jenna knew how Annabelle operated. She would toy with Jenna; offer her a seat at the cool table and then "accidentally" spill chocolate milk on her white pants.

At barely first light, Jenna got up and showered. The thought of being exposed made her almost choke on the billowing clouds of steam. The thought of what being exposed would do to her daughter made Jenna gag in earnest.

Bundling up Janie and running away was no longer

the option it had been when she was a baby. Jenna had run out of excuses for another sudden move. She had run out of money to finance a whole new life.

Jenna Welles Laine Black had run out of options.

Chapter Five

It took some very deep digging before Eric's private investigator found a woman named Jenna Black, a woman who hadn't existed prior to 2004, living in upstate New York. She owned a boutique called Rhapsody, and had an eight-and-a-half-year-old daughter.

"I'll stake out her house and shop and get some pictures to see if it's her."

"No." Eric was adamant. "I won't have you or anyone skulk around to get her picture. She's had enough of that. I'll go to New York myself."

Eric had no doubt the woman was Jenna. He knew it in the way an animal draws upon instinct to find water. He knew. He also knew she might once again slip into the shadows. It was rumored her story was going to be featured on a tabloid show that highlighted the lives of celebrities who abruptly abandoned their careers. It was his divorce that started all the "what happened to Angel" hype.

****

A week later, he was on a plane headed to a small airstrip in a town only a half hour outside of Manhattan. The private jet Bree insisted they needed sat idle at a hangar in Ventura, so he'd chartered another. The last thing he needed was to be photographed at a public airport, and for his wife to know where he'd gone.

A steward offered him a drink that he politely waved away. Distracted, he stared through the oval window as his mind constructed a bizarre telephone dialogue.

"Hey...you'll never guess who this is. It's me, Eric, the guy who ruined your life ten years ago. I've still got a few things that belong to you, actually a few million things and I thought I'd stop by and drop them off."

He lowered his face into his hands. "You are such an asshole."

His trip became an hours long melodrama that played in his head. In act one, a rowdy kid gets knocked around by a derelict father and ends up in an institution. In act two, a young man meets a beautiful girl who takes all his pain away. *If only it had ended there.* In act three, the young man fucks up so royally he loses everything. Eric called the steward back. He wanted that drink.

Hours later, weary and jet lagged, he checked into the Plaza, the shining staple of New York at the East Fifty-Ninth Street entrance to Central Park. The concierge quickly called for a valet to take Eric's bags to his suite. "A pleasure to have you with us, Mr. Laine."

"Thanks. I'm going to need a car. Can you have one here for me tomorrow morning?"

"Certainly, sir." The concierge was an image of alert consideration. "Just give me a time and I'll have a car and driver waiting."

"Um, no, I meant a rental, nothing fancy. Charge it to my room. Oh, and see if there are any hotels near a town called Cromline."

Clicking expediently at his keyboard, the concierge dulled. "It looks like there's a Micro-Motel and a Best Express a mile or two off the highway. If you give me a sec I can see if there's—"

"Best Express is fine."

"Very good, sir."

Eric nodded his thanks and headed to the elevator and his suite. He showered, climbed into bed, and pulled up the New York State highway map on his phone. Cromline looked to be about a two hour drive up the Thruway and not far from the town where Jenna had grown up. It made sense that after living like a Bedouin, she'd settle in an area close to home. He was more certain than ever that Jenna Black was his Jenna.

He put his phone aside. Cradling his head in his arms, he stared up at the ceiling. His heart was racing. What kind of reception would he receive he wondered. He'd only seen her twice in nine years—fleeting moments from his hospital bed after an on-set accident almost killed him, and for even less time in the lobby of The Metropolitan Opera House. Both occasions felt like losing her all over again.

The papers for Jewel Incorporated were arranged in a leather briefcase, but Eric knew they were simply a pitiful excuse to cast eyes on the face of the woman he could never forget.

****

Jenna attempted to make a new display of earrings and bracelets, but her hands were bloodless and unsteady. Worry clung to her like metal shavings on a magnet. She turned toward the sound of the door chimes tinkling as the source of her anxiety strolled through the entryway.

"Good morning," Anne said, light and breezy as springtime. She made her way down the narrow aisle, slowly, and plucked items from shelves to consign them to a basket. Twice she turned and grinned.

Jenna stepped over. "Annabelle?"

"Oh, so you *do* recognize me."

"Of course. Why wouldn't I? You look the…What I mean is…I…I was just so surprised to see you yesterday…" Trying to find a polite way to avoid mentioning Annabelle's weight gain was like struggling to escape quicksand. Each attempt at denial only made Jenna sink deeper.

Anne rested her hands on wide hips and gave Jenna a surveying once over. "You could have knocked me over with a feather when I saw you. Of course it would have to be a pretty damned big feather."

Jaw-dropped, Jenna stared. This was clearly not the Annabelle Walker who reigned imperiously over The Class of 99. That Annabelle would never poke fun at herself. Then again, *that* Annabelle would never have expanded her way out of size two, low-rise jeans.

She shook her head, her chin toddling like barely set gelatin. "Shut your mouth, Welles. I'll get to the point of why I'm here. No one in town knows about you. I've been back in Cromline for almost a month, and Cheryl hasn't said anything to me. If she doesn't know who you are then nobody does."

"*You* know who I am." Jenna's tone was a sober plea. "Do *you* plan on telling anyone?"

"God no." Anne lowered her basket to the floor, her expression humorless. "I can't imagine Cheryl's very fond of you. She's never been a fan, excuse the pun, of attractive single women. If she knew you used to be famous, or the scandal you were involved in, spreading it around town would be her personal crusade."

Disheartened, Jenna sighed. "So you know all about it then."

"I do."

"And?"

A gentle and surprising glow of compassion shone in Anne's eyes. "And nothing."

Jenna blinked her surprise. She remembered seeing nothing but malice sketched on teenaged Annabelle's face. Before Jenna could assign word to thought, Anne held up her hand to interrupt. "I doubt if there's one alum from Pinehill High who *didn't* follow your career. I've read everything that's ever been written about you."

"Not everything was true."

Nodding, Anne tightened her lips as if to blanket any emotion on her face. When she finally spoke, her tone was gentle and hushed. "I know all about what happened to you and your husband...his trial and all that. It was big news even here on the east coast."

The broken fluorescent light picked that moment to act up. It hummed from above, and white light flickered to pale yellow before the aisle was cast in a gloomy gray. Anne cleared her throat and resumed speaking. "After he was acquitted, those crap tabloids said you were pregnant. They claimed it was the result of an affair you had with the man your husband beat up. You were always too much a goody-goody, so I never believed it."

Chills broke out on Jenna's arms and she rubbed at her sleeves. It had been years since she'd had a conversation about the events that tore her life apart.

Anne gently reached for her hand. "Other stories said you had been ra..." Anne closed her eyes and released an onerous breath. "I can't even say it out loud." She dipped her head toward a bin filled with tubes of hair glitter and fingered the plastic containers as if they aroused a sudden interest. "It kills me to think that bastard never had to pay for what he did to you." Rubbing at her eyes she continued. "You were never my favorite person back in school. You or your friend, Randi Freed…both of you so blonde, so pretty." On a sigh Anne muttered, "jealousy…what a ridiculous emotion." She walked to the front of the store and placed her basket on the counter.

Jenna followed in disbelief. "Are you saying you came here today to tell me you're not going to give me away?"

"As far as I'm concerned, you're just another mom and the owner of this store." Anne snatched a pair of bright orange sunglasses from a rack to add to her purchases. "You can also consider me a customer. My daughter will love these things."

"Tell me about her," Jenna begged. "What was Cheryl trying to get at?"

Anne lifted her head at a proud angle. "My daughter is beautiful. My daughter is smart and kindhearted. My daughter has Cerebral Palsy."

Blindsided by the admission, Jenna fought to keep pity from altering her expression; but Anne stood looking unaffected and composed. "You don't need to say anything. It's classified as mild and she goes to recreational therapy when she needs it. The condition primarily affects one side of her body and she walks with a slight limp. Riley occasionally drops things, and her speech is a little slow when she's tired. Still, some people mistake the slurring for stupidity."

"People like Cheryl Baldwin."

"Exactly." Anne clucked her tongue. "And that nasty little brat of hers Tiffany. Ironic, isn't it? My daughter being the victim of the class bully. But whose

25

shoulders are better than mine when Riley needs a good cry? There isn't a soul on the planet with a clearer understanding of what goes on in the mind of a spoiled brat."

Appearing tense, angry almost, Anne took a beat before resuming. "My daughter understands that Tiffany and her bitchy, little friends aren't the only game in town. There are other children in the third grade, and my baby will make some friends. She's a good kid and doesn't care about being in the right clique." Smiling, Anne winked. "Kind of like a girl I knew back in high school."

Teary-eyed, Jenna grasped Anne's hand. "Let's go in the back and rummage through the new stuff I haven't put out for display yet."

****

It was both a relief and a happy surprise to learn Annabelle Walker hadn't grown up to be an adult version of the spoiled, insensitive teenager she had once been. Motherhood often taught a woman a life's lesson she could learn nowhere else.

Jenna met her for coffee the next day. They took a corner table at the gourmet shop in town. It was a place, brand new, but designed to transport customers back to their grandmother's kitchen. Antique coffee grinders and cannisters were on shelves, and a rainbow of color glinted off depression-glass creamers and sugar bowls in a display case. Chintz curtains hung from each window.

Jenna listened as Anne confessed to rebelling in college and hooking up with a boy her parents hadn't approved of. "The only thing he did quicker than get me into bed was disappear after I told him I was pregnant. You see, I had my own secret back then."

"I never heard anything about you having a baby."

After dumping a heaping spoonful of sugar into her coffee, Anne stirred with urgency. Dots of red bloomed high on her cheeks. "My mother hid the news like she used to hide her mad money from my father." Anne bit into a muffin fat with chocolate and walnuts. The angrier she looked telling her story, the more vehemently she chewed. "My parents made me leave school and sent me away as if I'd gotten pregnant during the damned Eisenhower administration. They wanted me to give my baby up for adoption. I still haven't totally forgiven them."

Jenna rested a comforting hand atop Anne's. "But you're married and happy now, right?"

"I am. I met my husband right after Riley was born and he adopted her. He also encouraged me to go back to school and get my degree. He's wonderful." Anne's smile returned, and she pushed her plate away. "What about you? Are you seeing anyone?"

It was Jenna's turn to let life and circumstance creep silent into her memory. Tearing a ribbon of pastry from a cinnamon roll, she gave her shoulders a glum shrug. "When you've moved around as much as I have, relationships never really stick." She slowly rotated her spoon in her coffee. "I haven't had a real date since forever, unless you count a couple of friendly lunches with Ash Baldwin. I'm going to the Chamber of Commerce dinner with him."

"*Really?*" Anne drew out the word musically. "Ash is the prime catch around here. He's pretty hot...richer than God, too. Just be careful of Cheryl."

Confused, Jenna tilted her head. "She's married to Teddy Baldwin. Why would she care who his brother dates?"

A Cheshire cat grin lit Anne's face, and the high school Annabelle made a guest appearance. She leaned forward resting on her elbows, her eyes widening as she proceeded to spill the gossip. "Cheryl dated Ash but couldn't drag him to the altar. She settled for Teddy and married him on the rebound. How could you have lived here for four years and not known?"

A waitress strolled over to refill their coffees. She looked directly at Jenna who smiled and nodded her thanks. As the waitress walked away, Jenna sipped the fresh brew and shrugged. "I guess the same way I've lived here for four years without anyone knowing my story. People only see what they expect to see."

Anne picked up her own cup and tapped Jenna's. "Touché."

Chapter Six

"Doesn't my mom look as pretty as a movie star?"

Ash nodded his agreement while Jenna fought the urge to react. She didn't smile at the compliment, nor did she shrink from it. "W...what a nice thing to say. You are such a sweet kid."

Janie's smile displayed a wide set of teeth that crowded her mouth. "So, can I watch Twilight on cable?"

"No."

"Damn." She grumbled and stomped off to the living room.

"Jane Marie!" Jenna faced Ash. "She's such a smart-ass. I should have known there was an ulterior motive for the flattery."

His eyes made a lingering journey from her feet up to her face. "She may be a smart-ass, but she's right."

In a breezy sweep, Jenna fluffed her hair toward her face. She'd been masking her appearance with different cuts, colors, hats, and sunglasses for almost a decade.

"Thank you, but I'm just a suburban mom in a fancy dress."

"Hardly." Ash handed her a bouquet of perfect white roses. "Something beautiful for someone beautiful."

"Oh. These are gorgeous." Jenna brought the velvety blooms close and inhaled the scent. "Let me put them in water before we go."

She rushed off to the kitchen. As she filled the vase, she caught her reflection in the glass insert of a cabinet. Her hair hung in golden waves to her shoulders, and black chiffon draped along her body. Jenna took a moment to study her image. She was fifteen years older than she'd been when she first became a presence in magazines and tabloids. The plump apples of adolescence no longer rounded out her face, and her cheekbones and jaw were more pronounced. Her eyes were no longer huge and curious spheres. They were ovals that followed the tilt of arched brows. At twenty-nine, her skin was unlined and creamy. At twenty-nine, she was still attractive. At twenty-nine, she was Jenna. Angel, a teenage pop star who'd enjoyed a fleeting career, was gone. Jenna dropped the flowers into a vase and returned to her foyer.

"I should be home by eleven," she called to the baby-sitter before she and Ash stepped through the door.

Outside, a stretch limo rested at the curb. Blue iridescence shone in its glossy black paint. The driver held the door and its passengers boarded. Ash reached for a bottle of champagne chilling in an ice bucket. As the car rolled down the street he poured, and sitting intimately close, made a toast to their *friendship*.

At the historic Cromline House, they made an entrance like celebrities at a premier. Inside, Ash was greeted with hearty handshakes. Stocks were discussed over cocktails, golf handicaps at dinner, and business during dessert and brandy. Jenna engaged in small talk with the women at her table—Cheryl and two other wives of the town's mucky mucks. Between courses Jenna and Ash danced.

By the end of the evening, Cheryl had sipped her

way through an entire bottle of wine and listed in her seat. Wagging hands that looked rubbery and boneless, she pointed at Jenna. "I hate to say this, but your window displays aren't in line with the rest of the shops on your street."

Ash shot his sister-in-law a warning look and stood. He offered his hand to Jenna. "May I?"

Once again, they stepped to the dance floor. A resonant strike of piano keys blended with the mellow hum of a sax as the band played a standard from the forties. "I apologize for Cheryl's comment. We only let her work at the real estate office because she nagged us about wanting to be involved in the family business. Being a Baldwin has gone to her head."

"Don't worry about it."

From over his shoulder Jenna stared out at the town's elite. As someone from middle class suburbia who'd also lived in the privileged world of celebrities, a small town with a defined hierarchy was a blessing. In Cromline, she'd found a niche somewhere between her wealthy neighbors and the generational townies. It allowed her to be a regular, a nobody.

Moving with grace, Ash led her around the floor. He wore refinement like a badge. Jenna supposed she should at least pretend to be impressed with his upper crust posturing. She'd sat in the limousine unfazed and detached, and it seemed to spark his curiosity. He'd asked too many questions about her past, but as always, she was vague.

They returned to the table for coffee. Cheryl added a long pour of cognac into hers and continued on about Rhapsody's display windows. When she pronounced the word tiara "taria," Jenna asked Ash to take her home. As they were leaving, he leaned toward his brother, and spoke clearly. "Keep that wife of yours in line."

****

The next morning, Jenna inspected the sidewalk in front of her store. Not so much as a gum wrapper littered the ground. Her window displays were frilly but not overwhelming in their aesthetic. As she was about to unlock the door, Cheryl clip-clopped out of the gourmet coffee shop with a gigantic paper cup in hand.

"I'll bet you need that," Jenna said under her breath.

"Excuse me?"

Years of straining to hear other people's conversations had apparently given Cheryl hearing like a safecracker with a stethoscope. Jenna smiled innocently to cover for the remark. "The coffee…I can't function until I've had some caffeine either."

"Hmm." Cheryl brought the cup to her lips and started to walk away then abruptly turned. "Before I forget, your lease is almost up, and I've made some amendments to the new one. We'll have to sit down and—"

"I've already signed my new lease. Ash has it."

"What?" Cheryl scuttled over, her thin heeled stilettos making her *thin* legs bend in awkward angles. "Ash isn't in charge of drawing up the leases on this block." She screwed her face into one of childish petulance. "Wow, you didn't waste any time cashing in on your relationship with him, did you?"

Jenna shot her an icy look. "I don't like what you're implying."

After blowing at her coffee, Cheryl took a sip. "Implying? No, sweetie, I'm stating a fact. My brother-in-law is the wealthiest man in Cromline. You aren't the first woman in town to try and get something from him."

Widening her eyes, Jenna smiled, honeyed and innocent. "That's true. From what I've heard…that would be you."

A sound like the squawk of a startled chicken tore from Cheryl's throat, and her body went poker stiff. She tottered from one foot to another. "Who…who told you that? Ash is my brother-in-law…I never…"

Jenna dipped her head. It was uncharacteristic of her to gossip, and she instantly regretted her words. In a tone barely removed from the warm lilt of a cartoon princess, she apologized. "I'm sorry. That was just some nonsense I heard. I'm sure no one believes it." She plucked her keys from her bag to open the shop. "Let's make a deal. I won't repeat any rumors if you don't start any. Don't spread stories about me and Ash that aren't true."

"Are you going to see him again?"

"Cheryl!" Jenna waggled the key in the stubborn lock. "I don't know. But if it will make you feel any better, I'll bring anything related to my store to you." She worked the key more forcefully until the tumblers disengaged. "You can start by fixing this lock." She opened the door with Cheryl still at her heels.

A man who appeared to come from nowhere, ambled close. He turned to Jenna, his lingering gaze as intimate as a caress. "Hello, Babes."

Jenna's knees buckled, and her legs almost collapsed beneath her. Again, what sounded like the cawing of a bird spat from Cheryl's mouth. She whipped her head around, her brittle blonde hair a blur. "You're. You're. Oh my God! He's…he's…"

Eric smiled and gave Cheryl a gentle shove. He removed the key dangling in the lock, grabbed Jenna's elbow and pulled her inside, locking the door behind them.

A jumble of questions bounced around in Jenna's head, but when she opened her mouth, nothing came out. Her heart throbbed wildly in her chest. Seeing Eric was like a visitation from a specter, something so unexpected it drained the blood from her head. Myriad emotions coursed through both her mind and body—shock, panic, sadness, and something too similar to passion to remain in her consciousness. The room tilted, and the brightly colored merchandise in her store started to turn gray. Strong arms caught her before she hit the floor.

"Jesus Christ! Jen, are you okay?"

She pulled herself away from his grasp and slapped at his chest. "Put your hands down. I'm not one of your fans about to faint at the sight of you."

"You could have fooled me." He dropped his chin to his chest. "I'm sorry I surprised you like that."

"Surprised? Shocked is more like it. What the hell are you doing here? How did you find me?"

"I was driving through town looking for your store when I spotted you."

He was still hovering too close, and Jenna fought a primal impulse to give him a shove. "I don't mean here on this block. I mean here, here in this town. How did you know about my store? Why…Why are you here?"

"We need to talk," he said as simply as if he were asking for directions to the library.

"Talk?" She rubbed her eyes to wipe away the swell of emotion that refused to loosen its grasp. "After all these years?"

He slid his hands into his pockets and stood staring. Jenna tried to look away but couldn't. She was like a planet caught in the orbit of the sun.

He was older, but the years had only improved his looks. His stance was casual and familiar, familiar yet different. It was as though a transparency of this Eric had settled over the one she knew so long ago and refined him. The same sandy hair that used to fall stubbornly across his brow was expertly trimmed. The hollow cheeks of a boy had filled out, replaced by angled, masculine planes. A smattering of fine lines crinkled at the corners of his brilliant, turquoise eyes, and a faded scar slashed faintly from one cheekbone to his temple. *The accident.* Jenna suddenly remembered the near-death fall that almost claimed his life. Memories, good and bad, began their battle with each other, and tears stung her eyes.

"Please go. I…I wasn't prepared for this."

"We need to talk. I have some things to—"

"No, I can't, not now."

Cheryl Baldwin was still outside tapping on the window with the palm of her hand, her rings clacking against the glass.

Jenna dabbed at her lower lashes. "Please, Eric, please get out of here."

"Okay. I'm sorry, Jen, but I will call you later. We need to talk. It's important." He unlocked the door and, head down, brushed by Cheryl who was still pressed against the window.

Chapter Seven

Bree Davis Laine stood by an open brace of French doors that led to tiers of shining pink granite. A breath of warm air caught the hem of her filmy cover-up, and it fluttered against her ankles. The terrace of her Pacific Palisades mansion was perfection. Cypress and exotic palms led to the crystal blue waters of an infinity pool, every inch of it a splendor of hand-painted tile. The house and grounds was one of her favorite places in the world, and she had no intention of losing it.

For all of her life, she believed her destiny was a life of red-carpet events, upscale homes, and first-class travel. But the lifestyle of the ultra-rich and famous had, for too long, been a whisper's distance away. She'd lived just at the edge, able to grasp only a scintilla of luxury until she'd turned a brooding, gorgeous young man into a star. Now, after six years of marriage, he was walking away.

Bree stepped outside and looked beyond her land to the hillsides. Golden swells and dips, dappled in sunshine, were simply dead grass, still, the vista was beautiful and enjoying it another part of her destiny. It was one she didn't believe in leaving to chance. She picked up her phone and dialed.

Less than an hour later, the man she'd summoned stood at the foot of her chaise. "Finding her might not be easy," he said. "She's been in the ether for a long time."

Bree slid nine-thousand-dollar sunglasses from her eyes up onto her head. "I know exactly how long she's been gone."

Private detective Stephen Powers took a seat on the ottoman near her chair. "Are you looking for leverage in your divorce? Do you think she and your husband have reconnected?"

In an unconcerned sweep, Bree smoothed suntan lotion onto her legs. "No. I'm trying to make sure they don't." She handed the detective an old newspaper clipping. "I also want you to find him." She rubbed more lotion onto her legs as the detective studied the sooty, black and white image.

He lifted his head, his eyes wide. "This is Mark Chambers, the guy your husband went to trial for almost beating to death. What are you up to?"

"Does it matter?" Bree snapped her pricey sunglasses back down over her eyes. Their business was done.

****

Eric paced the confines of his motel room. He ate chips and candy from the vending machine at the end of the hallway and drank three bottles of water out of restless boredom. He spent the day driving himself crazy thinking about Jenna. The last thing he wanted to do was hurt her. Though she'd begged him to leave, she appeared torn, as if battling with reason and emotion. He felt no such uncertainty. His feelings were crystal clear. It took only one glance for him to know he was still in love with her.

He paced more, dropped onto the lumpy mattress, and surfed the nineteen channels on the television bolted inside the particle board armoire. He needed to get out of the room. According to the paper he'd grabbed from the lobby, his new movie was playing at the multiplex in the local mall. It had gotten great reviews. *Why?* He'd filmed half the action flick in front of a green screen, and it was just one giant explosion.

He picked up his phone a dozen or so times but never dialed her number. Food eventually crossed his mind, so he took a shower he didn't need and shrugged into jeans and a sweatshirt. Plopping a baseball cap onto his head and slipping dark glasses over his eyes, he set off for the motel parking lot. He had no idea where he was going but supposed there would be a restaurant or diner somewhere along the road. Hopefully no one outside would notice him squeezing behind the wheel of the dinky subcompact. *Who said celebrities got everything they wanted?* He didn't have a divorce agreement, didn't have Jenna, and Discount Rental didn't have any midsize sedans available. He started the car and pulled out of the lot.

After doing a loop at the outskirts of the town proper, he pulled onto a grassy shoulder next to a place wrapped in weathered clapboard. Neon signs were in each window. A beer seemed to be in order. The clack of pool balls sounded from somewhere in the back, and classic rock played on the jukebox. The tavern wasn't exactly a dump but not nice enough to require the barmaid to wear a starchy looking white shirt and bow tie. Eric sympathized, remembering how he'd once hauled dirty glasses in tie and cummerbund. Like most actors, he'd ridden a carousel of jobs before fame struck—bar-back, waiter, construction worker, just to name a few.

He straddled a stool and asked for a draught and

order of hot wings. The server placed a chilled mug in front of him and rushed off to place his food order. With his elbows propped on the bar and his face shadowed by the brim of his cap, Eric slowly sipped his beer. He wondered when the girl behind the bar would recognize him. Although he managed to keep a grip on his ego, he had come to expect the fuss his presence usually created.

As he drank, he thought back to a time early in his career when he'd made the mistake of walking into an East L.A. bar in a tuxedo. He'd been arguing with Bree at an award's after-party because she claimed he wasn't "networking enough" and talking to the right people.

"You're my manager, you suck up for me," he'd told her, then abruptly left and hailed a cab. Within minutes of walking into the Verona Street cantina, he'd found himself surrounded by bikers. Their ink and leather jacket patches told Eric they were members of the Mongols, the Latino motorcycle gang so ruthless they'd run the Hell's Angels out of the area.

A hand had come down in a steely grip on his shoulder. "*Pinches gabachos.*"

The man attached to the hand had been huge, barrel bellied and tattooed. He shoved Eric down onto a stool. A woman had sidled over, her long sable hair trailing past a narrow waist. Her whisper had been silk at his ear. "*Eres guapo.*" The gang members hadn't appreciated her smile or her tone, and, menacing and leather clad, they'd surrounded him.

"I'll just be on my way," Eric said. But as he attempted to rise, he'd been pushed back down into his seat. A sea of gold teeth, chains, and spikes bore down, and he realized there was no way out of the situation he'd so carelessly placed himself in. As he waited to get his ass handed to him, the first commandment of all reform schools popped into his head. Having spent two years fighting for survival in juvie, he knew the philosophy well. *Take the biggest guy out and stand your ground.* A variation on the theme was a better idea in this situation, he'd quickly decided—*take the biggest guy out and run like hell.*

Leaning back as far as he could, he swung and hit the huge biker squarely in the mouth. Falling backward into the others, he and his *cabrons* landed like felled trees. Eric had been barely through the door when the mob was up and after him. As he ran down the street he'd almost collided with another large figure, Nick Lombardo, poised with a baseball bat and ready to do battle.

"I ought to use this on you, you stupid bastard!" Nick had roared. "What the hell goes on in your head going into a place like this, and in a tuxedo no less!"

"Later, Nick. In about ten seconds some very bad-ass bikers are going to turn that corner."

Looking around now, in a much safer space, Eric downed the rest of his beer and snorted a laugh. Even after all these years, he still wondered how Nick had managed to make a U-turn with a super-stretch on such a narrow street. Thank God he had followed him.

"Here are your wings…Another beer?" Eric finally raised his head and thanked the barmaid.

"Oh my God. I don't believe it. You're Eric Laine!"

He shushed her and bribed her with an exorbitant tip in return for her silence. He ate his food and had a second beer. When he left the tavern, Jenna was still on his mind.

****

The next morning, he was up and dressed early. He

drove to Jenna's house, a tidy structure with yellow siding and white, lintel topped windows. Hunkering in the rental car, he rehearsed what he planned to say. The door eventually opened, and a weedy little girl skipped down the drive. Her pale blonde hair was loose, long waves glinting in the morning sunlight as she ran to a minivan. She blew Jenna a kiss and got in the vehicle.

"Wait!" Jenna called out while waving a bright pink sack. The kid had forgotten something, probably her lunch. Scrambling back, the little girl grabbed the bag, hugged Jenna, and hurried back to the van.

A tightness pressed down on his chest as Eric watched the scene—Jenna bending to enfold her daughter, her hands tenderly sweeping over the length of golden hair, and the loving kiss. He'd played such scenes in his head a thousand times over the years, simple day-to-day things his stupidity had cost him. Piggyback rides, parental hugs, and bedtime stories were things he had never known as a child and rituals he took no part in as an adult.

He wondered how much the little girl missed having a daddy. Who fixed the chain on her bicycle when it broke? Who scared off the monsters in her closet? Who would knock the teeth down the throat of the first asshole to get out of line with her? *It should be me,* Eric thought sadly. Even though she wasn't his, he would have been proud to be her father.

If only he hadn't said such terrible things the night Jenna went into labor. If only he'd kept the demons of jealousy, anger, and hurt from rising up. *If only.* He shook his head, killed the engine of his car, and walked to the front door.

He gave a two-knuckle rap against the wood. As he

waited, his feet shuffling on the mat, time dragged into eternity before Jenna answered. Finally, the door opened to a narrow crack, and she peeked out. He felt tempted to wedge one foot at the opening like a pushy salesman, sure she would slam the door when she saw it was him.

"Come in." It was a reluctant invitation and she tugged the lapels of her robe tight about her throat. She cocked her head. "Kitchen's that way. There's a pot of coffee on the counter, help yourself. I'll be right back."

Eric stepped through, past the living room and into a space with honey-colored cabinets and shelves displaying jars, cups, and mismatched canisters. The house was welcoming with cushy furniture and lots of warmth. It was nothing like the austere box he and Jenna shared in Malibu, and nothing like any of the houses he owned with Bree. Jenna's home expressed comfort, something his current wife could never pull off no matter how high her decorating budget was.

In a short while, Jenna reappeared in jeans and a white turtleneck. Her sun-streaked hair was combed back from her face, a face still radiant in his estimation. Her eyes were different, still soft and golden but no longer wide and animated. They were pensive and held a glimmer of sadness. Eric longed to hold her, to draw her against his chest in a comforting embrace till the veil of sorrow lifted.

She poured herself a cup of coffee and sipped slowly, keeping her mug held high like a shield.

"Thanks for seeing me," he said.

"The sooner we settle whatever you think needs settling, the sooner you can leave."

"I know I deserve your anger…I wouldn't blame you for hating me." He let the words hang hoping she would deny the last part of his statement. She didn't. Discouraged, he raked his fingers through his hair and looked away.

Jenna sipped her coffee, willing herself to disregard the familiar gesture. Letting Eric's troubled body language spark any feeling would be too easy of a slip into the past.

He turned and spoke softly. "I guess I should start by apologizing for what happened the night you had the baby."

Jenna lurched as if she had been punched squarely in the chest. The impact of his words went straight to her heart. "Don't go there. I don't ever think about it. It isn't fair of you to remind me." She dipped her head so he wouldn't see how clearly she was lying. She'd thought of that night a thousand times, remembered how drunk he'd been and the sad tremor of his voice as he confessed he could never love her baby. *Our baby* her mind instantly corrected as her pulse started to race.

Had he somehow found out Janie was his?

Eric said "sorry" in a such a repentant whisper she knew at once he hadn't. *How could he?* He'd spent close to a decade in a whirlwind of fame and glamour, and all of it with another woman.

"Get to the point." Jenna held her mug high. It was ridiculously large, and almost masked her face.

"Could we maybe sit?" he asked.

Nodding, she crooked her chin toward the kitchen table. "Get to the point."

"I'm getting a divorce."

A tinge of annoyance replaced the thrumming anxiety beating at her insides. She narrowed her eyes. "I already know about it. It's not like you've kept a low profile all these years. The story is on the cover of every tabloid in the supermarket." Once again, she hid behind the mug.

"Can you put your damned coffee down so I can see your face while we talk."

Jenna lowered the mug and placed it on the table. She kept her back tight against her chair, her tone and glare steely. "Wow. Movie star temperament. I wondered if fame went to your head."

"You have? So…you think about me?" He smiled as if he'd won a prize.

Jenna's heart was back in her throat, throbbing now with ire. His A-list standing was the very last thing she wanted to acknowledge. She shut her eyes and pressed her fingers to the lids as if they burned or itched.

"Will you please just look at me," he begged. "I'm not temperamental, just more determined, a result of my age…not my star on the Walk of Fame."

Again, Jenna felt a weighty press against her breast. The mention of Hollywood prompted images of her former life to flash in her head like a cannonade—riots of screaming fans, disembodied hands grabbing at her, and the press never more than a yard away. Jenna let her eyes settle on the cozy simplicity of her kitchen till the chaos of her mind settled.

Eric sighed as if he knew he'd triggered bad memories for her. "Can we please just talk?"

"About your divorce? Why would I care about that?"

"It's about my assets. Bree is playing hardball."

"Your assets?" Jenna stood so abruptly her chair tottered before the legs came to rest on the hardwood. "What the hell do your *assets* have to do with me? That's between you and your *wife*." She watched Eric twisting in his seat and tapping his fingers against the table as if to stall.

"She's going after everything, including the house in Malibu."

Flinched as if stung by a bee, Jenna's voice tore from her throat in a high-pitched cry. "You kept the house? The house where Mark Chambers attacked me! The place where *you* practically attacked me!"

She flung the contents of her cup into the sink. Dark liquid splashed the white porcelain and spattered out onto the counter. "Dammit!" She pounded at the mess with a tea towel. "Malibu was another life. The house has nothing to do with me. I never want to even think about that place."

Eric got up and stood beside her, close, too close. "I'm sorry but I never took your name off the deed. In fact—"

"In fact?" She rounded on him. "Is that why you're really here? To tie up loose ends? How dare you compromise my privacy just to protect your money."

"Cut it out, Jen. Do you honestly think I give a shit about money?"

Her pulse was thunder in her ears. "You cared an awful lot when you didn't have any."

"Damned right. I cared about living above my head while my wife paid the bills. I came here to pay you back!"

"Pay me back or pay me off? You have one hell of a nerve to think I'd take anything from you. Let Bree have the fucking place. I only gave it to you so you could cash in the equity. I didn't want to leave you with nothing."

Eric froze. His steady stare was unreadable but to someone who knew him well. Jenna knew him more than well. She knew him intimately. She'd seen the same veiled look in his eyes a hundred times—anger, sadness, humiliation. He marched to the door and opened it.

Before stepping out into the morning sunlight, he turned. "Yet that's exactly what you did." She watched as he boarded a small car. And with tires screeching, he sped away.

Chapter Eight

"Damn it." Eric gripped the steering wheel as he burned down the street. *When did she become so stubborn? So damned cold?* He sighed. *Probably after the night you said you hated her unborn baby.* He depressed the brake pedal and flicked the turn signal. Getting a speeding ticket was the last thing he needed. With nothing better to do, he continued to cruise through town.

Eric made a left onto Baldwin Street, hung a sharp right onto Baldwin Court, and as he approached the town limits, he passed a strip mall, not surprisingly called Baldwin Square.

"What the hell?"

The woman he'd politely shoved away from Jenna's storefront had been arguing with her over someone named Baldwin. *Who the hell is this guy?* A half-mile down the road, Eric had his answer.

A large sign at the edge of a construction site read *Coming Soon Baldwin Ridge*. Smaller letters beneath the heading advertised the future site of an exclusive country club, golf course, and luxury town home community. *A Baldwin Development project, AEB Contracting, Ashton Edward Baldwin president*. Eric parked his car and walked over to a chain link fence. Behind it, mammoth excavating machines were digging in one area, while in others, rough framed structures were already standing.

Oddly, one house, an immense fixture of rotted wood and peeling paint, stood far back on the other side of the fence near the leveled trees and framework. Hanging on a lopsided post beneath a rusted mailbox, a sign said *Room for Rent*.

Eric's curiosity was at once piqued. Why was something so dilapidated so close to the lofty construction project? He stepped carefully onto the shattered ruins of a long concrete walkway.

The closer he got to the house the more obvious it was how desperately the massive old Victorian needed repairs. He looked up at decomposing clapboard, shutters hanging by a thread, and gaps on the roof where shingles were absent. Several windowpanes were missing glass. The monstrous house resembled the Bates Motel. The only structure Eric had seen in worse condition was his house in North Carolina. He rang the bell and waited to the tune of haunted house chimes that escaped from broken windows.

In true gothic fashion the heavy door creaked open. But instead of being received by a cadaverous butler from a horror movie, a cheerful looking, silver haired woman, no taller than five feet, stood at the threshold. Her smile abruptly vanished when she saw Eric.

"I thought you were the mailman. If you're one of Ashton Baldwin's lackies here to bother me about selling my house again, you can turn right around." She spun on slippered feet and made to slam the heavy door, but Eric flattened his hand against it. "No, ma'am." He coughed as he tried in earnest not to laugh at the squat little woman. "I'm here about the room for rent."

Pivoting back, she squinted, her gray eyebrows drawn low. "Sonny, I rent to veterans, old men with nowhere to go. Why would a young man like yourself want to live here?"

"Well, ma'am, I have some business in town, and I've been staying at a hotel. I stay in them a lot, and I thought it might be nice to live in a house for a change."

Flyaway silver hair framed her wrinkled face. "Nice try, but I think you're a bullshit artist working for that scum-sucking son of a bitch Ashton Baldwin. You'll move in here and set the place on fire."

"No, ma'am, I don't work for the scum-sucker." Eric tried to stifle a laugh, but it was futile, so he covered it with a cough. The old lady's aggressive stance and easy use of epithets was beyond funny. He was suddenly more curious than ever about Baldwin.

The woman puckered her face into a scowl. "So, what is this business of yours then?"

What the hell. Maybe this quirky, little-old lady was one of those people who believed truth was stranger than fiction. "Mrs.…."

"Cummings, Ina Cummings."

"Mrs. Cummings, my name is Eric Laine. I'm an actor, actually a movie star, a big one, very famous." He flashed a fawning smile and rattled his ridiculous monologue without stopping for breath. "My ex-wife lives here in Cromline. I've only seen her twice in nine years, but I'm still madly in love with her. I'm married to someone I *don't* love, but I'm getting a divorce. I can't leave town until I've had a chance to straighten things out with my first wife. If I stay at the Best Express, I'll be recognized, and I don't want the distraction. Oh, and I think my ex may be dating the scum-sucker, so I'm probably going to have to kick his ass."

Ina Cummings' alert eyes popped wide. "Movie

star! Well, that's the best one I've heard in years. Come on in."

****

Ash Baldwin barely lifted his head to greet Cheryl as she stepped into his office. "If you're looking for my brother, he's not here."

Appearing unfazed, she offered him the gushing smile of a schoolgirl with a crush. "I came here to see you, not Teddy. I thought we could grab some lunch."

"I'm ordering in."

Cheryl's cheeks were rounded, plump and pink and her mouth stretched wider. "Good, order me a salad, and I'll eat here also. I have something important to tell you."

"Important?" Ash finally lifted his eyes from the stack of papers on his desk and raised his head. His expression was stern. "After your behavior at the banquet, I'm not keen to listen to anything you have to say."

"My…my behavior? Ash I was simply—"

"Simply? Simply drinking yourself into a bitch."

"Ash!"

He stood and folded his arms across his chest. The bulge of shoulders and biceps beneath his Oxford shirt was a clear display of intimidation. "Listen to me, Cheryl, I like Jenna Black, and I plan on spending time with her. Keep that sharp tongue of yours in your mouth when she's with me."

A predictable jangle rang from her wrists, as Cheryl patted at her helmet of bleached hair. "But she's who I want to talk to you about. I know you like her, but I think she's already involved with someone."

Ash raised a brow. "Who?"

"This is going to sound crazy but I saw her with Eric

Laine."

"The actor?"

Ash tipped his head toward the fiberglass tiled ceiling and spat a robust but clipped laugh. The blush on Cheryl's cheeks deepened to scarlet. "Stop it. I'm serious. I saw them together in front of her store. Then he dragged her inside and locked the door. It was all very strange. They looked…intimate."

As he continued to laugh, the swell of his pectoral muscles also strained against his shirt. "Last month you swore a broken-down Creamy Cone truck was really a car bomb. You called the state police and all they found inside of it was melted ice cream." Shaking his head and still chuckling, Ash ambled into the outer office. He passed his receptionist diligently clicking away at a keyboard. "Have you heard? Cromline is the new Hollywood." Still sniggering, he called over his shoulder, "Cheryl, my brother better see to it you lay off the sauce. Eric Laine, here in Cromline, of all things."

"It was him," she insisted. "And they looked very cozy."

****

On hands and knees, Jenna picked up bottles of lime green nail polish. She was lucky they hadn't broken into a million shards of enamel-covered glass. It was barely noon, and the display was the third thing she'd knocked over or dropped. Her nerves were getting the better of her. Or was it guilt? Maybe it was both. She placed the nail polish in a box and shoved it behind the counter to arrange later. A small picture of Janie was taped to the register. Even in the wallet-sized photo, her daughter's eyes were bright, lambent blue. Eric's eyes.

Jenna had suspected the truth of her daughter's

paternity, but it wasn't until she'd rushed to a local hospital after hearing about his accident that she knew for certain. While crying at his bedside she'd discovered he and Janie shared the same uncommon blood type.

Jenna picked at more items but only ended up making an incompatible display of merchandise. She sighed. She'd factualized a hundred reasons for not telling Eric Janie was his. For four long years, Jenna sliced away till those reasons were pared down to a single pretext disguised as the truth. She couldn't bear the thought of being away from Janie—not for a summer, a holiday, a weekend, or even a day. It had been just the two of them for too long.

But Jenna knew her decision hadn't been fair. Janie had a right to know she had a father. The child was at an age where vague dismissals on the subject of *daddy* no longer held up.

A pain settled behind Jenna's eyes. It was blinding. What *would* happen if she told Eric? He had the money and influence that came with being famous. What would he do when he found out Janie was his? And what would Jenna do if he wanted to share custody? The thought had her backing absently into another display, a tall rack that swayed and almost came crashing down.

"Watch out!" Anne, for all of her bulk, came running from the doorway in time to warn Jenna that a stand of merchandise was about to topple on her. Steadying it, she answered with a shiver and shake of the head.

"You look colder than a block of ice. Here." Anne handed her a disposable cup. "I came by to say hello. I brought you a latte."

"Thanks." Anne's studious regard made Jenna's

anxiety ramp up a notch. "Is something wrong?"

"I need to tell you something Cheryl's spreading around."

Dipping her head again, Jenna sighed. *Things couldn't possibly get more complicated.* But Anne's lead-in of "don't panic," told her they could.

"At her last liquid luncheon, Cheryl told everyone she saw you with Eric Laine. She said you two looked very cozy, and that if a married movie star was one of your conquests Ash had better watch his wallet."

Jenna gagged on her latte. "Did anyone believe her?"

"Not after I poked some holes in her story."

Anne's smile was a simpering grin that took Jenna back to high school. She sucked in a relieved breath. "Thank you."

"I'll run interference for you any time…but…"

"But it *was* him," Jenna admitted. "I guess you know that."

Anne set her coffee down and made order out of the items Jenna had indiscriminately set on the counter—receipts, earrings, and pots of lip gloss. More things slanted in uncharacteristic disarray on shelves. "How did he find you? Why is he here?"

Dropping onto a stool set behind the glass showcase, Jenna shook her head. "I'm not sure. But now that he is here, I'm going to have to tell him something I should have told him a long time ago."

****

Over homemade muffins, Ina told Eric all about the dirty dealing Baldwin Family. They had been swindling people out of their land since the early twenties when Addis Baldwin cheated Ina's grandfather out of the property that was now Baldwin Square.

"His golf course is on land that was part of my little farm here, and Ash won't be satisfied until he's driven me off my last few acres."

Eric took an automatic glance toward the window. It was a grid of wavy panes of glass, peeling paint, and glazing putty curling away from the wood. "How much land do you have?"

"Enough for him to build another section of ugly condos instead of the detached houses he was supposed to build." She pushed the plate of muffins closer to Eric, but he waved away the offer. "Ash promises me market value, but he's never really offered me anything fair. I won't sell anyway. I've lived in this house all my life." Ina stood and motioned for Eric to follow. "Come on, let me show you something."

In sharp contrast to the front of the house, the back was an explosion of color. Shoots of spring perennials were reaching through the soil. In the center of the yard, a circle created by a low hedge housed railroad-tie boxes. In each box, a variety of budding herbs grew. A large greenhouse stood in the distance.

"I've been doing this as a business for more than twenty years, but I've tended my gardens all my life." It was a proud declaration and the old woman's smile was a wide crescent. "In the spring I sell flats of flowers and herbs, in the fall sugar pumpkins that I grow in that field over there."

She and Eric traveled the verdant yard, the sky above the blue of a lupine. A shed, in as much need of repair as the house, listed beyond a tilled section of earth. Ina's hands were at her back as she played tour guide and roamed her gardens. "I sell jams and pies, too. Make them from fresh peaches and apples I buy in bulk from an orchard the next town over. I do a very good business when folks vacationing in the mountains travel through on their way back to the city."

It wasn't hard for Eric to figure out how a businessman like Baldwin felt about having the run-down house situated so close to his stately country club.

Ina continued, looking more frustrated than angry. "Last year I had three veterans living here. The VA paid their board and, hand to God, I used the money on meals and keeping the place warm. Whatever was left over I used for repairs."

Eric gazed more at the charming splendor of the grounds, and then back at the house, a gnarled collection of boards and banking shutters. It was obvious there hadn't been much "left over."

"With no warning the town council pulled my gentlemen out…some bullshit about building codes and my back stairs being hazardous. But it was Ash. He got those spineless bastards to do his dirty work. I'm sure of it. Mark my words if you move in, he'll see to it that you're thrown out, too."

A budding grimace that worked its way to Eric's lips was replaced by a half smile. "Are there any laws in this town that prevent a long-lost nephew from visiting?"

****

Eric returned to his motel to collect his things. He made three phone calls. One was to his agent to tell him he was declining an offer to star in yet another action flick. The next was to his law firm. They gave him the news that Bree's attorneys were moving full force in their pursuit of Jewel Incorporated. Eric told them to give her sharks access to whatever they wanted, then he asked them to find out what they could about local zoning laws in New York. The third call was to Nick. "Any news for me?"

"None of it good." A hard sigh preceded his disclosure. "*True Hollywood Scandals* is planning a feature on Jenna. The producers offered me a king's ransom for an interview. They also contacted Alan Stark, but he gave me his word he won't have anything to do with it."

Eric muttered a curse. The news was bad, but it was the mention of Alan Stark that prompted the epithet. Every time Eric was reminded of Jenna's former manager, the man who'd embarked on a desperate quest to ruin him, it was like cracking a tooth, the pain swift and sharp.

"You sure about Stark?"

"Yeah," Nick answered. "He might be scum, but whatever creepy fixation he had with Jenna was never meant to hurt her. He won't want to now."

Chapter Nine

At the gym, Ash added weights on the bar for his last series of bench presses. After finishing with a primal grunt, he wiped sweat from his forehead and strode to the locker room. He stripped out of his nylon shorts and stepped to a mirror and flexed. He ambulated to the steam room in a scanty towel. An impromptu business discussion evolved as it always did in the bath.

He spoke first to a local official whose campaign he'd heavily invested in. "I want Ina Cummings off my golf course."

"I'll do what I can. But if you plan on putting up condos there, I can't zone the property nonresidential."

"I want her out." Ash rubbed his chin. "The damned house is falling down around her ears. She can't be safe living there."

With shaking hands, the assemblyman dabbed at his brow and repeated, "I'll do what I can, but she's a stubborn old girl."

Billowing blasts of steam flooded the space and when it cleared the veil of concern was gone from Ash's face. "Stubborn is no longer my problem. I offered her a good price and pulled strings to get her bumped to the top of a senior housing list. I'm through negotiating with her. Get her out."

The assemblyman took an arduous gulp of steam and again mopped his head with a towel. "I had a hell of a time getting rid of her borders. The town council members weren't keen on making veterans homeless. They agreed to let them come back if she makes repairs. She'll need a loan. You have enough clout with the bank to see that she doesn't get one."

"You can get a loan on the internet." Ash's matter-of-fact tone was worse than a threat. "Have a conversation with the building inspector. Remind him the lease is almost up on his wife's little muffin shop. I'm sure he'll find enough wrong with the Cummings' house to have it condemned."

****

The vanity in Bree's ensuite bath was a grand length of white stained rosewood. Everything in the room, from the walk-in shower, Venetian tub, and hand-fired tiles was as high-end as anything found in a palace.

Peering into the mirror she studied her aesthetician's handiwork. Her lips were augmented plump and lush, but the collagen injections for her laugh lines failed to mask the somber parentheses framing her mouth. Miserable was an inaccurate illustration. Bree was angry—chew glass-and-smile-as-it-sliced-her-tongue angry.

Damn her ungrateful husband. He should be off somewhere filming, reaping the rewards of the life she'd handed him; while she should be at the clinic in Switzerland, having the full treatment instead of a half-assed one at a day-spa on Wilshire.

Stepping into the bedroom, she rifled through her mail. Not so much as a single summer holiday invitation was in the mix. She damned Eric again. He was the star and would be getting the parties and the red-carpet events in the divorce. "Fuck him and his sad little broken heart," she muttered as she wandered the room.

Her eyes coasted from one item of luxury to another, and another. The suite in the Pacific Palisades house was the most elegant of all the bedrooms in their various homes. It was a vision of pale-pink and cream colored damasks and brocades. Satin pillows with silky tassels rested on the chaise, and a carpet as dense as a lamb's hide cushioned her feet.

Bree stepped close to the bed, a massive four-poster with inscribed columns that swirled toward the high ceiling and ended at an open canopy. Yards of gossamer silk wrapped around the frame and draped like a pour of shimmering water to the floor. The bed was designed for lovemaking—a sultry vessel where she had spent the most ardent moments of her adult life.

Bree brushed her fingers over the luxe fabric covering the bed while wistfully remembering nights shared with Eric. He had been an artful lover, far better than any she had taken to idle away the time while he'd been away on location. Her extramarital flings had been poor substitutes and a cliché testimony to the bored Hollywood wife—one on ones with her tennis instructor, personal trainer, or whoever was young, attractive, and eager to please on any particular afternoon. None of her lovers came close though, not in looks nor prowess. Eric Laine was a virile lover whose performance was unrivaled.

Sitting on the bed, she gripped the heavy duchess satin in her fists. *Performance.* Bree should have appreciated the irony. The talent that afforded them the trappings of Hollywood entitlement didn't live exclusively on reels of film. In bed, he had also performed. He had taken her, hot and desirous, *performing* as a dutiful husband. But he never spoke of love. His eyes never probed long and lingering, into hers. His breath was never the thready sigh of a man fallen lost in the depths of passion. He had carried the torch for another woman, a woman Bree grew to resent more and more as the years passed.

"Fuck him and his broken heart," she repeated. "Fuck the both of you." Bree was either going to get Eric Laine back, or she was going to get even.

Chapter Ten

Ina Cummings scraped another helping of fricassee from the pan. "Here, have another piece of chicken."

Eric gladly obliged. He couldn't remember ever having a meal this good. During the years of his childhood, sustenance was whatever slogged from a can, and *Nouvelle* cuisine, what he generally ate now, an over flavored burden on his tongue. He did as his landlady ordered and cleaned his plate. There was nothing better than an old fashioned, home cooked dinner.

As he swiped the last bit of gravy with a biscuit, Ina smiled. "As much as I've enjoyed feeding the gentlemen who've lived here, it's a lot easier making meals for someone who doesn't have ulcers or high blood pressure." She leaned across the table and whispered. "You don't have a spastic colon, do you?"

Eric shuddered at the suggestion and then laughed. His new landlady was on the quirky side, but he got a real kick out of her.

"Well, I'm off to bingo. There's pie in the fridge. Just help yourself."

From her window, Eric watched her old pickup sputter down the dusty drive. He stepped outside and eased comfortably low in an Adirondack chair. The night was clear and stars were quickly gathering in the evening sky like old friends. The lingering warmth of daytime air crept low, but night's chill was pressing at the edges. He rolled the cuffs of his flannel shirt down to cover his wrists. A howl of something, baby fox or nocturnal bird, jarred him from drifting into sleep. A glance at his watch told him it was only 7:30.

What the hell. Why not. He rose from the chair and headed to his car.

****

Jenna heard a light tap at her door. Before opening it, she took a breath and drew her lips into the smile she'd at one time reserved for interviews—a wide faux gleam that showed no gums. She'd agreed to another date with Ash and hoped the night ahead would spark some deeper interest in their friendship. She pulled the door open, prepared to greet him, but her smile departed as Eric stepped inside. "What are *you* doing here?" She gave an anxious glance toward the stairs praying her daughter, her eyes a wide and unmistakable azure glow, wouldn't come running down.

"I…we…we still need to talk."

She brushed at the red *crepe de chine* fabric of her dress with her fingertips. His stare was unnerving…intimate.

"You were in that color the night we met," he said on a breath. "It still looks great on you."

"Same color, completely different style." Jenna's mind flashed to a night a lifetime ago, when she'd dared to venture out dressed in a sexy scrap of scarlet. She'd stepped out of her "good girl" image and gotten drunk. Eric found her asleep in a nightclub lounge and rescued her, and she'd fallen in love with him that very night. Looking down, she continued to smooth her hands along a much more modestly cut dress. "I have a date."

His eyes stayed upon her. "I figured as much."

Unsettled by the gaze, Jenna fingered her hair as if to straighten a wayward lock. "You have to leave. He'll be here any minute." As soon as she spoke the words, the gentle motor of Ash's roadster purred outside.

"That him?"

She gritted her teeth. "No, it's someone else I *don't* have a date with. Will you get out of here?"

But Eric made no move to leave. "Are you and he… I mean…It's none of my business, but is this just a date or are you in a relationship?"

Jenna's heart dashed into a heavy and awakened beat. "You're right. None of your business."

Head down, he shuffled his feet, his eyes still raised and upon her. She peeked out her sidelight to see her date slipping from his car. "Seriously, you have to get out of here. Go out the back door before Ash sees you."

Eric's head snapped up. "Ash Baldwin?"

"Yes. How do you know his—"

"You were arguing about him in front of your store with the woman with the big hair. Remember?"

The doorbell rang, and Jenna gave Eric one more pleading look. "Just go out the back door…please."

Looking handsome, looking wicked, he shook his head and smiled. "Back door? Uh, uh. Haven't you heard? I'm a big shot now."

Jenna balled her hands into fists, her arms stiff at her sides. "How the hell am I supposed to explain you, 'Big Shot?' You need to leave."

He shrugged. "I would, but my car is in your driveway, and your *date* just blocked me in."

The bell rang again, and Jenna had no choice but to open the door. Eric took a sideways step and then moved away. He scrubbed at his head and created a mussy confusion of hair that fell across his eyes.

Ash's lips were stretched wide as he stepped inside, but his smile departed as he spotted Eric. "Did I mistake the time?"

"Oh hey." Eric offered his hand, but Ash ignored the greeting.

Frozen in place, Jenna watched the exchange. Though Eric was grinning, his eyes were steely. "I just stopped by to say hello to Jen. I didn't know she had plans. We go way back...Name's Mike."

Ash's lips remained fixed in a steady line that was neither smile nor frown. His blond brows lowered over gray eyes. Jenna wrapped her arms around one of Eric's and led him to the door. "Mike was just leaving."

"Well then, I guess I'll be on my way." Before stepping through the doorway, he called over his shoulder. "If you need me for anything, Babes, I'll be around." As she was about to shut the door he shouted, "Hey, pal, you're blocking me."

Sweeping past, Ash strode into the driveway and aimed the alarm remote at his car. After the two chirps sounded, he climbed behind the wheel and backed out of the driveway. Jenna gripped her porch railing, watching Eric amble down the drive and lean into the window frame of the shining sports car. Voices rang clearly through the quiet evening air.

"This is a sweet little machine...Jag huh? What year?"

"It's a seventy-five, a classic."

Eric grinned and tilted his head at his rented subcompact. "Sweet, but my car's brand new." With that, he boarded the tiny vehicle, screeched out of the driveway, and burned tire down the street.

Caught between wanting to laugh or cry, Jenna shook her head as Ash took out his handkerchief and wiped Eric's handprints off his car.

Janie vaulted over. "Who was that guy, Mom?"

Stepping back inside, Jenna drew her daughter close to avoid her wide, inquisitive eyes—Eric's eyes. "Oh, he's someone I used to know a long time ago. He showed up, out of the blue, a few days ago." The lie of omission clawed hard at her throat.

"He sounded funny."

"He was trying to be, but I don't think Mr. Baldwin thought so."

The sitter arrived and Jenna instructed her to make sure Janie was in bed by nine. It was a directive that wouldn't happen. She kissed her daughter and left for her date.

*****

Slouched once again in an Adirondack chair, Eric swigged down a beer. The sky had deepened to indigo, and the opalescent brilliance of a million stars sparkled against it. He threw his head back and emptied his mind of all thoughts except the stars. As he charted the constellations, a vision of Jenna smiling at Baldwin from across a candle-lit table sauntered slow and easy into the frames of his thoughts. "Fuck," he whispered.

Eric hated Ash Baldwin the minute he saw the man, all pumped up like he'd eaten a double helping of steroids. With his close-cropped blond hair and white-blue eyes, he looked like someone who would show up at Central Casting when the call went out for Nazis. *And the car thing, what the hell was that?* Only a true dipshit would set the alarm in a date's driveway.

Ina arrived home at ten and proudly announced

she'd won a seventy-five dollar Round Robin. "I can finally get those leaky sinks fixed."

"Ina, why don't you let me pay for it."

The elderly woman drew her mouth into a smile that revealed small, discolored teeth. "Why that's right, I almost forgot. You think you're a rich movie star." The smile ripened to a hearty laugh. "Best one I've heard in years."

****

Jenna and Ash dined at the Heritage Manor. Though she had been there before, entering the elegant foyer with him added an unnerving and familiar spin to the experience. A fawning greeting from the *maître d'*, and servile behavior from both wine steward and waiter reminded her of another time and another man—Alan Stark and life in Los Angeles. Both of which she'd rather forget.

Once Ash seemed to have had his fill of the bootlicking, Jenna enjoyed her dinner. She and her date engaged in light conversation and Ash never questioned her about "Mike." It was later, while sipping dessert *apéritifs,* he laughed and said, "My sister-in-law thinks your friend is Eric Laine the actor. Comical, isn't it?"

Jenna returned an uneasy shrug. Even to her own ears, her nervous chuckle sounded forced. "Comical," she echoed the word back to him.

Reaching across the table, Ash lay his hand on hers, his thumb making a gentle pass along her skin. "I don't mean to sound like a snob, but your friend doesn't seem the type of person who would be in your circle."

This was far from the first time someone voiced such an opinion of Eric and it still blistered. "I don't exactly have a circle. But if I did, it would be wide."

"No offense meant. It's just that the man comes off a little rough around the edges."

Jenna lowered her lashes and her eyes stayed closed for more than a blink. Rough around the edges was an apt description of the Eric she once knew. He ambled into her head as surely as if he'd stepped into the room—mussed hair falling over a sun-kissed complexion, work-worn jeans, and eyes, though soft and dreamy, that could easily flash danger. Ash's hand, covering her own, felt noticeably soft and impotent.

"Where do you know him from?"

Slipping her fingers away, Jenna fiddled with her napkin. Outright lies had become a complication during her years of hiding, and sticking to shades of the truth made it easier to keep her stories straight. "I met him out west years ago, but we lost touch. I'm actually pretty shocked to see him here in Cromline."

"What does he do?"

It was the standard question among the affluent, and again Jenna was truthful. "He was a bar-back when I met him, then a carpenter. I don't think he's working at all right now."

Ash ran his fingers along his jaw and nodded as if satisfied. "Movie star, ha. I knew as soon as I saw him, Cheryl was mistaken."

An easy breath spilled from Jenna's mouth. She was familiar with the mindset of people who were rich. Ash's ego clearly didn't grasp the possibility of anyone else being successful enough to drive in his own lofty lane.

He was still laughing as he slipped his platinum card from his billfold and signaled for the waiter. "Eric Laine, of all people. Your friend probably has a good five inches on him. The movies always make actors look bigger than they really are."

"I read somewhere that Eric Laine is actually pretty tall." Jenna angled her lips into another lukewarm smile and damned herself for the impulse that made her rush to correct an unflattering, yet insignificant opinion of him.

Without looking at the check, Ash placed his card inside the vinyl sleeve. "They all lie in their biographies. Most movie stars are really pretty ordinary."

"I suppose."

As they were leaving the restaurant, the toadying manager rushed ahead to hold the door for them. At Jenna's house Ash parked and walked her to the door. He set his car alarm. Gracious and polite as always, Jenna thanked him for a wonderful dinner. "I'd invite you in for a nightcap but it's late, and I have a daughter who will have me up at dawn."

"I understand." Still, Ash lingered, drawing her into more conversation and slowly inching close. She offered her cheek as he closed in for a goodnight kiss. Though she'd expected a friendly peck, he pressed close, and a dry thickness plunged into her mouth.

The kiss was stingy, and he didn't explore too deeply. He closed his eyes and made a low moaning sound as if he were giving her his most passionate effort. Jenna's hands lay on his shoulders, but her own eyes remained open. She didn't push him away, nor did she loop her arms around him to draw him closer. The kiss persisted, never wavering in intensity. It was a long and mechanical pressing of one mouth to another. It hadn't repulsed nor impressed. When it ended, he gave Jenna a slow-eyed and lingering smile.

"I'll call you tomorrow," he said, and paced back to his car.

****

Eric pulled onto Redbud Lane just as Baldwin was ushering Jenna from his car. Neither of them appeared to hear his rental since its motor was no louder than a small swarm of bees. He cringed as he watched the scene on the porch—Baldwin holding Jenna awkwardly, his thick arms like overfilled sandbags.

Sulking, Eric hunkered low in his seat. *There are places for men who stalk their ex-wives—mental wards and prisons.*

He frowned as he watched the two bodies press close and the space between them disappear. He watched Baldwin's hand slide down Jenna's arm in a drawn out pour. He watched Baldwin travel back to his car striding proudly and smiling. Eric fought the urge to screech forward and broadside him.

A moment later, a vehicle with ramped-up hip-hop screaming from the windows pulled to the curb, a girl ran down the drive, hopped in the car, and it sped away. Eric loped to the porch and knocked on the door.

****

Thinking the sitter had forgotten something and returned, Jenna rushed to the door. "You," she whispered.

Eric stepped into the foyer. He took her waist in his hands and pulled her close. Jenna didn't try to wriggle away. She didn't shove or make any attempt to escape the steely grasp. Spellbound, she found herself caught in the blue fire of his stare. He walked, obliging her to match his easy footfalls but backward. Their stride was like a tango, slow and graceful, their bodies fitted perfectly together as they stepped along the floor. Their journey ended only when Jenna's shoulder blades came to rest against a wall.

The length of Eric's body made contact with hers at every plane. His chest, abdomen, and thighs pressed close as he held her against the cool plaster. Her heartbeat matched the pulse she could see beating at the hollow of his throat. She had never been more aware of the surging rise and fall of her own breasts.

He stroked her face with his thumb, starting at her temple and glancing from cheek to jaw. "Your boyfriend doesn't know how to kiss." Eric slipped his fingers through her hair and covered her mouth with his.

The slow and sensual mingling of lips and tongues seemed to last forever. His hands slid down her ribs and around her back, and he pulled her closer. Womanly softness molded easily against the muscle of his taut frame. His mouth was warm. The taste and fragrance of him was a sweet persuasion that roared into a fiery memory. Jenna put up no resistance and melted into him. When it ended, she could feel his heart pounding hard against her breasts.

"I'll never let another man kiss you again."

Then, as quickly as he entered the house he left.

Chapter Eleven

The ten o'clock church service seemed to freeze time as the minister rambled on about her journey from some personal crisis to God. It was meant to be uplifting, but Jenna paid little attention. Her thoughts were a mile away—two point three to be precise. In her mind she was still in her house, still pressed up against the wall near the stairs, Eric's hands and mouth upon her. She hadn't been kissed intimately in too long a time to even remember, and last night, she had been kissed by two different men within minutes of each other. She was still reeling from the last.

How could she have let herself respond to Eric like a love-struck schoolgirl? She was supposed to be over him. This wasn't *supposed* to happen.

It had been nine years, and he'd been married to another woman for six of them. How could he possibly believe he had any claim on her? He was obviously not the same man. He was Eric Laine the star now, a self-absorbed, arrogant son of a...Jenna pushed the curse word from her mind. She was, after all, in church.

The organist began the introduction for the next hymn and, books in hand, the congregation rose. Forgetting herself, Jenna sang *Lift High the Cross* in such clear tones she far surpassed the sound coming from the choir loft. When the hymn ended, a dumb-struck cluster of her fellow parishioners, the minister, and even her own daughter looked at her as though a halo had suddenly materialized above her head.

****

Ina Cummings was busy rolling out piecrust when Eric jogged down the stairs whistling. "Pour yourself a cup of coffee. There's biscuits and gravy on the stove, help yourself."

As Ina continued kneading and rolling out dough, Eric piled his plate high with food. "I'm going to get fat if I keep eating like this."

"You can have your personal trainer pound you into shape when you get back to Hollywood."

The fork dripping with the creamy sausage mixture stopped halfway between Eric's plate and his mouth.

Ina lifted gray eyebrows. "Supermarket, sonny. I go shopping after church." She wiped dough residue from her fingers and picked up a copy of *The Inquisitor*. "That *is* you on the cover, isn't it?"

Eric intentionally stretched his mouth wide enough to expose his back molars. He winked. "I told you I was a big star."

"Bah. You're no Troy Donohue, but I suppose you might look passable up on the screen."

Shrugging, he winked again. "It's a living."

Ina picked up a coffee pot, an old-school percolator with a glass bubble on top, and poured. "So, do you want to tell me what the hell you're doing here?"

Sobering, Eric looked at Ina. He studied the abundant integrity in her eyes and the discerning wisdom sketched into every line and fold of her face. "I already did." Then he told her more of the story. He told her all of it.

****

Jenna pulled into her driveway to find her childhood, best friend Randi Freed-Stouffer hauling enough clothes from the back of her minivan to last a month.

"Randi!" Jenna screamed, rushing to embrace her friend. "What are you doing here?" She pushed her an arm's length back, as concern momentarily replaced her delight. "Is everything okay?"

"Fine, everything's fine…with me. I came here for you."

"It's under control."

"Hmm." Randi huffed before turning to sweep Janie into her arms. "There's my girl." Hugging tightly, she swung her in a circle. "Be a pal and bring that bag in for your old auntie. Careful, it's heavy."

Janie rolled her eyes and scrunched her nose. "It's got wheels."

As the child trundled the bag to the door, Randi turned to Jenna and crossed her arms like a sentry. "Well?"

"Well, what?"

"You know very well, well what."

The two friends were so close they spoke in a personal code, one in which the topic of conversation never needed to be referenced by name."

"Why, Jen, why did you…"

"I didn't. He did."

"But you did it back, and…"

"Oh, for God's sake, it was a kiss, one lousy kiss."

Randi shook her head. "A kiss you babbled on about for two hours on the phone last night."

Reaching down, Jenna lifted a small carryon. "It was late and I had some wine at dinner. You know how I get."

She opened and closed her empty hand like a shadow puppet. "I ramble. It's no big deal."

"The man who broke your heart just barged back into your life. It is a very big deal. And FYI, wine doesn't make you ramble. It makes you curse like a sailor."

In the guest room, Randi dumped her things onto the bed. Jenna wondered by the amount of clothing going into the closet and dresser if her friend ever intended to leave.

"My mom will be watching the kids during the day. She's usually at my house telling me how to raise them anyway, so she'll be right at home. She'll probably redecorate while I'm gone."

Once Randi was settled in, the two friends spent the rest of the day doing the usual—talking about their children, trolling social media to look at pictures, and catching up on hometown gossip.

"Annabelle Walker lives here? And she's fat! There is a God," Randi said.

"She's nice, not like the Annabelle we knew. And by the way, I said she was heavier than in high school. Fat is offensive."

"Jesus Christ! Eric Laine *and* Annabelle Walker?" Randi stabbed the end key on Jenna's laptop to close out the Pinehill High, 1999, Good-bye 20th Century page. "I didn't get here a minute too soon."

****

The next morning, dragging tail from too many glasses of wine and too many lectures from Randi, Jenna crept into the kitchen. At the stove her friend was mixing pancake batter and humming. "You're such a lightweight," she said as Jenna plopped into a chair.

"It's barely *light* out."

"I have two kids under the age of five. Not getting up before six is like sleeping in."

Tired and grouchy, Jenna shuffled to the coffee maker. Two kisses, two nights of drinking, and a night of tossing and turning had resulted in only *two* hours of sleep. Back in her chair, she slouched and sipped, glaring through one eye at her friend. Petite, perky, already-showered-and-dressed-at-six-am, Randi Freed-Stouffer was humming, cooking, and at the moment, pissing Jenna off. But it wasn't her friend's energy that rankled so much as the very valid points she'd made the night before.

"Eric Laine is not the same person you were married to, Jen. He's a big star and probably has a big ego to match."

"As soon as he became famous, he married another woman."

"Don't ever forget the things he said to you the night Janie was born."

Throughout her lecturing, Randi never seemed to have a problem with the fact that Jenna never told Eric he was a father.

How were you supposed to tell him? By writing a fucking fan letter?

Randi, still humming what Jenna identified as a nettlesome song from a children's show, served pancakes and took over the job of getting Janie off to school. Jenna kissed her daughter goodbye and trudged upstairs to shower.

Later, through a downpour of spring rain, she and Randi drove to the shop. Around noon, Eric walked through the door.

Jenna introduced him to Randi, who for all of her

tough talk, still acted like a smitten fan and fidgeted like a schoolgirl when he took her hand to shake it.

"Jen used to talk about you so much, I feel like I already know you."

"I…I'm just going to have a look around the store," Randi said. As she walked away, she made a gesture with her fist that said, "be firm, hold your ground." Jenna put on a serious face and answered by making the okay signal with her thumb and forefinger. She and Eric walked to her office in the back.

With her arms folded, she leaned against her desk, her posture intentionally stern. *The kiss meant nothing. It meant nothing.* She cleared her throat and swept the "nothing" from her mind. "Eric, don't you realize if you stay here people are going to notice you? Someone is going to make the connection and realize who I used to be. I value my privacy. You have to leave."

"Not until we settle up."

"All right, but now isn't the time. There's too much media focus on you right now. Go home. *Settle* your own affairs first, and let me worry about mine."

His head pivoted around the room. Jenna's office was an intimate space with a velvet couch similar to the one he'd found her sleeping on the night they met. She saw his eyes settle there and moved as far away as possible. "Wipe the grin off your face."

He nodded. "I'm here strictly for business. I've been sitting on a lot of money that belongs to you. Money for your daughter, too."

His daughter. Jenna felt her eyes expanding to the size of hula hoops. It was how she'd look when her body was found after her stress-induced heart attack.

"My…my daughter, why?"

"Because she was born Jane Marie Laine and I have a legal responsibility toward her."

A legal *right* to her was what he actually had. Jenna's stomach cramped. A stiff collar that restricts the ability to both breathe and swallow was suddenly tight around her throat.

She fought the pressure and willed herself to speak calmly. "I already told you, I don't want anything from you. I may not be as rich as I was, but I can take care of my child. I put money in a trust for her right after she was born." Jenna, the actress, was a model of serenity even though her conscience screamed. *Good God what the hell is wrong with you? You have to tell him the truth!*

She opened her mouth, her confession ready at her tongue, when Eric groaned and plowed his hands through his hair. The gesture was a foreboding of bad news. "I didn't come here today just to discuss money," he admitted. "*True Hollywood Scandals* is planning a feature about you."

Jenna felt her whole body chill as if hit by an arctic blast. Eric stood uniformly still and didn't resume speaking till she blinked. "The producer got it into his head to do a story about your disappearance after I announced I was getting divorced again. I'm sorry."

Poised stiff as a doll anchored to a display stand, she stood frozen except for the steady curl and uncurl of her fists. "Let me get this straight. I'm going to be the topic of a 'whatever happened to' documentary because of you? Some sleaze cable show is going to report everything that happened a decade ago. They're going to drag up Mark and the whole filthy mess because of you?" Jenna slapped him. "Get out of my life. Once and for all please just get the hell out of my life!"

Chapter Twelve

Eric felt as pained and exhausted as if he'd been beaten up. The only person in the world he truly cared about was the person he always managed to hurt. He didn't blame Jenna for slapping him.

He pulled into Ina's mud-soaked driveway. Rain that customarily cleared away soot and grime from country roads did nothing to improve the appearance of the Cummings' residence. The downpour splattered mud and crumbling concrete into her flower beds and soaked a good part of the foundation because the ancient gutters leaked. Old, rotted wood absorbed the moisture like a sponge, and he had to push forcefully on the front door to open it.

Ina was at her desk, a massive block of oak, old and magnificently detailed. By a window a steady plink of water dripped from the molding and into a large glass bowl. She was intently studying a piece of paper in her hand but looked above the wire-rimmed glasses perched on her nose when she saw him. "How'd it go?"

"Not real well. She threw me out of her store."

"Today's not your day then. Looks like I'm going to have to throw you out of here too."

Eric stepped around a puddle accumulating at the base of another window to make his way to where his distracted landlady sat. He glanced at the paper in her trembling hand. "That bad news?"

"The bastards have condemned my house."

He carefully pried the notice from her wrinkled fingers to read it. *So, Ash Baldwin was a scumbag of the first order*. He'd gotten his good old boys to do his dirty work for him. Ina would have no choice but to sell the land, and Ash, Eric was sure, would not be offering top dollar.

He knelt at the foot of her chair and took her hand. The palm was callused but the back thin-skinned and blue-veined. It was cold. "Listen to me. They can't force you out until you have a chance to make the repairs. They have to give you some time. Let me—"

"No." Wisps of white hair escaped bobby pins as she shook her head. Her remarkably clear green eyes met his. "Son, my family has owned this property for more than a hundred and fifty years. We've never had to resort to charity to keep it. I won't start now."

"What about your children? You did say you had kids."

"Two." She began to sniffle. "My son has four little ones and a big mortgage. I can't ask him to help me out. My daughter is divorced and has a son in college." Ina bowed over in her seat and sighed. "I don't imagine I'll be leaving any of them anything to speak of…not even this run-down place."

Eric rubbed the hand enveloped between both of his gently. He looked toward one of the tall windows and at the rain beating against the glass. It was a dreary day, gray and bleak…fitting. The town's big wigs, cowards all of them, were going to let self-interest and greed run a little old lady out of the only home she had ever known. An entire family legacy was going to be leveled so the upwardly mobile could improve their scores on the back nine. *And golf is supposed to be the sport of gentlemen.*

Eric watched more rain patter against the window and sighed. He was unsure of what lay ahead between himself and Jenna. He was even less sure of his divorce's outcome. One thing of which he *was* certain was that next year, when the golfers finished their day on the links, they would be bringing home fresh herbs and apple pie from the quaint little farmhouse *next* to Baldwin Ridge.

****

Randi rushed back into the store with a cup of chai tea she bought from the gourmet café two doors down. "Drink this, you don't need any more caffeine."

"*True Hollywood Scandals.*" Jenna scrubbed at her face and groaned as if needles were jabbing the backs of her cheekbones. "They'll have a truckload of old footage from ten years ago and will report every bit of dirt—my assault, Eric's trial, Mark's lies about our supposed affair… How the hell am I supposed to shield Janie from all of that?"

"Tell her the truth. All the sacrifices you've made were for her. She'll understand."

The bell over the door chimed and a customer stepped in. Jenna called out a fainthearted welcome. A woman, wearing the Cromline mom uniform of beige slacks and cardigan, grabbed a basket and padded far down the aisle.

"Will she?" Jenna's whisper was barely audible as she tugged Randi behind the counter. "Will she really understand that I ran away because I thought her father was a rapist. Will she understand that even after I found out the truth, I still kept her from her real dad?"

Randi placed her arm around Jenna's shoulder and

squeezed. The two friends stood with blank expressions on their faces as the customer approached. The woman set pink sunglasses edged with crystal beads and a palette of iridescent eyeshadows by the register. Jenna tallied up the sale, wrapped the items in tissue, and nodded her thanks.

Rushing to the door, Randi engaged the lock. "You know how I feel about Eric Laine, but you have to tell him the truth. You have no choice. Janie needs to be protected. Mr. Hotshit A-lister doesn't deserve her, but you have to let him acknowledge her and end all the speculation."

Overcome by trembling, Jenna wrung her hands. "And then what? I share custody of her with him? Pack her up to spend Christmas in California with a man she doesn't even know? Expose her to an invasion of paparazzi?"

"It would be more devastating for Janie to think Mark Chambers is her father."

The hair on Jenna's arms stood on end. Though nine years had passed, the mention of the name still made her skin feel like it was crawling from her bones. Her windpipe was suddenly collapsing from the pressure of her esophagus contracting, and she gagged.

She bolted from behind the counter and ran to the bathroom where she retched her tea into the sink. Randi stood behind her, smoothing her hair back as she continued to heave. Blindly Jenna reached for the faucet and rinsed her mouth. She spat, still shivering, dread still clutching at her stomach. Outside a car door slammed, and Jenna quickly splashed cool water on her face and dried it with a paper towel.

"Do I look okay?"

"Fine, fine...just..." Randi pantomimed fluffing her hair, and Jenna gave a toss of her head. She wiped beneath her eyes with her knuckles.

Janie was rapping at the door. "Why is the shop locked?" she called out while continuing to tap her small fists against the glass.

Randi opened the door, but Janie, who usually skipped, animated and cheerful, everywhere, walked in with her head bowed in a solemn arc.

"Hey, kiddo, you okay?" Jenna asked.

The child's glum expression was telling, and what little warmth Jenna felt faded away as she noticed faint blotches of red on her daughter's nose and cheeks. "What's wrong? You look like you've been crying."

"Am I a bastard?"

"A what!" The expression "jaw dropping" was an accurate illustration as Jenna stood with her mouth agape. "Where did you get an idea like that?"

"T...Tiffany Baldwin."

On a solitary and angry breath, Jenna rounded her fingers into fists tight enough to make her hands cramp. "What exactly did little Miss Tiffany say?"

Janie angled her head at the floor. "She said kids who are born without fathers are bastards."

Could the day get any worse? Jenna relaxed the steely curl of her hands and folded her arms across her chest. "Janie, kids born without fathers are only bastards in old movies and Charles Dickens' novels. It's the twenty-first century."

"But Tiffany said—"

"Screw Tiffany!"

"Mom?" Janie's sniffling turned into a laugh of delight and her eyes popped wide. "Can I say that to her the next time she's mean to me? Can I? Can I?"

"I'm afraid not, baby." Jenna pulled her daughter into her arms and rocked. "When someone is mean to you, you don't make it worse by sinking to their level."

Snorting her frustration, Janie shrugged out of her mother's arms. "So I'm supposed to just let Tiffany, Amber, Britney, other Britney, and new Britney all call me names?" Janie marched off to the office, dragging her backpack behind her. "Maybe if I at least knew something about my dad I could shut them up."

****

After dinner, Jenna left her daughter in Randi's care. Though looking at Randi, sipping wine, teary eyed and angry, Jenna wondered who was caring for whom. She drove to the Baldwin Estate, her fingers holding tight to the steering wheel as she passed between tall pillars. At the top of a long driveway, the house sat in graceful splendor amid huge oak and maple trees. It was a monolith of white clapboard, scaling windows, and glossy black shutters. Gas lanterns flickered on both sides of the double doors. Still seething, Jenna strode to the entrance and jabbed the doorbell with her thumb as if she were poking out an eye. Chimes rang out like high mass at Notre Dame.

Declining an announcement, Jenna brushed past the maid. The Baldwin family, Ash and Mother Baldwin included, were gathered around the dining table.

Cheryl began to rise. "I beg your pardon?"

Her mother-in-law held up a wrinkled hand laden with jewelry and motioned for her to stay seated. She addressed Jenna. "Young woman, do you make a habit of barging into people's homes and disrupting their dinner?" The elderly woman articulated each consonant like the snap of a whip.

Unfazed, Jenna snapped back. "Only when one of those people spreads nasty rumors that make my daughter cry." Jenna shot Tiffany a loathsome glower before returning her attention to Cheryl. "Did you know your daughter is telling her friends Janie is a bastard?"

"A...wha...what? Tiffany!" Cheryl appeared genuinely shocked. "Why would you say such a thing?"

Lifting one of the three silver forks at her place setting, Tiffany Baldwin stabbed a baby carrot from her salad plate and tucked it into her mouth. "I heard it from you." She pointed to Cheryl and gnashed the tuber between her teeth. "You said it at your luncheon the other day. You said Mrs. Black didn't seem to have an ex-husband and that Janie Black was probably illegitimate, a 'bastard' baby."

Jenna crossed her arms and aimed fire at Cheryl. "Don't you ever say anything about my daughter to your gaggle of gin swigging friends ever again. Or do you want the entire PTA to know what a vicious gossip you are?"

Mother Baldwin's salad fork hit her plate with an angry clatter, and she turned toward Cheryl. "I do hope there is an explanation for this." Her aim then settled on her younger son. "Teddy, I've warned you to keep your family in line. I'll not have these embarrassing scenes."

Ash also fixed heated eyes on his sister-in-law. He slapped his linen napkin onto the table and rose from his seat. "Jenna, let me see you to the door."

She offered a curt apology to his mother and walked with him. "I'm sorry I interrupted your meal. I didn't mean to make such a scene."

In another lifetime, she had been the focus of many,

and had promised herself never to be at the center of one again. Blinding anger had made her break that vow.

Ash inched closer and laid his hands on her shoulders. "Tell me what I can do?" His voice was steeped in concern.

"It's all right. I think I made my point."

He exhaled a tired breath. "I'm not going to let my sister-in-law ruin our friendship. I value it." His hands were still lightly resting on her arms, more caressing than touching. "I apparently didn't make myself clear the other night. I guarantee she'll never say anything about you or your daughter again. And as for my darling niece…I'll leave her to Mother."

Chapter Thirteen

If Eric added up the price of his suit, tie, imported shoes, sunglasses, and wristwatch, it would amount to a higher figure than the one Ina needed to borrow. Stepping into the First National Bank of Newton, Eric Laine was in full-successful, no-nonsense, I get what I want at once, regalia. With his expensive clothing and a clean shave, there would be no mistaking him for a redneck named Mike. A woman who was sitting at a desk and sifting through a stack of papers, looked up as he approached. Her mouth yawned open into a slack O.

He smiled. "Excuse me, I'd like to speak with a loan officer."

A robbery would have caused less of a commotion as all the tellers gawked in his direction. Customers did the same, their eyes widely regarding him as if he were the grand finale at a fireworks display. The manager rushed over and led him into his cubicle and away from the dumb struck group.

"Have a seat please. Sorry for the stares, but I don't think we've ever had a celebrity just wander in here. Have you moved to the area?"

"No, but I have business to discuss. I'd like to secure a loan for a friend over in Cromline. She's having a tough time getting one at the bank there. I'm going to transfer funds to an account, and I'll act as guarantor. I want it kept confidential though."

Eric's next stop was to a car dealer. He made a quick call to the agent handling the insurance for Nick's limousine company; and in less than two hours, Eric drove off the lot with a brand new pickup truck. After a shopping spree at The Home Warehouse, he returned to Ina's with enough plumbing supplies, hardware, and power tools in the bed of the truck to not only repair a house but to practically build one.

The next day, more supplies were delivered, and he set to work at once. Though climbing a forty-foot extension ladder was not really where he wanted to be, he decided to assess the roof's condition anyway. Heights had never bothered him until he almost fell to his death while performing a stunt in a movie. Remembering the near fatal accident turned his thoughts to Jenna and how he'd awakened to find her at his bedside. He'd been in such pain and so lost he'd embraced slipping into the shelter of death. Then he heard her begging him to stay and he forced his eyes open. It was her face, her beautiful face that offered him hope.

Why the hell didn't I look for you after I got better? Why did I let another four years pass?

He stepped from the top rung of the ladder and on to the roof. It was a disaster. Moisture had rotted the wood beneath the slate, and he'd have to re-sheath as well as shingle. The house was one hundred percent Victorian in design, complete with peaks and turrets, and framing that went every which way but straight. Sitting at an angle that aligned his body with the steep pitch, Eric eyed more of the roof. Green moss and chalky lichen gathered in the seams, and chimneys listed like a Jenga tower. He smiled. Working with his hands would be a gratifying reminder of the job that had given him his first taste of self-esteem.

He climbed down to inspect the rest of the house, but he already knew it was in no better shape. Pipes leaked, the plaster was a web of cracks, floorboards creaked, and the foundation was crumbling. *You'll be in Cromline for a while, pal.* It wasn't an unhappy circumstance. He'd be near Jenna even if she wasn't speaking to him.

****

Bree swept through the doorway of her Sutton Place apartment while a lobby attendant, carrying her travel bags, followed. Bree had sets of posh luggage in every designer flavor. Once in her apartment, she folded onto one of four sofas in the airy living room. The flight from L.A. and the limousine drive from LaGuardia through midtown traffic had been a drain. She called to her maid and demanded a drink. "Martini. And make sure you chill the glass."

She picked up her phone to make some calls. The first would be to her New York masseuse. His hands were like steel, and he knew the exact spots to touch to ease her anger-born tension. Other than treating herself to life's finery, there was nothing Bree enjoyed more than giving her husband's hard earned money to another man.

She often traveled East and was a fixture at both Spring and Fall Fashion Week, The Met Gala, and the opening of every new Broadway show that proved difficult to get tickets for. A position in the Hollywood hierarchy was always boosted by an appearance at exclusive spots in Manhattan, though for the love of

God, Bree could never understand why. She hated New York.

A prickle of irritation worked its way into anger. Without Eric at her side, any events she attended wouldn't include a red-carpet visit. She paced the apartment looking for signs of him, but their building's doorman already told her he hadn't been there lately. Their pilot hadn't deposited him in any of the nearby private airports, and his manager hadn't heard from him.

Still, Bree suspected Eric was nearby. Her investigator had a possible lead on Angel living in a town north of the city. If Bree knew anything at all about her husband, it was that he still carried the torch for the former teen queen. He was also intent upon giving her the money from Jewel.

She scrolled the contacts in her phone. In it she had the numbers of photographers she occasionally tipped off so she and Eric would be spotted coming and going from L.A. hotspots. Most found them without her intel anyway, but Bree left nothing to chance. It was PR gold to be seen.

"Which one?" She stopped tapping her finger against the screen and smiled. The choice was obvious— Larry Belka, a sneaky little shit who'd jumpstarted his career by harassing Angel. Bree hit his contact number, and after two rings the loud hack of choking sounded in her ear. "Belka photography."

The scratch of a match ignited, and she could hear him dragging on a cigarette. "This is Bree Laine."

"Well I'll be damned. It's been a while. To what do I owe the honor?"

"I'd like to hire you."

A draw of smoke and wheezing laugh stalled the

conversation. Larry eventually cleared his throat and spoke. "I have a pretty tight schedule, lots of photo shoots on my calendar. But I guess I could squeeze in some freelance work."

"Don't play hard to get, Larry. Your photo shoots are taken with a telephoto lens from behind a bush. I don't want to use you for your critical eye. I want to hire you because you'll go anywhere and do anything to get a shot."

A tide of liquid audibly bubbled in his chest, and Larry laughed again. "And I always do."

Bree shuddered as the oily whistle of his lungs traveled through the line. "You also have a knack for getting pictures of people at their worst."

"Not you and your hubby. I sold nothing but beefcake shots of Laine to the tabloids. I made him look great, real handsome."

"He is handsome, you ass." Bree shifted her eyes to her dresser and to an early headshot of Eric she'd framed. Of the thousands of movie star images she'd seen through the years, none had ever glowed so brilliant as his.

"I read that you two split up. You plan on setting him up? You want me to catch him in the act with some broad?"

Gritting her teeth, Bree seethed. "No, Larry, I absolutely do not want pictures of Eric and another woman. What I want Larry, are pictures of his ex. You remember her, don't you? Angel, your one-time favorite subject."

Even with the obstacle of cell phone static and the gummy burbling of Belka's vocal cords, the shift in his tone was immediate and direct. "She's been in the wind for a long time. Any idea how I'm supposed to find her?"

"I'm working on it. I'm also working on finding her baby daddy."

"Chambers?" Larry almost sang the name. "You planning a little family reunion?"

"Just make sure you can be ready to travel at a moment's notice. I'll be in touch." Bree ended the call.

Chapter Fourteen

A waiter in starchy apron and bow tie approached Jenna's table to tell her that her lunch tab had been taken care of. From the bar, Ash Baldwin raised his glass, smiled, and nodded.

"Very handsome," Randi whispered, tipping her head close to Jenna's.

There was no disputing the eye-catching appeal of the fine features and square boned symmetry of his face. Still, Jenna shrugged. "He is, but I wish he hadn't picked up our check. I don't want him thinking there's more going on between us than there is."

Though smiling, Randi's eyes were the same narrow slits all mothers use to wordlessly scold their children. Jenna returned the silent glower and stood. "You know why. Things are just too complicated right now to start something new."

"Your life has been complicated since you were fifteen. You can't keep postponing it."

"Thanks for the reminder."

"Ladies, join me for a drink," Ash insisted, as they approached. "I just had a business lunch and have some time to kill before I head back to the office."

"We'd love to," Randi answered before Jenna had a chance to decline. They ordered drinks, and Ash placed his hand, warm and easy, against Jenna's back. He nattered on about his country club, detailing the particulars to Randi as though she was a potential investor. In turn, she hung on his every word while nodding her approval. Jenna stood silently by with a half grin on her face. Her interest in Ash was quickly waning.

"Ladies, you've made a lonely bachelor's day brighter, but I'm afraid I do have to get back to work."

His hand remained comfortably assigned to Jenna's back as the threesome exited the bistro. Outside, looking as untroubled as the valances fluttering at the bottom of the window awnings, Eric stood leaning against a small white car.

"Isn't that your *friend* over there?" Ash's tone was so abrupt his teeth clicked together.

Jenna sent Eric a wide-eyed glower that he returned with a quick wink and lopsided smile. He was dressed in jeans, mud caked at the hems, a plaid flannel shirt, sunglasses, and a dusty Tractor Warehouse cap.

Ash's stride was a deliberate march as he crossed the lot to Eric resting against the subcompact. "Do you have business here?"

"Nothing that's any of *your* business."

Ash swept one arm wide in a suggestive piss on his territory. "On the contrary, I own this building, the whole block to be exact."

Eric lifted his shoulders. "Am I supposed to care?"

Two knotty lumps formed below Ash's ears as he gnashed his teeth. "You're a 911 call away from being removed from my street for loitering, so yes, you should."

"Standing on a city road isn't a crime *or* an emergency as far as I know." Eric crooked his head in the direction of the restaurant. "I was thinking about going in for a bite."

Ash's stormy gray eyes sparked pleasure. "I doubt if you can afford the place."

As Eric opened his mouth to respond, Jenna put an end to the chest thumping. "Okay, boys, put them back in your pants." She tugged Eric away so they were out of earshot. "What the hell are you doing here?"

"I saw your car and wanted to say hello."

"Didn't it occur to you," she asked, aiming her gaze at Ash's convertible, "that I might be with someone?"

Eric coughed as if to suppress a laugh. "Um…no, no it didn't."

"I'm late for a meeting," Ash called out brusquely. He started his car and made a sharp U-turn, screeching to a halt inches from where they stood. "There's a town ordinance that prohibits cars from parking curbside overnight. This is an upscale town, and we don't want rinky-dink economy cars littering our streets. You might want to rethink hanging around where you don't belong." After waving to Jenna, he revved the motor and sped away.

She watched the car's departure, then turned to face Eric. Smiling, she offered him a limpid gaze, and sighed. He responded with an easy grin, but as he was about to reach for her, she slammed her hands into his chest. "Are you out of your fucking mind!"

He blinked and burst out laughing. "I see *someone* had wine with lunch."

Seething Jenna brought her fingers up close to his face as if she might claw at it. "Now I'm convinced you've been blasted with flashbulbs too many times. What the hell was that?"

"Jen, I was just—"

"Just what? Stopping by to ruin my afternoon?

Maybe announce your presence to a few more of my neighbors?"

He rocked on his heels, his hands stuffed in his pockets. "I was just going to turn this car back in to the rental place."

Jenna made a sound like a growl. "Here's an idea. Keep it and drive it back to Los Angeles." She grabbed Randi's arm, stormed over to her own car, and drove away.

****

After his lunch, Ash went directly to the weight room at his club and bench pressed till his shoulders and lats bunched tight. Once done, he went to the steam room to wait for his cronies to arrive for his meeting.

A town board member, whose ancient muscles were withered by time, sat swathed in terry cloth and gasping for breath. "I can't stay in here for very long."

"Then tell me what I want to hear and you can take your shriveled carcass out of here."

The elderly gentleman pulled his towel tightly around his wizened frame and took another shallow gulp of fog before speaking. "We agreed to condemn the Cummings house. But before the building is razed, she has to be given an opportunity to make repairs. State law." He settled back against the wall and panted, his face a shade of violet so close to blue, death would barely alter it.

The bank manager, the man whose lips were always in close proximity to Ash's butt, spoke. "We turned down her loan application."

"Good." Ash pressed the tips of his blunt fingers together as if deciding on his next chess move. "Has she been given an eviction notice?"

Chief of police Willy Parks pressed a towel to his face. "Process server got her in the market just the other day." The former high school jock and longtime chum of Ash's moved his towel to the current of sweat running down his thick neck. He leisurely dabbed the drops of perspiration beading on a shaggy matting of chest hair. "She's only got thirty days to complete the repairs and we hit her hard."

The building inspector nodded. "She'd have to come up with a ton of money to fix up the place."

Ash smiled his victory. "Excellent. Boys, you've made my day." He turned to the elderly board member who sat wilted against the sauna's teak wall. "Christ, get the hell out of here before you have a stroke."

"Thank you, Ash," the little man said as he skittered away.

The building inspector chimed in. Despite the sweltering vapor, he looked pale—the messenger about to be killed. "You may still have a problem. I stopped by your development yesterday. When I passed the Cummings' place, I saw some guy up on her roof. He had a compressor revved up and was shooting nails into the roof like he was a house on fire."

Ash fixed his eyes into such an angry stare, he never blinked when salty beads of sweat leaked into them. "Did you ask to see his contractor's license?"

"You don't have to be licensed in New York."

"What about a permit?"

"You only need one for new construction or additions."

Ash stood and walked the steam room in the slow trudge of an ogre stomping everything in its path. "I've got every damned contractor in the area working on my club. Who the hell is this guy?"

"I don't think he's from around here," the inspector said. "Something familiar about him though."

"Well. Do you know him or not?"

The building inspector tapped his hands against the wooden bench, then snapped sweaty fingers together though they made no sound. "The movies!"

"You saw him at the movies?"

"No. I saw him *in* the movie. The guy fixing the Cummings house looked like the actor in the movie."

"God damn that son of a bitch." Ash cursed in a voice final and condemning. "He's going to be one sorry bastard if he continues stepping on my toes."

****

An hour later, Ash was in his construction trailer, one hand steadily slapping against his desk. Willy Parks stepped through the narrow doorway, and a clamor of noise accompanied him—the roar of compressors, steady thwap of nail guns, and the strident cry of power saws slicing through lumber. Yards away, similar sounds indicated another project.

"This is my town, and no one crosses me. That guy is either a ballsy son of a bitch, or just plain stupid. What did you find out about him?"

Willy stepped around a small table stacked high with brochures and dropped into the swivel chair across from Ash's desk. "I snuck around back. There's a brand new pick-up loaded with equipment in the yard. I ran the plate. Truck's registered to a limousine company in Brooklyn."

Ash snorted. "Brooklyn? That redneck doesn't strike me as a guy from Brooklyn…or someone who's ever seen the inside of a limo."

Leaning back in the chair, Willy stroked his jaw. "Could be a scam artist. Guys hit up small towns pretending to look for work. They get their marks to pay for equipment, make a few repairs, and then disappear with a whole lot of gear to hock. Seniors are the easiest targets."

Ash nodded at the chief's suggestion. "You might be on to something. Anyone can file for an LLC, and the limo company could be a front." He stabbed a finger onto his desk blotter. "But if it isn't, I still have a problem. I want you to find out who the guy is. I also want you to find out what his relationship is with Jenna Black. Something about the two of them doesn't add up."

****

Day-drinking was not an activity Jenna had ever mastered. She sat behind her counter close to nodding off. From tip to toe Eric lingered—a sweep of sun-streaked hair, worn jeans snug over taut thighs, broad shoulders, and as always, his crystal blue eyes glowing in the afternoon sun. If she were to fall asleep in her chair he'd slip into her dreams.

The door to the shop opened and Ash walked in. "I don't suppose you expected to see me again so soon." His ready smile and words seemed a forced spill of charm.

Picking up a mug from the counter, she raised it. "No...actually I didn't. I'm still trying to clear the cobwebs from the drinks I had at lunch."

Ambling close, he straightened his tie and shrugged. "I have to admit this isn't just a social call. I hate to ask, but how well do you know your friend Mike? What's his deal?"

Jenna's heart began to power walk, and she took a

long breath to slow the escalating rhythm. "Deal? I'm not sure what you mean."

Ash dipped his head as if he was unsettled by his own curiosity. "He's um…doing some work over at Ina Cummings' place."

"That little farm by your development? I…I don't understand. What do you mean work?"

"He's fixing the place. Or at least making it look as though he is. I'm only asking you about him because I'm fond of the old girl. I'd hate to see her become victim to a con artist."

Jenna laid her cup on the counter. Food, wine, an aperitif, and now coffee were all fighting for space in her stomach. "What would make you think he's conning her?"

Ash's expression softened more, his complexion almost glowing an earnest, boyish peach. "Targeting senior citizens has become an epidemic. Grifters find a vulnerable senior, offer to do some 'work,' collect the money, and disappear. Your friend's appearance fits the narrative."

While forcing herself to appear indifferent, Jenna instinctively wanted to spit on Ash Baldwin for having the nerve to think Eric would steal from anyone. "My friend isn't a grifter or a thief. He's probably just trying to help her."

"But he isn't." The statement was firm. "She's way behind on her taxes and is going to lose the place anyway. I offered her a good deal and now your friend is making her squander what little money she has left."

Yawning moments of silence created an uneasy atmosphere. The air seemed charged with it. Jenna steered her sight to anything but the challenging glint in

Ash's eyes.

"Why Ina?" His concerned tone blanketed a demand.

"I don't know."

But Jenna did. Her heart knew why. Rich or poor, movie star, bartender, or carpenter, Eric was still trying to save people. It was his nature, and he'd been doing it since he was a kid.

****

Over midmorning coffee the next day, Jenna explained the idiosyncrasies of her cash register to Randi. "It has a mind of its own sometimes. If it rebels against you, just hit this button on the side and the drawer will open." She gulped the remains of her double mocha latte and scolded herself for getting so caffeine-buzzed right before her errand.

"Are you sure you know what you're doing?" Randi asked.

"Yes, I have to convince Eric to leave Cromline. I have to tell Janie everything, and I don't know how she'll take the news. It would be best for her sake if he isn't around so she doesn't feel any pressure. After it all sinks in with her, then I'll tell him." She crossed her fingers. "Wish me luck."

The ten-minute ride to the Cummings house gave Jenna a small opportunity to rehearse what she would say, but when she arrived her nerves still pricked the surface of her skin. She'd spent half her life plagued by the anxiety fueled muscle spasms that made goosebumps cover a person's body. She cranked her car's heat to fight the chill and then pulled into a driveway so bereft of asphalt someone could fall lost into the gaps. Slipping quietly from her car, she followed the sound of rock and roll to the back.

Eric was hunched over a rotted stairway and pulling at the treads with the claw end of a hammer. As Jenna watched him work, a decade easily faded away. He was dressed in overalls but wore no shirt beneath. His strong arms and shoulders were sun kissed copper. The familiar sight was like a flash of seductive memories that almost made Jenna forget her reason for being there. "Hi," was all she could manage to say.

A smile lured the corners of his mouth upward, and he leaned back on his haunches, his hammer dangling from his fingers. He stood and wiped dirt from his hands on the thighs of his pants. "Hello. I was just thinking about taking a break…as long as that slave driver I'm working for doesn't mind."

Ina Cummings hovered close by, half hidden behind a forsythia bush. Unfurled yellow blossoms and green buds weren't in bloom enough to disguise her busy pink housecoat. Eric winked and her face scrunched into an embarrassed looking pout. "I wasn't eavesdropping," she insisted. "I came over to offer your guest some of my freshly brewed iced tea. I put mint leaves in it, and it's very refreshing." She glared at Eric and crooked her head toward an outdoor faucet with a steady stream of water spilling from it. "You can suck on the end of that rusty spigot over there if *you're* thirsty, wise ass."

"You're lucky I can work with the limited rations I'm on," he teased.

Feathery brows lifted high on her forehead. "Humph, I'll bet your dear old mama never fed you the way I do." She stalked away and Jenna wondered if the elderly woman knew how true the remark was. Eric's parents had never made caring for him a priority.

Sliding his hands into his pockets, he followed Ina's departure with his eyes and laughed. "She's a character, but I'm totally in love with her." He turned to Jenna, his expression wistful. "It's really good to see you."

"I can't stay long, but I need to speak with you. It…it's important."

"Good. It's time we talked."

Eric led Jenna to the patio, past rows of herbs and blooming perennials. The smell was intoxicating, the space as beautiful as anything featured in garden magazines. They stopped under a grape arbor, the knotty vines pinched back and just starting to sprout new growth. He inclined his head in the direction of a set of fussy wrought iron furniture.

"This was one of my first projects." He pulled one of the lacy patterned chairs out for her. "I scrubbed this stuff for hours with a wire brush. It's amazing what a little primer and some paint can do."

Given the care to the property, Jenna couldn't help but wonder if Mrs. Cummings really planned on selling the land. "It's beautiful. In fact everything back here is beautiful."

"It's a lifetime of work," Eric said. "Ina began her first garden with her mother when she was three. Every tree in the yard has some significance…milestones in her life—her christening, wedding, and the birth of her children. That huge maple on the far side of the house was planted after she lost her first tooth."

Ina returned with a pitcher of iced tea and cookies that were sugar coated drops fluffy as cotton balls. Her expression was that of a besotted girl, and Jenna could tell how fond the old woman was of Eric. Then again, his appeal touched most females. She watched Ina rush away and disappear behind a tall box hedge.

How out of place the house looked, Jenna thought. It was like the wreckage of an old fighter plane lost on an unchartered island—rusted and ruined—a black stain on an otherwise perfect piece of paradise.

"It won't be so bad when I finish fixing her up," Eric said. He'd answered her thoughts like only he could, and her stomach did a little flip. Everything about him was still so painfully familiar—his half smile, his posture, the way he held the glass as he brought the iced tea to his lips. Even the small bead of sweat glistening between his collarbones and trickling into his overalls stabbed her heart with a memory. His stare stayed fixed on her face, his eyes capturing hers for too many breaths, too many heartbeats. She took a sip of her drink and looked away. "How did you end up here?"

"Just driving around. Ina rents rooms, and it's a good place to lay low."

"Does she know who you are?"

He slowly nodded. "I told her about us…I guess I needed someone to talk to, and I trust her. She's like the grandma I never had."

Shaking her head, Jenna pinched between her eyes as though a pain had cuffed her from ice cream brain-freeze. "Being here doesn't make you as inconspicuous as you think. Ash knows you're fixing the house."

"Baldwin again huh?" Eric's expression dimmed like clouds that disappoint the day. He leaned back in his chair and crossed his arms. "I guess he's not too happy I'm helping her."

"But you aren't. He said she can't afford the taxes. So even if you fix her house, she's going to lose the land anyway."

Eric answered with a sound that was almost primal, a guttural hum. If he were an animal he'd be snarling. Jenna had witnessed an Eric who simmered with anger, his jaw clenched and fists rounded as he fought to restrain himself. She also knew there were times he'd lost the battle and fought. There had been a time in his life he'd needed to.

He cupped his iced tea, his fingers knotted around the glass. "Baldwin is lying. He had his boys in town hall take away her agricultural exemption and he made the bank manager turn down her loan." Eric glared and Jenna felt suddenly included in his ire. "Is Baldwin the reason you came over here? Did he ask you to tell me to stop working on the place?"

"No. Of course not."

"Good, because I'm not going to. He's trying to steal the property and that's the only reason she's in danger of losing it."

Jenna was silent, remembering the warm sincerity in Ash's voice when he declared his concern for the old woman. "Are you sure?"

"Very. Baldwin isn't a good guy. You might want to rethink your relationship with him."

Jenna's nervous hand wringing became a sudden and impatient finger tapping. "Relationship? With your track record? Bree Davis…Mark? Do you honestly think you're qualified to talk *relationships*?"

Gaging his expression Jenna knew she'd struck a nerve. Still, it was her own stomach that twisted as she imagined what characters filled his circle now. Was another version of Alan Stark a daily presence at Eric's California mansion. Was there a roll call of Hollywood hangers-on coming and going—suits, actors, militant PR reps…the press lurking at the gates? *My baby can't be a part of that.*

"Hire a contractor to finish up here. I need you to leave!"

Eric flinched as if her words were bits of debris blown by an unexpected gust of wind.

"What…is…wrong with you?"

"You…your life…my old one. It's all too complicated. I haven't told Janie anything about the past. She doesn't know any of it."

"Nothing?"

"Nothing."

He stood and walked around the small table to reach for her, but Jenna stood and took an immediate step back away from him.

"That's all the more reason I should stay," he said. "I was a part of everything that happened. I should be there to help you explain it all to her."

"No, no. I can't count on your help. Please just stay away."

She hurried down the crumbling drive. "Thank Mrs. Cummings for the cookies."

****

Eric rolled up the cord of his skill saw, set it aside for his next task, and swept a few errant nails into one of the pockets of his tool belt. Hours after Jenna scrambled out of the yard, he was still pounding away and going from project to project. Ina ambled over to where he was working and inspected the newly finished set of steps.

"All equal and up to code," he said.

Nodding, she smiled as a tender swell of pride lit her face. "You do nice work."

Though deflated, he managed to smile back and

wink. "I have a thing for my client."

She blushed scarlet. "Go on with your flirting."

Eric loped over to where he planned to dig a drainage ditch with Ina trailing after. "You plan on watching me all day?"

"If I'm in your way just say so, but it looks like you could use some company."

Removing his baseball cap, he slapped it against his leg and a shower of sawdust fell to the ground. His hands were calloused, and his overalls caked in dirt. Brand new work boots already showed wear. "I've had better days. I've had worse."

Ina eyed him head to toe. "I don't imagine this is how a movie star typically spends his days, good *or* bad."

"I guess I'm not a typical movie star."

A bit of warmth filled him. While still in a funk over Jenna's hasty departure, Ina's comment reminded him of how happy he was to be away from L.A. and anywhere else celebrities congregated. A-List clubs and events were asylums of bad behavior, and he'd viewed it from both sides. Most luminaries balked at paying for anything, bitched if they weren't seated at the right table, and treated staff like indentured servants. Now, as a part of the elite, Eric would sooner break his fingers than be a typical star and snap them for attention.

"Earth to Eric," Ina called. She was still standing next to him, a shovel in hand. "Where did you go? You looked lost in thought."

"Lost." He shrugged. "I suppose I am."

"Well then, knock off for today. You've earned a good meal." She laid the shovel down and reached over and gently placed her hand against his back. "And maybe a bit of advice from someone who's of an age to have some to spare."

****

"Is he packing his bags?" Randi was quick to ask as Jenna inched through the doorway of the store.

"No."

"Did you tell him about Janie?"

"No!" On the verge of tears, Jenna shook her head. "He thinks I'm crazy. Every time we come close to having a rational conversation I freak out and—"

"Hmph." Tapping a foot on the tile, Randi crossed her arms in a show of anger. "Maybe if he hadn't *freaked out* the night Janie was born, the two of you would still be—"

"All right." Jenna retrieved a bottle of ibuprofen from behind the counter and popped it open. She tossed two tablets into her mouth and swallowed. Looking bewildered and somewhat repulsed, Randi asked how she could swallow the pills without water.

"Ten years of tension headaches," Jenna answered while rubbing her temples.

"Why don't I run next door and get you some coffee."

Jenna waved the offer away. "I've had enough caffeine."

Randi flipped the "Closed" sign and locked the door. "Then let's talk."

The two friends went in the back and sat on the small couch in the office. Jenna's legs were curled beneath her, while Randi's were stretched out on a carton, recently delivered and unopened. "I'm going home for the weekend to see my husband and kids, then I'm coming back and staying until this mess of yours is resolved."

"Then you'll be staying with me forever."

Randi snorted. "As much as my mom loves my boys, I don't think she's up for that."

"More guilt. Thanks."

Jenna sank into the cushions. Her gaze wandered from the brass coat rack covered with boas and hats, to her desk piled high with boxes of makeup. Handbags and headbands, all covered with a rainbow of glass beads, were in cartons stacked against the wall. She had her own personal wardrobe department, all the trappings of a little girl's fantasy. Ten years away from the frames of celluloid and bright lights, and she was still surrounded by make believe. She dropped her face into her hands.

"Oh, Jen." Randi put her arms around her and hugged. "It'll be all right."

"How? I ran away like a coward and made a mess out of everything."

"You were not a coward. It took a tremendous amount of strength for you to go out into the world all alone with a tiny baby and—"

"—And I'm still alone." Jenna gulped back tears. "There were times I've been so lonely I couldn't stand it."

Patting her friend's head, Randi began to sniffle. "No. You have your family, and me, and Janie. You are *not* alone."

Jenna looked out through a wavy blur of tears. "But I'm still lonely. And Janie is too. I never let either one of us get too close to anyone. I've been so unfair to her." The words settled into hopeless sighs. "Janie is all I have, and she's going to hate me when she learns the truth."

Chapter Fifteen

Bree lit a cigarette and took a long drag as she sauntered out onto to the terrace of her New York penthouse. Her day would have been most women's dream—lunch at *LaVié*, and a private showing at a 7th Avenue design house so new and chic Milan was envious. Bree had her recently lifted butt kissed more than any other woman on the island of Manhattan. Her mood, however, was wretched. There was still no one who knew where her husband was.

She peered out at the oppressively gray, New York sky. Steel and mortar contained within a twenty square mile piece of rock was unnatural. How could Eric even think about abandoning his life at the top of the magnificent SoCal hills? "You're out there somewhere looking for her, aren't you?"

She flicked her cigarette over the balustrade. "Why the hell couldn't you ever get over her and love *me*?"

Bree's conversation with herself grated against her teeth, and she paced the terrace to calm herself. Her grudge against former teen idol Angel went bone deep. It propagated like mildew nurtured in some damp chamber, one long denied fresh air or any form of light. Years of jealousy had ripened to hatred.

Bree lit another cigarette, taking a deep drag and exhaling through her nose. She looked out at the water and the long span of the Queensboro Bridge. The terrace was her view from the top, and she swept her arm wide as if she alone owned the air. *I didn't spoon feed Eric Laine a lifestyle of fame and luxury so he could give all of it to another woman.*

Stepping inside, she picked up the burner phone she had her maid buy downtown on Canal Street and dialed.

Stephen Powers answered, his tone all business. "Mrs. Laine?"

"Tell me something I want to hear."

"Your hunch was right. Your husband checked into the Plaza weeks ago, but since then he's been off the grid…no credit card action and no one has spotted him. No one at the hotel will say whether or not he's still a guest."

Bree huffed. "They wouldn't. They protect the privacy of their celebrity clientele." Outside her window, sunlight glinted against the red bucket of the Roosevelt Island tram making a slow journey across the East River. "Do you have *any* good news for me?"

"I have a lead on Chambers."

"Follow your lead and find him." Bree snapped the cheap phone shut and grinned. Her day had just gotten better.

****

Three days later, private investigator Stephen Powers cruised down a South Side Chicago street of row houses separated by narrow, litter filled alleys. The houses were old, neglected, shingled in asphalt, and the windows on most, covered by boards. The area had all the ingredients for another great Chicago fire.

He parked his rental car and stepped quickly to number fifty-five, pivoting his head as he walked. Inside, the hallway was strewn with filth—cigarette butts, fast food cartons, and disposable, hypodermic needles.

Door numbers were long gone, but enough of the shadows remained for him to find 204. He knocked. There was no answer, but a shuffle of footsteps scraped from inside the apartment. "Mark Chambers?" Powers called out.

No answer.

Powers identified himself. "I flew in from Los Angeles. I have a client who's asked me to find you."

The sound of locks turning preceded the creak of the metal door opening a few inches wide. Eyes, red rimmed and creased by bloated lids stared out through the sliver of space. A chain was in place. "Who?"

"Bree Davis Laine. She has a proposition for you."

A death rattling cough lasted an eternity before the door closed and the chain scraped open. "C'mon in."

Powers stepped inside. He touched nothing and refused the offer to "have a seat."

Lighting a cigarette, Mark sucked a long lung full. His once glacially white implants were stained yellow and old scars intersected the skin of his face. Blue eyes were rheumy and unfocused. "I'm interested. Talk."

"Like I said, she has a proposition for you. Of course it's on the DL. Understand?"

Mark dragged deeply, wheezing as he exhaled. "I heard my old buddy Eric and she split up. Is she back in entertainment management? I'm an actor, y'know."

Powers huffed and slowly inched back toward the door. Mark Chambers' gaunt body and scar-seamed face would cause even the most stoic person to shudder. "She's trying to arrange a meeting between you and your daughter. Consider it an act of benevolence."

Mark's eyes popped wide. "She found my kid?"

Powers nodded. "You stay put and when we're ready for you, I'll come back and bring you to her."

A siren blared, the high-pitched peal rushing through a cracked windowpane. Muffled voices accompanied plodding footsteps on stairwell treads in the hall.

Mark sniggered. "Bree doesn't know the meaning of benevolence. She needs me for something…you get me out of this crack den today."

He swept bony fingers from his shoulders to his legs. "And I can't meet my baby looking like this. I'm going to need some cash."

Chapter Sixteen

Once again, Jenna sensed something was troubling her daughter. She'd been quiet since coming home from school and didn't seem anxious to go to gymnastics' practice.

"Spill it, kiddo," Jenna demanded later that night. "What did the delightful little Miss Baldwin do now?"

Janie dropped her chin to her chest and admitted to a scene at school with Tiffany and her crew bragging about going to a concert in the city.

"Concert? Aren't they a little young for that?"

"No, Mom. It's Kylie Harte. She's the prettiest and best singer in the world."

She isn't, Jenna mused. Kylie Harte was a former child star with an autotuned voice and generous butt who gamboled on stage in revealing outfits. At fifteen she topped the pop charts and was idolized by both adolescent girls and middle-aged men.

"Tiffany talked about the concert all day, like she wanted me to feel bad because I wasn't invited. Why does she have to be so mean to me? I never did anything to her."

Jenna let her eyes flutter shut and took a cleansing breath to cool the scrape of anger. She readied herself to speak in the incidental tone of a parent imparting the life lessons of high-roads and being the better person. But when tears rolled down her daughter's cheeks, she sincerely wished Tiffany Baldwin would crap her pants in front of the entire school the next day.

Jenna swept Janie into her arms. "I hate to simplify it baby, but some people, for whatever reason, are just not nice."

"Mmm." The child burrowed close, and Jenna hugged tight as if the circle of her arms could act as a bulwark against "not nice."

She had a repository of memories of what "not nice" meant and where "not nice" lived. More and more often her mind slipped back there to Hollywood. The Industry was a road littered with alcohol and drugs, producers who were borderline rapists, and a blood-thirsty media. Its glamour was simply a beautiful veil covering a disfigured face.

Jenna willed away a shudder and forced her thoughts back to the present. She wouldn't project her own hurt and past trauma onto her daughter. She ruffled Janie's hair. "You did kick her butt at the last three gym competitions. Maybe Tiffany is a little jealous."

"Of what?" Janie exhaled a long sigh. "She lives in the nicest house in town with a built-in swimming pool. She has all the best clothes, and her own horse."

Jenna stroked Janie's back. Tiffany had much more than the trappings of upper-class entitlement. She had the one thing Jenna had denied her daughter. Tiffany Baldwin had a daddy.

****

An hour later, Jenna tucked Janie into bed. She studied her face, the face of the person she loved above all else. She hated to see such beauty and innocence touched by childhood confusion and hurt. She hated to see even an insignificant dilemma wipe away her daughter's smile. Jenna knew how happiness and trust could be taken in the blink of an eye. She hugged her again. "Night, baby."

"Night, Mommy."

As she slowly descended the stairs, she tried in earnest to convince herself it was just a concert, and her daughter would be fine. Disappointment was part of life. Then a thought struck. Janie would have to endure the post-concert bragging, and oh how Tiffany Baldwin would rub the experience in Janie's face.

Line cutting, table stealing, and obnoxious, celebrity barging were the things about her former life Jenna missed least. When the time came to tell Eric the truth, she would insist he never use his position to Janie's advantage. Jenna foraged in a cabinet for an old copy of the White Pages, long hidden away, and proceeded to break the vow.

The listing for Ina Cummings was in the book and Jenna dialed. She wasn't sure if her hand shook from anger or from an attack of nerves, but there was little time to think before a ringing sounded in the receiver. She took a breath and waited.

****

Ina Cummings' telephone was an old Ma Bell rotary black and heavy as an anvil. Though Eric was sleeping, his face mashed into a pillow, when the phone rang, the shrill jangle woke him. Jarred, he sat up to find Ina staring down at him. "What the fuck! What happened… Where…What?"

"Oh, my." Ina stepped back from her groggy tenant. "I'm going to have to get a bar of soap for that mouth of yours."

"What's going on? Is the house on fire?" Eric's

chest rose and fell as if he had just run a five-hundred-meter dash.

"She's on the phone."

"Who?"

"Your nice young lady. I told her you were out on the porch. Now get your ass downstairs before she hangs up."

Scrubbing at his hair and then rubbing bleary eyes, Eric rooted around the end of the bed for his jeans.

"Oh for Heaven's sake, don't worry about your damned pants. I was married for forty-six years. Whatever you've got down there isn't going to shock me. Get to the damned phone."

In only briefs, Eric trotted down to the telephone and spoke, his voice still lowered to the baritone of someone just waking. "*Hullo*."

"Oh…were you sleeping? I'm sorry."

"No…No. I was um…" Hovering close, Ina nudged his arm and pointed to her front door. "Out on the porch."

"I need to ask you for a favor."

He was at once alert and attentive. "Sure, name it, anything you need, Jen."

"It's actually a favor for my daughter."

Eric listened as Jenna stumbled over her words. They staggered into the phone's receiver like spurts of water from a crimped hose. "I would never ask, but…there…there's this girl at school with concert tickets. She's taking a bunch of Janie's classmates but Janie wasn't included and…and she…she's so disappointed and um…"

Eric interrupted her stammering. "Do you want me to get concert tickets for you?"

"Well, I thought…that…you know, because of who

you are, you'd be able to." Her voice faded away.

Eric took a gladdened breath. *Finally*. There was finally something he was able to do for her. He could get front row tickets to anything, anytime. *Victory*.

Then shame swiped at his moment of satisfaction. He traveled back to a foggy night in San Francisco where he'd waited outside of a concert hall for *her*. He'd stood among her fans, a nonentity without enough influence to get a seat on a city bus. What he had brought upon her hit home once again. She had been reduced to groveling for a favor, something for her child. He felt like the biggest bastard alive.

"Sure, whatever you want. I'll call my manager. He can get tickets to anything."

"It's Kylie Harte. Her concerts sell out as soon as the box office opens. If it's possible, I'd like four tickets. Oh and…and I insist on paying for them."

Eric rubbed a hand over his eyes and didn't immediately answer. To Jenna, his silence must have yawned into eternity.

"I've imposed. Forget I called."

"No, Jen, wait. Getting the tickets isn't a problem. I can get backstage passes too if you want. I just have to tell you something first." Eric stalled and took another long breath. "Alan Stark is Harte's manager."

Chapter Seventeen

Anne Mills held her daughter's hands to spin the child in a merry circle. Riley returned her mother's enthusiasm with a lopsided smile, then turned to hug Janie. "I can't believe it! You're asking me to go. *Me*?"

Riley Mills was clearly more excited by being considered a first choice than attending the concert. The tiny girl with the slight limp and crooked mouth; the child who on occasion dropped things and finished last at field day races, was often included in things as an afterthought.

Anne silently mouthed the words "thank you" to Jenna while wiping a tear from her eye. In the scant few weeks since the women became reacquainted, Anne proved to be a good friend. She was the one person living in Cromline who knew about Jenna's past life, and it was a blessing to have someone to confide in.

Clearing her throat, she sent the girls upstairs to play. "I can't thank you enough for this. I've never seen Riley so happy. I owe you one."

Jenna waved away the statement. "You don't owe me anything. Janie really likes Riley. I had nothing to do with it."

"Yes, but you got the tickets." Anne's tone was more sly than curious.

"I suppose you're wondering how I got them."

"Hmm. Most people don't have eighth row seats and

backstage passes for a sold-out concert just fall into their lap."

Jenna's cheeks grew warm, and she scrunched her nose in the manner of a child caught pilfering a cookie. "I confess. I asked Eric to get them. I told Janie I won them from a radio station, so that's the story."

"My lips are sealed. But how the hell do you plan on going backstage without anyone recognizing you? It might be hard explaining to the kids why you're wearing a wig and dark glasses, don't you think?"

Sunlight filtered through Anne's sheer curtains like golden rays of optimism, and Jenna took a deep breath. "I know what these backstage things are like. I should be able to blend into the background and you can mingle a little with the girls."

"Are you sure? What if there are people there who knew you from before?"

Jenna stretched her arms wide. "There will be. My old manager for one. I'll be keeping my head down and my fingers crossed. Besides…I don't think my secrets are going to be secrets much longer anyway."

****

Thinking it wise to be in the city and near Jenna, Eric returned to his suite at the Plaza, the digs he had been paying fifteen hundred a night for and hadn't used in weeks. He retrieved an endless list of messages from the desk—seventeen from his lawyers, and about fifty from his agent. If Eric had wanted to talk to them, he would have answered his cell phone when they called. He crumpled the mass of paper in his fist and ambled to the elevator. He checked his watch. It was two-thirty, and Jenna should be on her way to the city by now.

After wolfing down a room service sandwich, he

called the front desk and asked to have a taxi waiting for him. While playing carpenter, he had worn some pretty serious holes in the knees and the backsides of all his jeans, so he decided on a trip to the penthouse to pick up more clothes. He had complete wardrobes in the various places he and Bree owned.

Saturday traffic in the city was its usual crawl, and it took more than fifteen minutes to travel the seven short blocks from 5th Avenue to York. The doorman greeted him and held the door. Getting into the apartment was another matter. His key no longer worked.

He heard sounds coming from within and knocked. A maid, someone new, answered the door, standing firm and blocking it. She said something to him in fractured English. From the distance of the long entryway, he saw Bree standing with her arms folded and her eyes narrowed.

"My apartment," he explained to the maid.

She turned and appealed to Bree. "Missus Laine?"

"You can let him in, Natalia."

With her arms still twined and pressed tightly under her breasts, Bree padded over. "Do you mind telling me where you've been?"

"Does it matter? And what are *you* doing here in New York?"

Her tone softened marginally. "You left L.A. weeks ago. I got worried and decided to look for you. You are still my husband."

"For now."

"For now? Marriage is supposed to be forever." Her expression was downcast, veiled in sorrow, eyes wide and lips aquiver. "Why are you doing this, Eric?" She spread her arms wide at an expanse of luxury that stretched forth like food at a Bacchanalian feast. "All of this is because of us…because we're a team. We should be working things out. It isn't too late."

Eric shook his head, genuinely sorry for his part in entering and leaving the ill-fated marriage. His words were measured and soft. "Working things out isn't a realistic goal. It's been too late for us for about three years now. Don't you think it's time we made it official?"

Dropping her hands to her sides, Bree clenched her fingers into something resembling French manicured talons. Tears clung to her lashes. "No. I don't. Things were fine. The whole world knows how perfect we are for each other."

Eric slanted his mouth into the pained half-grin of a person finally conceding defeat. "We were far from perfect. I ignored everything wrong between us, while you turned a relationship into soundbites and headlines. The only place we were a happy couple was in the press."

Bree scraped her tears away, and her eyes settled back into their natural shape, narrow and appraising. "The press is very powerful. Public opinion is swayed by it all the time. Celebrities rely on a good Q Score."

Tired and defeated, the tang of failure bitter on his tongue, Eric looked at his wife. This was the true Bree, glacial and imposing, a woman whose ambition blanketed any humor or kindness. He slumped his shoulders. "You know I never cared about popularity polls or stats. And all I care about right now is packing up some of my clothes. Excuse me."

Brushing by her, he headed for the bedroom. He walked down a hall as wide as an average room and tugged at the collar of his shirt as if it was suddenly too tight. For all of the apartment's airy space, it still made him feel cloistered—shuttered and alone.

"Fine! Disappear again," Bree shouted. "When it comes down to it, the court will side with me. I'm not the one who abandoned us."

"And I'm not the one who slept with a twenty-year-old who waxed my skis."

Bree's response was a smoky laugh, a deep and mocking lilt that made Eric stop and turn. His comment hadn't made his wife falter or gasp her shock. Instead, her rigid stance relaxed into a languid lean onto one hip. Her pupils dilated amorously, and her voice was a dark utterance. "You have no *proof* that I've ever been unfaithful. But it is a shame you can't seem to find a wife who doesn't end up with another man's dick inside her."

The reference to Jenna's assault made Eric's heart pound, the rhythm quick and heavy, his lungs burning. His body stiffened and his hands rounded into such tight fists the veins in his hands bulged. "You're lucky I would never hit a woman." He continued on to his bedroom, grabbed four pairs of jeans and strode from the apartment.

****

During the two-hour drive to the city, Jenna and Anne were entertained with a personal concert. At the top of their healthy little lungs Janie and Riley sang every Kylie Harte song they knew. They knew all of them. The performance ended only when Anne slowed her minivan and exited the East Side Drive at 60th Street. Eric had provided a night's accommodation at The Plaza, one room for Jenna and another for Anne. "Regular rooms," Jenna had insisted, "and in Anne's name."

Easing the van among a line of hansom cabs,

limousines, and taxis, Anne gave her car to a valet and the foursome entered the lobby. While Anne registered, Jenna contained the two wide-eyed kids. The girls looked like baby birds in search of their mother—necks stretched, heads up, and mouths yawning wide.

"Look at that chandelier!"

"Ooh…look at all the gold on the ceiling."

Janie nudged Riley and they both stared, struck mute, as two women, pencil thin and towering, glided past. "Models," Janie was finally able to whisper.

"Okay, we're in 705 and 703," Anne said. "We only have a couple of hours to get our things up to the rooms, have dinner and get to the concert."

"Let's go, then," Jenna added. But after taking only one step, she abruptly stopped.

There was an almost imperceptible change in the buzz of voices and patter of footsteps in the lobby. Motion stilled a mere fraction, a change no one would notice except someone who had experienced such a phenomenon. Her ears pricked like an animal sensing a sudden storm. Eric was walking through, and for a brief moment every person he passed abandoned all speech and movement. It created a domino effect of silence followed by murmurs. He turned toward Jenna and smiled.

"Mom," Janie whispered. "Do you know who that was? That was Eric Laine, the movie star. Eric Laine just smiled at you."

Chapter Eighteen

Framed by fountains and gilded statues, the Plaza rose in timeless splendor against the backdrop of Central Park. Across the street on Fifth Avenue, a grid of buildings spanned east. Some were old, their stone facades capped with carved entablatures, while newer, glass structures glinted like beacons in the afternoon sun.

The eager group headed across 58th Street in search of a restaurant, their pace swift enough to match the pedestrian traffic they walked among. Both mothers vetoed fast-food and decided instead on a bistro with a sidewalk cafe. After a quick dinner Jenna hailed a taxi and they headed downtown to Madison Square Garden.

Hundreds of people, mostly adolescent girls, lined West 34th. Vendors selling Kylie Harte paraphernalia wove through the flow of ticket holders. Scalpers lurked in corners. Jenna and company were swept up among the crowds going through turnstiles and down ramps until they reached their section.

Throughout the concert, Janie and Riley bounced and danced in front of their seats. They joined in with twenty-thousand other voices and screamed for the entirety of the performance. Anne danced along with the girls for part of the two-hour concert, but by the second half of the show, she huddled in her seat, hands over her ears.

Jenna watched her daughter singing and smiling,

clapping hands and doing a remarkably precise mimic of Kylie Harte's dance steps. They were so close to the stage Jenna could see the sheen of sweat covering the singer's body and how tight the scanty costumes clung to her generous curves. Transfixed, Jenna watched. Transported, she remembered. She knew how hard the pretty girl's heart was beating. Jenna knew how blinding the lights shining into her eyes were. She knew how the stage shook from the powerful amplifiers and earth-shattering screams of the audience. Jenna knew. She knew all of it.

She twisted her head around at the crowded venue and felt an oddly hollow space inside of her. A flicker of regret. Then her daughter's delighted voice filled the void. "Mommy, that was so cool! Did you ever see anything so cool?"

"Never," Jenna answered.

"It was the best!" Riley added. "I love her, that's what I want to do when I grow up."

"Kylie Harte isn't grown up, she's fifteen," Anne was quick to remind her daughter.

They squeezed up the aisle to the lobby, where the girls hurried to a souvenir booth. "T-shirts and programs are my treat," Anne said, as she rushed after. Jenna approached an usher for directions to the rooftop terrace while her friend parted with her money.

Janie and Riley both let out the shriek of someone discovering a dead body when Jenna told them about the backstage party. There was almost no keeping pace with them. Anne tugged Jenna's arm and told the girls to stop for a moment. "I need to catch my breath." Her face was pale, her mouth a worried slash.

"Are you okay?" Jenna whispered. The girls stood

by untroubled as they examined their bags of loot.

"I think someone is following you."

Ice was an immediate press against Jenna's spine. "Are you sure?"

Anne murmured from one side of her mouth. "I noticed him when we got off the escalator. He was staring at you. We've passed several exits and he's still behind us."

"Does it look like he's carrying a camera, maybe one hidden under his clothing?" Jenna lowered her head and brought one hand up to cover her face.

Anne automatically mimicked the action. "Wait, why the hell am I hiding *my* face?" She turned to glance in the direction of the man. "Shit, I can't tell. He's wearing a jacket."

"C'mon girls." Anne shuttled them ahead to block them from view of the man who trailed behind. "He's walking faster. I think he knows we spotted him."

Jenna pulled at her daughter's hand and increased her own tempo, not daring to look behind. "C'mon, c'mon. That's the entrance up ahead, hurry up." Her voice was a sharp command even though she labored to disguise the tremor in her voice.

As the four turned the corner Anne gave a fretful shake of the head. "Hey!" she yelled as the man turned and bore down on Jenna. He bumped into her, throwing her off balance, then gripped her arm to prevent her from falling.

The hulking figure held her close, and Jenna stared openmouthed as Nick Lombardo steadied her. "Sorry for being so clumsy, miss." He spoke loud enough for the others to hear. "I have a security job to do backstage and I'm running late."

He further closed the gap between them and whispered. "Your little girl is a real beauty, sweetheart, just like her mother. I'll be keeping an eye on both of you tonight, so you relax and have fun. No one is going to bother you." He lumbered ahead and disappeared down the hall.

Anne gasped. "Are you all right? I thought he was going to tackle you to the ground."

"I'm fine. That's New York for you…everyone in a hurry. C'mon, girls, let's get inside." Jenna showed the passes to the security guard, and they all entered into the clamor.

Swiping two glasses of champagne from the tray of a passing waiter, Anne handed one to Jenna and downed the other. "What was that all about? No one is that clumsy. That man was aiming for you."

Jenna whispered behind her cupped hand. "It's okay. He's my bodyguard."

"Body-what!"

"Shh. His name is Nick Lombardo and he used to be my bodyguard. My guess is Eric sent him to babysit."

"My *guess* is your movie star ex-husband still has a real case for you."

Anne's diagnosis was cut short by the appearance of a beautiful young girl with a wealth of long blonde curls that trailed to her waist. She slipped through the crowd hugging and kissing people, a wide smile effectively drawn on her face. Anne snuck a few pictures as Jenna inched her way to the corner.

Nick stood nearby, one of a dozen or so bulked up men, standing sentinel—quiet, unassuming, but ready to pounce should the need arise. Jenna was enormously grateful for his presence.

As she expected, the party was the usual Industry schmooze-fest. Backstage affairs were part lavish feast, part command center. Corporate suits shook hands, pitched ideas, and forged alliances. Celebrities and power brokers mingled. Jenna stood alone in a corner, her collar pulled up high, and her hair mussed toward her face. She watched as Kylie Harte autographed Janie and Riley's T-shirts. Then, feeling as if the activity in the room stilled, oxygen seemed to thin. Looking trim, tailored, and a bit grayer, Alan Stark stood nearby, his eyes riveted upon her.

He didn't break his stare and the possessive glower peeled away ten years. Jenna almost heard him directing her every action, telling her where to go and what to do…who to talk to. As a flight response of adrenaline sped through her bloodstream, she moved away to escape. Then she remembered who she was and stood firm. He had no power over her.

Nick blocked the path as Alan stepped forward.

"It's okay," Jenna said. "I'm sure he just wants to say hello."

Nick leaned close. "Keep your conversation short," he warned and moved no more than a yard away.

Alan stared expressionless, his features looking forced into an intentionally blank canvas. Still, his chest rose and fell as if breathing was a struggle. "You look beautiful, very different but still beautiful."

"I'd like to say thank you, but I'd prefer it if you didn't compliment me."

"Fair enough."

Jenna looked at her former manager as if seeing him for the first time. For all of his Hollywood power and connections, he was still a slight and inconsequential man. She angled her chin toward Kylie Harte. "I hope you aren't smothering that kid, controlling her…treating her like you own her the way you did to me. Let her have some space and live her life."

Alan huffed, and his face melted into folds. He brought his drink to his lips and sipped. He appeared already drunk, his shoulders slumped forward like a crestfallen child's. "No one tells that brat what to do. I'll be chasing her all over Manhattan tonight to get ahead of whatever trouble she gets into."

Jenna shook her head. "Maybe you should manage the careers of adults instead of exploiting children."

Music pounded the air and a steady line of people brushed by. Voices and laughter rode along as guests circulated.

"Goodbye, Alan." Jenna disappeared into the crowd.

She didn't look back. She'd said all she had to say.

Chapter Nineteen

Eric shaved and ran a brush through his hair. He grabbed the towel from around his waist and mopped up the residual shaving cream from his chin. The sweep of the soft terrycloth on his naked flesh roused him into a semi-erection. "Down, boy."

It was a command to the part of his body of which he had very little control. He laughed at the irony. The biggest "heartthrob" on the screen couldn't even remember the last time he'd had sex.

He'd had the opportunity, but not the desire—not for his wife, or for any of the actresses, models, lawyers, producers, waitresses, or even high-end escorts he met. His desire was for only one woman. He'd known it for years, but had been too busy, afraid, or too plain stupid to do anything about it. He was going to do something about it now and straighten things out between them once and for all.

Nick had driven Jenna back to the hotel and overheard her say her daughter would be spending the night in her friend's room having a pajama party. Eric knew Jenna was downstairs in her room alone. He threw on gray trousers and a plain white shirt and rolled back the cuffs. He went back into the bathroom and brushed his hair again.

****

Jenna sat at the table by the window and looked

down. Her room was on the Fifth Avenue side, its view of the park's greenery blurred by the lights of the city. Cars, streetlamps, and the steady glow in windows created an illusion. Orbs of radiance seemed to hang suspended in the night's air. It was magical. She spotted a man whose hand was gallantly extended to help a woman step from a hansom cab. She was dressed in something Jenna might have worn herself if she'd the occasion for such an outfit—a dress with fitted bodice and full skirt that was layers and layers of pearly tulle and chiffon—a romantic outfit. Jenna watched, eyes moony and longing as the couple locked arms and strolled into the warm New York night.

She went to the bathroom to brush her teeth, gathering her hair into a ponytail as she slowly walked. Her face was scrubbed free of makeup and wisps of hair fell from the elastic band. Shaking her head at her reflection, she sighed. She was at the Plaza, alone on a Saturday night, wearing a huge T-shirt that hung close to her knees. On it was a picture of a green and orange dinosaur with the words Mommy-saurus written in bright purple letters.

"You are one hot babe, Jenna Laine." In an instant, her fingers were at her lips. She'd barely claimed the name long enough to put it on her driver's license. "Black, Jenna Black," she corrected.

Ambling from the bathroom, she grabbed the remote and clicked on the television. She fell into bed, hoping to get drowsy enough to sleep, but a rap on the door disturbed her. *Janie*. Jenna sprinted over and pressed her eye against the peephole, but when she saw who her visitor was, her heart began to pound. Slowly, breathlessly, she opened the door no farther than the security bar allowed. "It's after midnight."

"Nick just dropped you off ten minutes ago."

"I…I'm…I'm not dressed."

Eric offered no reaction other than to smile and slide his hands into his pockets. She turned from the liquid stare, her back against the partially opened door. Admitting to being undressed wasn't the way to dissuade a man or cool his passion.

"I know it's late but, I…um…wanted to know how the concert was."

"You wanted to know about the performance of a fifteen-year-old pop star?"

"C'mon, Jen. I just want to talk to you. Don't make me beg. Open the door…please."

"Okay." She answered in a whisper because the thready breath was all she could manage. Her eyes fluttered shut, and she inhaled and exhaled, slow and easy, until her heart's rhythm calmed. She slipped the bar from the slot and opened the door.

Eric stepped inside, but weeks of fleeting encounters had exhausted his willpower and his eyes touched her everywhere. Though she was blanketed in an oversized T-shirt, the memory of gently swelling curves and sun kissed skin heated his blood. He brought his sight up and away from her body, but as his eyes settled on her face, he felt a deeper stirring. Tendrils of golden hair escaped a band and tumbled around her face. Her soft lips, slightly parted, whispered to him in his imagination. He blinked and swallowed hard, willing himself to break what he knew was a forlorn gaze.

As if feeling the intimacy of his stare Jenna tugged at the shirt. When she spoke, her words rolled across her tongue in a stammer. "S…sit."

"Thank you." His arm accidentally brushed her shoulder as he walked by, and it caused a shock to pass between them. "Sorry. It must be the carpet."

"Of course," Jenna agreed. "Static." She brushed her hand up and down her arm as if the tingle persisted. "Let me go put some clothes on."

He tilted his head and smiled crookedly, his eyes again sweeping over her. "That's a pretty big shirt. Besides, it's not like I haven't seen you without your…Oh hell, I didn't mean to say that."

They stood face to face, moments long and uneasy, their eyes locked as if some hypnotic force connected them. The blue pools of Eric's glinted in the dusky light and the wide golden gleam of Jenna's shone like polished topaz. Eric grabbed one of the chairs at the table, turned it around and straddled it. He leaned his arms on the back and smiled again.

The masculine yet graceful way he moved made Jenna's breath skip into her lungs. No one walked the way he did, his shoulders slowly dipping with each easy step. No one leaned against a wall, or just sat, giving off an aura of pure maleness the way he did. Jenna wished to hell she still didn't see him that way. Before her insides turned liquid and she fell into a boneless swoon, she pulled a chair close and sat, her shoulders rigid against the back, her hands folded in her lap. "Why are you here?"

"So many reasons," he said with a shrug.

The truth about Janie lay suspended on Jenna's tongue, and her heart once again began to race. She pressed tighter against the chair's tufted upholstery and dropped her sight to her clasped fingers.

Eric wished to reach for her, to pull her close and

shake the stiffness from her body, to let the heat of his hands spread over her till she fell warm and curving against him.

"Us," he said. "We need to talk about us."

Jenna's eyes were wide and pained. "There hasn't been an us for almost ten years."

"Money then." Bringing up memories, going back to a place that had shattered both their hearts seemed an unwise path to take. "I need to sign control of a portfolio to you. I could recommend someone to handle it."

"I don't need you to recommend anything." Her words were a sudden flow of ice. "I run a business and know how to handle money."

Jenna felt her face flush and angry tears were building behind her eyes. His talk of money stung. The Eric Laine she was married to had carried his net worth in his pockets. The sting became the quick slice of a blade. How would they ever be able to share Janie when she couldn't shake her anger and be civil to him for more than a moment?

Standing, she tightened her ponytail and tugged at the edges of her T-shirt. She wished for a thousand other things to feel other than how much it hurt that he had done so well without her—that he had accepted Bree Davis's help and never her own. In the short time Jenna and Eric had been together, she'd offered him countless business opportunities, and each time he'd flatly refused. Anger over his stubborn pride, she decided, was the easiest to grab on to. "I think you should go."

He stood and pushed the chair away. "Jesus, Jen, ten seconds into a conversation and I've already pissed you off. I can't seem to do or say anything right."

"Then stop trying and just go." She walked to the

door to escort him out. She couldn't sit calmly in a beautiful hotel room, wearing a big stupid T-shirt while talking to the only man in the world who had the power to turn her life upside-down. "Thanks again for the tickets. We have a long drive tomorrow; I'd better get to bed." She aimed her eyes at the carpet so he wouldn't see the glassy sheen in her eyes. "If you'll excuse me…"

"No," he said softly. "You'll have to excuse *me* because I'm not leaving. I've been trying to talk to you for weeks, and every time I do it turns into an argument." He clasped his hands behind his head and stretched in frustration. "If you want me to go, you're going to have to call hotel security, because I'm not leaving until you hear me out."

He walked to the window and pressed his hands against the glass. Staring down, he fixed his eyes on the blur of traffic while his heart searched for the words he had waited too many long years to say.

Slowly, he turned and spoke. "I know I hurt you the night you went into labor. The press had been all over me and I got drunk. That punk kid I'd tried so hard to bury came alive and raging. I said things that were unforgivable." His stare never faltered. He was too intent upon making her understand. "I've never regretted anything more in my life."

Jenna angled her head high, her face a resolute picture of pride that failed to mask her wounds. "Regret? Really? According to the tabloids, you and your *regret* were filming in Monte Carlo a few months ago." She bit down on her lip as the heat of embarrassment made her skin flush. "That was rude. Your career is none of my business."

"Stop it." His words were a whisper of misery. "Just

stop it. Please. I didn't become an actor to spite you. I became an actor so I could earn the money to try and find you. It was all I thought about."

His words hung in the air like a fleeting curl of smoke. He raised his arms overhead and linked his hands behind his neck. "But after three years, I had to face the fact that you didn't want to be found. It became such an unhealthy obsession I had to give up."

"So you moved on with your life and married my manager's assistant. When I read about it in the papers, I wasn't all that surprised. I might have been young and naive, but I wasn't stupid. I always knew she had feelings for you."

He shook his head. "Feelings? No. She saw me as an opportunity, so I did as *you* asked in your letter. I made a fresh start—new career, new marriage, new life. The career was the only thing that seems to have worked out though." He moved closer to reach for her.

"Don't," Jenna said, backing away. Her eyes burned. Memories of the love they'd shared and lost were like hands around her throat.

"Don't what? Don't say that even after all these years I can still feel what's between us. Admit it, Jen. You feel it too."

She shook her head, her tears clinging to her lashes. "I...I don't know what I feel. We're not those kids anymore. You and I are...are..."

"What, Jen? What?"

"Strangers."

"Strangers? Then why did you come to the hospital four years ago, when I was hurt? Why did you cry at my bedside?" Droplets fell to her cheeks. "Why are you crying now?"

He took her hands in his, the grip tight, warm, irredeemable. Still, he wasn't letting go. "What happened to you was the worst thing that could happen to a woman. I was too young and too plain stupid to be there for you the way I should have been, the way a husband should have been. Beating Mark half to death was what I needed, not what you needed *from* me."

Jenna's hands trembled in his and he squeezed tighter. It was wrong to force her back to the most painful time of her life, but worse to allow trauma and shame to keep them apart.

"Guilt tore me up and I made mistakes, said and did things I'll always regret. I've wanted to make it up to you every day since, but you were gone." He drew her closer and took her face in his hands. "Look at me," he commanded. They stared eye to eye, his deep and sad, hers a golden, glittering pool. "You were my wife and I loved you. I fucking adored you. When you left you broke my heart. It's still in pieces."

More tears slipped down Jenna's cheeks. She couldn't continue to keep her heart safely locked behind an iron gate. She couldn't continue to pretend she didn't still love him. He gently wiped her tears with the pads of his thumbs. Time stopped and nine years slipped away.

Their lips grazed softly, barely touching as he swept her into his arms and carried her to the bed. Ardently they kissed, their hands twined in each other's hair then slipping lower to shoulders and ribs. Eric kissed her neck and the hollow slope above her collarbone. When his hand slipped beneath the dinosaur shirt to caress her breast, she stopped him. "I can't. I'm sorry." She smoothed the T-shirt back down over her thighs. "I-I just can't do this."

He sat up, and his head fell back against the headboard with a thump. "It's okay." Spreading his legs, he pulled her to him so her back rested against his chest. She could feel the tympanic rhythm of his heart, and the insistence of his ardor pressing steely against her back. He settled his chin on her shoulder and brushed her cheek with his jaw. His breath was a warm tingle that floated by her ear. "It's okay," he repeated.

"Eric, it's been so long…and there are so many things that…and besides…you're still married. That would make me the other woman."

He laughed, a low sexy chuckle that made her almost change her mind and give in to desire. "Babes, you could never be the other woman. You're the *only* woman."

"Nice try."

Edging away from her, he stood and tucked his shirt in his pants to adjust the bulge behind his zipper. He stood arms open wide, and she politely cast her sight away from the evidence of his arousal.

"I've sowed my wild oats and been married twice. Believe me, you are the *only* woman I want…the only woman I will ever want." He glanced down below his belt and shrugged. "I hope there's no one in the elevator. This could be embarrassing."

"Then maybe you should wait until…y'know."

"You're just too damned enticing in that T-shirt. A cold shower should do the trick."

He reached down and gave her a brotherly peck on the top of her head. "Goodnight, Babes. Sleep well. We'll talk more back in Cromline."

Chapter Twenty

A roll of blueprints for a Baldwin Ridge outbuilding was spread out on a table in the construction trailer. Ash jabbed his finger on a shaded area that indicated the Cummings' property. "This is supposed to be a club house for the condos, not a fucking pumpkin patch." He turned toward his police chief. "Get rid of that son of a bitch."

Willy Parks sat in a swivel chair, scratching lazily at his chest, his legs propped up on a sawhorse. "I was going to have a little talk with him over the weekend, but I didn't see him around."

"Well he's back up on her roof right now. I don't care if you have to shoot him. Get him off there before he fixes anything else."

With a groan and a creaking of knees, the chief sat upright. "I can't grab him in front of the old lady. It'll look suspicious. As soon as he drives into town, I'll stop him and convince him to leave. Don't worry, he'll be out of your hair."

Ash leaned over the table and planted his palms flat on the surface. His half-smile was more dire than a threat. "He had better be, Will. Because if you can't get rid of that redneck drifter, I'll call the Simpson brothers to do it for you."

"Jeeze, Ash, Jake and Harley Simpson? You can't actually kill this guy. I'm a cop for Christ sake. I didn't hear you say that."

Ash ambled to the trailer door, straightening his tie as he walked. He spoke over his shoulder. "You'll only be top cop for as long as I need you to be, and for as long as I'm willing to pay to shut up the next stripper you 'accidentally' sleep with. Get the drifter out of my town."

****

As promised, Jenna took the memory card that contained pictures from the concert to the drug store to have them printed. Janie was eager to have them and Jenna, try as she might to be adult, couldn't help but feel a bit of satisfaction knowing her daughter would be getting even with darling little Tiffany Baldwin. Jenna would love to be a fly on the cafeteria wall when Janie showed her classmates pictures of Riley and herself at the backstage party. *I hope Anne got good shots.*

Later, as Jenna walked back to her car, a voice rang out. She turned and forced a smile. "Hello, Ash."

"I called you this weekend. Did you get my message?"

"Afraid I didn't. I was in the city with my daughter."

Relaxed, ever a picture of charm, he grinned and folded his arms, his weighty biceps evident beneath the silky linen of his sports coat. "Ah, that's a relief. I thought you were avoiding me."

Jenna tapped her fingers against her thighs. The passion of kissing Eric cooled whatever small attraction she felt for Ash. "No, I've just been busy."

The pharmacy parking lot wasn't the place for a detailed explanation of why she wouldn't be accepting any more invitations to any of the pricey restaurants where Ash Baldwin was a front-row, season ticket holder. She smiled and said she had to run.

"Wait." His eyes were softly appraising, his grin amiable. "I thought we might have dinner one night this week." His request sounded like more of a dictate than an invitation.

"I'm sorry I can't." Her reply was too quick, and she saw the ease escape his posture. "I'm expecting my friend back tomorrow night. It would be rude to go out and leave her."

"I'm sure your friend won't mind if you take a night for yourself. I'll call you." He hopped into his convertible, giving her no time to argue the point.

****

Another spring shower halted Eric's work for the day. Since returning from the city, work seemed effortless. Kissing Jenna, having her respond the way she had, suffused him with energy. She'd set the almighty chemicals of happiness flowing in his veins. The schoolboy grin on his face was a giveaway, and Ina commented on his happy mood, fluttering around him at dinner, ladling food, and swamping him with advice.

"Now, you give her a gentlemanly call to show you're interested."

Eric swallowed a hunk of a potato whole so he wouldn't spit it across the table while laughing. "Ina, I told her she was the love of my life. I'm pretty sure she knows I'm interested."

Reaching across the table, she scraped more spinach onto his plate. "Iron. A young man, especially one in love, can't have enough iron in his blood." She winked at him and dove into a long discourse. "Flowers would be a nice gesture, nothing showy, she already knows you're richer than Midas. Courtship is very important…you don't want to blow it, not this time around."

The elderly woman continued to counsel him on affairs of the heart while refilling his plate. Her advice ran out only when the supply of food was depleted.

She plucked her bright red raincoat from a hook by the front door and shrugged into it. "Well, I'm off to bingo." She bustled out the door and it slammed behind her.

Eric was still laughing as he cleared the table and washed the dishes. After, he sat on the porch as he did most evenings. Outside it was warm, and mist caused by the evaporating rain rolled along the ground. Moonlight glittered through the breaking clouds. Propping his feet on the railing, he looked out at the night. Hazy ribbons of fog turned into Jenna's hair, the brilliant gold of the moon her eyes. She was everywhere, all around him, but mostly inside, locked away in his heart.

"I'm never letting you go again," he vowed as he gazed up at the stars. He went inside to take Ina's advice and call her.

****

Jenna picked up the phone.

"Hi, Babes."

The sound of Eric's voice made a thousand tiny butterflies beat their wings against her skin. "Hi," she answered on a breath. "How are you?"

"A little achy, I finished Ina's roof today."

A vision of him sprang instantly in her head—tool belt low on his hips and jeans snug against his thighs. Sunshine highlighted the flaxen streaks in his hair, and his eyes were, as always, a rich sea of blues and greens. "It's a really nice thing you're doing for her," she said eons after he'd asked.

"I'm glad you see it that way. I can't leave until it's all finished. Hope that isn't still a problem for you."

Jenna retreated to a corner and spoke quietly into the receiver so Janie wouldn't hear. "No. In fact, I've been thinking about things. Maybe it is best if you stick around for a while. I have some things I need to say also."

"Babes, I'll stay around forever if you want me to."

For Janie. He would stay for his daughter. But his feelings for her might be less than kind once he knew how long she'd kept the truth from him.

"How about dinner tomorrow night?" he asked.

Jenna stretched her neck to see into the living room where Janie was busy amid scattered papers and textbooks. "Not on a school-night. The weekend?"

"Okay."

Jenna Welles and Eric Laine made plans for Friday night. Two people, who had in another lifetime been consumed with love for one another, were in a new life, going on a first date.

Chapter Twenty-One

Randi arrived back in Cromline with enough clothes for a month, though she insisted she'd be going home again for the weekend. Jenna told her about the concert, purposely leaving out the intimate moments she'd spent with Eric. Her friend had very little objectivity where movie star Eric Laine was concerned and rightfully so. Too many of Jenna's tears had rained down on Randi's shoulders because of him. Jenna cleared her throat and moved on to her friend's second least favorite subject, their high school nemesis Annabelle Walker.

"I…um made plans for us to have coffee at Anne's later today."

Randi thrust her arms in front of her body like a cop unhappily demoted to traffic detail. "Whoa, whoa, whoa. We're doing what? Going where, later today?"

"To Anne's. I have a girl coming in to cover for me at the store. It'll be fun."

Randi's lips dipped into a petulant frown, and she scrunched her nose like an angry five-year-old. "Are you sure she'll be serving coffee or pouring *venom* into the cups."

Jenna laughed and slung her arm around her friend. "You should have been the actress, Ran. You have a real flair for drama."

Later, after lunch, and under much protest, Randi sat in Jenna's car with her arms tightly folded. "I still don't believe she's suddenly Mrs. Nice Guy and not the same bitchy princess she was in school."

"She's been through some stuff, and it changed her."

"I'm sure whatever *stuff* she went through, she deserved."

Jenna leveled a final cautioning glower before getting out of the car. "Be nice. She's the only friend I have in this town."

At the door Anne greeted both of her former classmates with a wide smile. She grasped Randi's hand. "Randi Freed, my God you haven't changed a bit."

Jenna remained close enough for a pinch if it became necessary, but Randi smiled and gave Anne a cordial greeting in return.

"I won't bore you with a tour of the house. C'mon in the kitchen and sit. I have a pot of French Roast and homemade beignets. Who would have guessed I'd learn to bake." She hustled to the counter for the coffee and pastry.

"See," Jenna whispered. "She's nice."

"Hmm." Randi's eyes were still reptilian thin. "So, Annabelle…"

"Ugh, call me Anne, please. Annabelle sounds like I should be wearing a hoop skirt and big floppy hat."

"All right, *Anne*." Randi simpered and once again wrinkled her nose. "Your house is lovely."

Jenna couldn't help but notice how the compliment scraped grudgingly past Randi's lips. Anne's home was a showcase, clean and bright as if fingerprints or dust were magnetically repelled. Randi, on the other hand, had never mastered the fine art of neat and tidy.

"Uh, oh, now you are going to have to stand the tour."

"If we have time." Randi added another faux smile and nose wrinkle.

The three women drank their coffee and talked about the old days in Pinehill.

"So how is the crew from up on Birchwood Lane? Do you keep in touch with them?" Randi asked.

Jenna rolled her eyes knowing her best friend was trolling for an argument. She had hated the Pinehill High A-listers—girls bent on bullying her. Anne answered, counting on her fingers. "Married…separated… divorced…on her third marriage…and dabbling in lesbianism."

"Great, glad we're all caught up." Jenna said. Her tone was breezy as she steered the conversation away from past grudges. But Randi was standing firm on institutional tile edged by a row of lockers. "You know, back in school Jen and I had a really funny nickname for you and your besties. We called you the Snotty Six."

"Randi!"

"It's all right." Anne gave an apologetic lift of her shoulders. "We earned the title."

Jenna gnashed her teeth together as she spoke. "Well that was then. Randi, get your phone and show Anne pictures of the boys."

It shifted the conversation momentarily to children, holidays, and vacations. But the *détente* lasted only until Anne mentioned strapping, six-foot-two, blue-eyed movie star Eric Laine. "I'm telling you he still cares for you," she insisted as she bit into a beignet.

"You don't know the man. How can you say that?" Randi argued.

Anne defended her position. "Well, for one thing he's here in town. And I saw the way he looked at Jenna at the hotel. He still wants her."

"Of course he wants her." Randi threw her hands in the air. "She left him. It's a male ego thing. Men all want what they can't have."

"Don't be ridiculous." Anne's expression softened like a teenager spying a crush, eyes dreamlike and lips slightly parted. "They were married and in love; and now he's come back for her. It's the most romantic thing I've ever seen."

Randi's countenance was the polar opposite, teeth gritted and eyes ablaze. "Oh you have no clue. No idea what that man did to her."

"I do too. Jenna told me everything. She still has feelings for him, and I think she should give him a chance. If not for herself than for Janie."

"She shouldn't give him the time of—"

"Hey!" Jenna shouted. She'd been quietly listening to the exchange and had enough. "I'm still in the room."

Both women said the word "sorry" simultaneously while continuing to glare at one another. Before the subject of past love and loss had a chance to get cold, they resurrected the argument. Randi insisted Eric was scum and should be drawn and quartered. Anne contended he was Jenna's true love, and she should ride off into the sunset with him.

"You're the same know it all you were in high school, *Annabelle*."

"And you're just jealous because your best friend has a hot movie star in love with her, *Freed*."

Chairs scraped against wide planks of pale stained oak as both combatants stood.

"That's it, fat girl!"

"Watch it, shorty!"

Jenna brought two fingers to her mouth and whistled loud enough to almost shatter the crystal fruit bowl resting on the center island. "Knock it off! I can't believe you two. I'm having a hard enough time with all of this, especially after what happened at the Plaza."

The need to hear an explanation for the statement took an immediate back seat to the name-calling and threats. Anne and Randi both leaned toward Jenna, eyes wide and ears perked.

"I knew something happened. You were smiling the entire ride home."

"Spill it," Randi ordered with a hard rap on the table.

Jenna pushed at her cup. "Damned caffeine."

Anne and Randi closed in more, their heads poking forward like turtles reaching for raw hamburger. They dropped back into their chairs and waited.

Sunshine sliced through glass sliders in the already bright kitchen, and a beam of light fell across Jenna's face, the glare apropos for her interrogation. "He came to my room after the concert."

Anne clapped her hands in delight while Randi muttered a stream of profanity.

"You didn't. Jenna Welles, please tell me you did *not* sleep with him."

"I didn't…but I wanted to."

Racing to the counter, Anne grabbed the coffee pot. "Details, I want details!" She poured more of the brew all around.

"We kissed, that's all."

"Kissed?" Randi puckered her lips like a guppy. "Or kiss kissed. Did you make out with him?"

"Oh for Heaven's sake, they aren't thirteen," Anne scolded. Then she sighed and her expression, once again, turned adolescently wistful. "Was it wonderful? Did he tell you he still loves you?"

"Not in those exact words."

"I knew it!" Randi slapped her hand on the table hard enough to make coffee quiver in all three cups. "He's using you."

"For what? Do you think Eric Laine has a problem getting laid?" Anne turned and patted Jenna's hand. "Sorry for being so blunt." She whipped her head around to redirect her ire at Randi. "What would he possibly be using her for?"

"To get even, to soothe his ego, who knows? Jenna walked out on him. Big stars like that can't stand the rejection."

"He wasn't even famous back then," Anne corrected. "He was a busboy."

Jenna jumped up from the table, her fists balled tightly at her sides. She and Eric had tolerated two solid years of the media attaching "Busboy" to his name as if it was a royal title. "He wasn't a busboy! He was a bar-back, and a carpenter, and a lifeguard, and a waiter. He was never a fucking busboy!"

Startled, Anne blinked, and Randi apologized for her negativity. "I'm sorry, Jen. I'm just so afraid he'll hurt you again. Especially after you tell him about Janie. I just don't think you should get too involved with him yet."

"If he loves you, he'll get past it," Anne said.

Jenna folded back down into her chair, wondering which one of her friends was right.

Chapter Twenty-Two

Ash Baldwin called The Highland Casino, a hotel an hour away from Cromline. The place was a beacon of steel and smoky glass settled between a gorge in the nearby mountains. Rooms were luxe with thick carpeting, sconces aglow against pearly wallpaper, jet tubs, and layers of silky linens on plush, king-sized beds. "I'd like to book a room for Friday night. I also want a plate of chocolate covered strawberries, chilled champagne, and a dozen red roses in the suite."

After finalizing the reservation, he stripped out of his jacket, and hung it on a hook in the corner of the construction trailer. Stopping in front of a mirror, he tightened his pectoral muscles so they danced beneath his shirt. He smiled. "She'll be sending *me* roses after I'm done with her." He dialed the number of Jenna's store.

"Rhapsody," she answered.

"I hope we're still on for Friday night. I made arrangements for something special."

A length of silence yawned through the line. "I'm sorry. I have other plans."

He gnashed his teeth together but steered his voice into an easy register. "Anything you can get out of?"

"Afraid not."

"Another time then. We're still on for the hospital benefit next week, right? You wouldn't cancel on me and break my poor lonely heart, would you?" Not waiting for a reply, he laughed and said goodbye. His next call was to Willy Parks.

Ten minutes later, the police chief was at the construction office rolling his tongue around a double-dip, chocolate ice cream cone.

"You were supposed to arrest him." Ash hammered the words into Willy's face, and it almost caused the top tier of the ice cream to topple onto his uniform shirt.

"Be reasonable. I said I'd find a way to hold him as soon as he drove into town, but he never leaves the Cummings' place."

"Well, if my guess is correct, he'll be leaving it Friday night. You have him picked up." Ash stepped behind his desk and sat. An e-mail confirming his booking at the Casino opened up on his tablet. Stabbing at the screen, he pressed "cancel reservation." He turned to Willy. "By the way, the next time I call you to my office don't make any pit stops. You don't need that ice cream. You're getting fat."

****

Over the phone, Bree gave instructions to photographer Larry Belka. "Book a flight into any New York airport and get a rental car. From the city you've got about a two-hour drive to a place called the Trails End. It's right outside of a small town called Cromline. Write it down."

Bree listened as he mumbled while jotting his instructions. "C...r...o..." and so on. "Got it."

"Get her routine down, but make sure she doesn't see you."

The strike of a lighter clicked and Larry made a sucking sound. Bree wondered how he was always able

151

to get such clear shots with a cigarette perpetually dangling from his lips.

"Not my first rodeo," he said.

"Don't pull an attitude with me, Larry. You're going to be paid very well for a very easy job." She waited as he dragged more smoke into his lungs. "I want you to leave as small of a paper trail as you can, but unfortunately no one flies these days without identification. Same goes for rental cars or I'd have booked everything for you. The motel, however, won't care what name you use."

"So, what you're saying is it's a dive."

Bree's tongue scraped at her palette audibly. "It's in an obscure location. I can't have you bumping into her or my husband."

The register of Larry's voice rose in excitement. "Laine is there?"

"Possibly, but I don't want you to take any pictures of him with Angel. I don't want the whole damned world to think they're an item." Bree was iron girder firm, then her tone eased into the fluid notes of an inspirational lecturer. "My husband's picture is in the paper all the time. But…Angel and Mark Chambers? Sell those to the tabloids and you won't even need the money I'm paying you."

Bree's next call was to her private investigator, Stephen Powers. "I'm ready for Chambers."

"There's a problem."

"Problem?" Her fingers seized viselike around the phone. "You were supposed to have him ready for me. Fix it."

There was a tinny snag of static through the speaker of Bree's burner phone; she had to make Powers repeat himself several times.

"It wasn't easy finding him. He doesn't have a job or a driver's license. After I found him, he demanded cash to stay put."

"And?" Sound squealed through her phone like feedback, and she had to extend her arm away from her ear. "What the hell is that noise?"

"Sirens. I'm in the dregs of Chicago and like I said…there's a problem."

"Enlighten me."

More words were repeated, the connection lost, and entire sentences recapped before it became understood that Mark Chambers had been arrested after roughing up a prostitute.

"Even hookers find him repulsive. You might want to rethink this plan of yours."

"I didn't ask for your advice. Pay off his hooker, post his bail, and bring him to New York."

Chapter Twenty-Three

The muscles in Eric's shoulders burned from the chore of carrying cinderblocks to the back of the yard. Working on Ina's property was a better workout than any he had ever had in his private gym at his Pacific Palisades estate. Although he wasn't overly fond of the house, or how a wrong turn required search and rescue, he did miss his spa tub. A good soak would do his aching body a world of good.

Now that the roof was done, it was on to grouting the foundation. Being on *terra firma* would be a welcome change. The place was starting to shape up. After the foundation was sealed, the plumbing replaced, and new wallboard plastered, it would be just a matter of cosmetics. Ina had gotten her loan and hired an electrician. Wiring was the one thing Eric wasn't sure he could tackle on his own. He worked tirelessly into the late afternoon and then got ready for his date.

"Well, these won't do," Ina said, holding up a pair of jeans with a hole in the seat. "And this shirt! Good Lord, haven't you ever heard of an iron?"

Eric dug through his leather satchel and proudly pulled out a fresh pair of jeans and an Oxford shirt as wrinkled as the one in Ina's hand.

She shook her head, her gray hair fluttering. "It's no wonder nobody around here believes you're a movie star. You're a slob. It wouldn't have killed you to go out and buy something decent to wear."

Eric smiled and winked at Ina. "Darlin', everything I need is right here."

His flirtatious teasing never failed to bring a blush to her face, and she waved her hand across her cheek. "Save all that charm and bullshit for your young lady."

****

Loaded with a sleeping bag, pillow, and knapsack, Janie kissed her mother and hopped into Anne Mills' minivan.

"Have fun tonight," Anne shouted from her window. She winked and blew exaggerated kisses, then drove away.

Charged with energy, Jenna rushed through the house picking up whatever items were strewn about—junk mail on the kitchen island, laundry yet to be folded, and hoodies draped over the newel post on the stairs. Chills nipped her skin and a buzzy sensation trailed from her throat to her stomach. She poured herself a glass of wine and went up to bathe. Goblet in hand, she sank into a froth of bubbles, the heady essence of vanilla settling her nerves.

Hopefully the night would tell her what she needed to know. Her heart insisted Eric was the same man she had loved, but hearts were too often misleading. They enticed, and lied, and swept away reason. Hearts told you what you already wanted to hear.

Jenna stepped from the tub calm enough to grapple with the buttons on the blouse she'd picked out. She applied makeup, smearing and blending to make the cosmetics look like the result of nature. A little less gloss, she decided as she blotted her lips. Nature only made them *that* wet in the rain. She fluffed and flattened her

155

hair and changed her outfit three times.

"What are you doing?" she said into the mirror. "He isn't the captain of the football team, and you aren't sixteen." She took a deep breath. "That's better." Then the doorbell rang and she felt an urgent need to pee.

Eric was there on the porch. He was wearing jeans with knife sharp creases, a shirt starched into an origami project, and topsiders. He shrugged. "Ina ironed me."

Jenna burst out laughing. "I'm sorry. I've just never seen you look so...so—"

"Much like the big nerd on campus. Keep laughing. There's a corduroy blazer in my truck that belonged to her husband. I'll put it on if you don't stop."

Jenna continued to giggle, and Eric winked. "You said we had to go somewhere low-key or I would have worn a suit."

She brought a finger to her bottom lip. "Nah, jeans are a better look for you."

He dipped his head and made a slow journey from her feet to her face. The ardent appraisal stopped at her eyes, but the heat of his stare pushed past the simplicity of flesh and bone. Jenna felt his gaze meander deep and intimate.

****

A static interrupted voice bleat through the police radio at Willy Park's house. "That pickup you wanted is parked on Redbud Road."

"Damn it," Willy swore under his breath before pressing the button to answer. A two-inch thick sirloin sizzled on the barbecue, and a vat of potato salad sat on the patio table. He ground his words into the mike. "You were supposed to radio me when he first left Mrs. Cummings, not after he already made it through town."

"Sorry, Chief, but I got a call…kids loitering in the park."

Five pale ales were already slogging behind Willy's "Kiss the Chef" apron. He snapped at his officer. "Kids are always loitering in the damned park. I wanted you to stop him."

"Should I pull him over and hold him for you now?"

Willy belched into his hand and flipped his steak hard against the grill's grate. Hot fat sprayed his arm. "Shit!"

"Should I keep tailing him?"

"No. Just do your fucking job, next time."

****

Eric pulled into what was more of a field than a parking lot. His truck's thick tires crunched over gravel as he pulled between another pick-up and a grassy shoulder. Neon beer signs lit the area blue and orange.

"The place isn't very fancy, but they have great wings, and it's dark inside. I ate here my first night in Cromline."

Jenna's expression held a look of unease. "Did anyone recognize you?"

"Just the barmaid. I called and promised her a hundred bucks for a private table in a dark corner. She guaranteed no one will bother us."

"That's a pretty big tip."

"I used to work for tips. Remember?"

"Of course I do." Jenna's voice dropped and she lowered her head, her sight at her twined fingers. "What's it like for you?"

"What's what like?"

"Being famous."

He slipped the gearshift into neutral and cut the

engine, his hands resting idly on the steering wheel. "Nothing like it was for you. You were a phenomenon. I was just one of a half dozen kids on a really bad teen drama." He reached over and gently swept away the hair falling across her face. "You don't really need to hear this."

"I do," she insisted. "I need to know who you are."

His hand was still a warm caress against her cheek, his eyes falling lost into hers. They'd had a version of this conversation a lifetime ago. It was the night they'd eloped. Eric had insisted she listen as he admitted to his humble childhood and troubled adolescence. At first, she tried to deny him his confession, but he begged until she agreed. Now, she *wanted* to know about his life, and he could hardly refuse.

"I'm still me." He shrugged, never relishing the attention that was part and parcel of fame. "The press is a pain. They push and get too close hoping I'll react…lose it. I still have a reputation for being a hot head even though it's been a decade since I've raised my hands in anger."

The reference to the day he beat Mark Chambers bloody stalled their conversation and they sat quiet and still in the car's dark interior. Eric eventually spoke. "I'm not mobbed everywhere I go like you were. No one grabs at my clothing or tries to rip locks of hair from my head." He took a heavy breath. "I should have protected you from all of that."

"That wasn't your job."

"It was." He drifted into silence again and peered through the truck's windshield. Stars were a milky blur against the ribbons of steam rising from the tavern's chimney. Sparks of light glinted off cars, and a black silhouette of trees was in the distance. Eric hopped out of the truck and jogged to Jenna's door.

They stepped through the entryway of the bar and eased their way to a corner table in the back. Its wood was scuffed with age and a candle flickered in a small clay pot. They ordered burgers. But as they shared more tidbits about their lives, the more prone they were to gaze, eyes locked and lingering, their food eventually discarded.

The tavern was dark and clamoring with the sounds of a bar—plates and silverware rattling, the sharp clack of pool-balls, and the humming of voices. It became an external buzz. Sound and motion, even the bright shock of neon over the bar blurred, tuned out by two people who only had each other in their sights.

Eric took her hand. "We've wasted so much time, so many years. Give me another chance, Jen. Give us another chance."

Jenna slipped her hand from his and laid it against his face. It felt good to touch him, for her palm to rest against the hard contours of his cheek and jaw, so good and so familiar.

"I love you, Jen. I never stopped."

He paid the tab, adding three crisp hundred-dollar bills instead of the one promised. They walked out into the balmy spring night. Her hand was still in his as he drove back to her house, his declaration of love playing over and over like a perfect refrain. He brought her hand to his lips and kissed her fingers. "I mean it. I never stopped loving you. Not for a moment."

Jenna smiled, tears filling her eyes. She had never stopped either. The best she had ever managed to do was wrap her loneliness and heartache into a tolerable burden, one she ferried as she and Janie moved from place to place, disconnected and alone.

She gripped his hand tighter, wishing he would never let it go. An oldie about lightning striking again appropriately drifted from the radio as he pulled into the driveway.

****

Ash Baldwin sat in his car, well hidden behind the overflowing greenery of a blooming seasonal shrub. A pickup truck pulled into Jenna Black's driveway and the sound of doors slamming broke the quiet night air. Ash's car crept along the street as two figures in silhouette stepped through her entryway.

He tapped his fingers on the steering wheel as the duo disappeared behind the front door. Illumination moved from window to window followed by darkness. The path of light ended upstairs. When the last rays of yellow blinked to black, he picked up his cellphone and called Jake and Harley Simpson.

Chapter Twenty-Four

Jenna stood in the bedroom enveloped in shadow, her eyes picking up the low flicker of a candle. They shined like fiery twin jewels, glittering amber, topaz, and peridot, a prism of color that reminded Eric of the sun setting over an autumn glade. Even in his imagination, he couldn't recall a more alluring sight. He stepped close without touching her and lowered his head so their lips gently brushed. "I thought I'd be giving you a gentlemanly peck on the cheek and going home."

"Is that what you want to do?"

He swallowed hard. "No, Babes. Now that I'm here, I have no intention of being a gentleman." He pulled her close and kissed her. The demanding press of his lips was payment for all the years they were apart and all the kisses and moments they had missed. Eric swept her into his arms and laid her on the bed. Her hair, glowing golden, fanned around her face. He leaned over and pulled the satin ribbon at the neckline of her blouse. Silk fluttered open and slipped from her shoulders. Jenna lay there, her skin pale and luminous. Shadows accented her features and transformed her into a lovely portrait.

"You are so beautiful," he said, and he kissed her again, and again, and again.

His blood became fire, Jenna's touch the wind making it burn and rage hotter and wilder. "If you want me to stop, tell me now."

She slid her arms around his neck and drew him closer. "Kiss me," she whispered. "I don't want you to stop. Love me."

Straddling her hips, he sat up to unbutton his shirt. All thought abandoned him, and his body became an entity drawing on pure instinct.

Jenna stared, from beneath heavy lids, as he shrugged out of his shirt. Her eyes trailed from his wide shoulders to the swell of his arms, and the hard rippling of muscle on his stomach. A dusting of hair, unfamiliar, and a reminder of the nine years that passed, stretched across his chest and down the center of his abdomen. She reached up and undid the top of his button-fly jeans, and with a bold tug the rest gave way.

He threw his head back and took a deep breath. He kissed her again and then drew her filmy blouse from the waistband of her pants. His hands trailed along her bare ribs, and with a pinch he released the fastening on the front of her bra.

Jenna shivered as he cupped one of her breasts. The pad of his thumb was callused and rough against her nipple and she shivered more. She arched her back in offering. He peeled her blouse and silken bra from her, and they fluttered away like dandelion seeds on a breath. Then his mouth was on her bare skin, warm and wet, as he moved from one tight peak to the other. She ran her fingers through his hair and down his neck to his back, languorously glancing over ridges of muscle.

Then the smooth seductive ritual of foreplay became a sudden clumsy grappling—shoes thumping to the floor and more of the whooshing of clothing being removed. A ball of denim, silk, and cotton collectively hit the carpet. In one fluid motion, Eric was between Jenna's thighs and deep inside of her, her legs tight around his back. She pressed her hips to his, thrusting against him, sliding over the steely thickness inside of her.

Eric rose up on his arms, his body shaking, and his chest heaving. "Stop, Jen."

"I can't." She panted her response and writhed, rotating her hips beneath him and drawing him deeper into the heat.

"It's been too long. I won't be able to hold back. Stop wiggling, dammit! Christ, I feel like some clumsy teenager."

Jenna looped her arms around his neck and pulled him back down for a kiss. Their mouths melded together as his body tightened and broke into a series of palpitating shudders. He went heavy and still.

"I'm sorry…I just couldn't hold back…I've never felt anything like…" He collapsed once again into silence.

She continued to tease the back of his neck, her fingers feathery touches against his skin. She giggled, her breath warm at his throat.

"Laughter is the absolute last response a man wants from a woman after lovemaking."

"You call that lovemaking?" Her voice was a sultry taunt.

Sliding his arms beneath her, Eric rolled to his back and reversed their positions. He was still tightly coupled to her. "You be in charge then. Let's see if you can do better."

They made love again, their bodies a slow and leisurely press. Jenna rode Eric in long strokes, pulling almost completely away and slipping, warm and easy, onto him. She bent over, her breasts grazing his chest and her hair pouring down gossamer light. Eric whispered words of love and she returned the declarations, gasping his name as her pleasure built. There was no arm, no leg, fingertip, or strand of hair uninvolved in their passion play. Desire bound them tightly together, pleasure, earth shattering and transcendent released them. They lay spent, wrapped in each other's arms. In a while Eric's breathing became steady and even with sleep.

Jenna studied his face, taking in his perfect features—his finely arched brows, and the dark lashes she knew accented eyes the color of an island pool. In slumber, he sprawled on his back, one arm carelessly thrown over his head and the other reaching for her.

You should have told him, the niggling voice of her conscience scolded. You should have told him before letting him make love to you. "I'm so sorry," she whispered, then curled into the warmth of his body, and joined him in sleep.

****

In the morning, Jenna left Eric lying comfortably in her bed and stepped into the shower. Not long after, he sauntered naked through the steam and joined her. Air caught in her lungs as he scrubbed at his face, water running down his neck and torso. The steady flow was interrupted before it reached his legs.

"Happy to see me?"

"That?" He looked south. "It's the morning." He winked and moved close enough for the object of her interest to press against her. "I didn't actually wake up this way, but I heard the shower running and thought…naked and wet works for me."

Eric turned her in his arms so that her back was to him. He poured a dollop of shampoo into his hands and ran it through her hair. Leaning back against him, she groaned as he slowly massaged her scalp. Heady scented foam slid down her neck and back. His hands moved from her hair to her nape, his fingertips teasing her soap-glazed skin. He rubbed her shoulders and breasts, spreading the silky bubbles lower and lower.

She moved to the showerhead, and a cascade of water pulsed against her. "Your turn," she said as she picked up a bar of soap, pink and sweetly scented. She rubbed it across his chest.

"Mmm, won't I smell pretty," he murmured.

"Shut up." She discarded the bar and reached down to stroke him. Her hand was warm and slick, and his low moan told her he was not going to be able to tolerate the erotic milking for long. He picked her up and drew her legs about his waist, spearing her in one hard lunge. Smooth tile was against Jenna's back, Eric's chest and thighs warm and hard against her. The water rained down upon them as he began to move, his hips grinding rhythmically. Her climax was immediate and intense, her cries of pleasure muffled by the sound of water splashing against the shower door.

****

Wrapped in a terry cloth robe, Jenna sat on the edge of her bed watching Eric dress. It brought back memories, pleasant ones. Damp hair fell into his eyes as he bent over to tug on his jeans. He walked barefoot toward the bed to retrieve his shirt and give her a kiss. After shrugging into the garment, he took her hand and urged her from her seat.

"Do you want to go grab some breakfast somewhere?"

Half joking, Jenna pointed to herself and then at

him. "Former popstar and currently famous actor? A dark bar is one thing but a bright café…?"

"Ina's then?"

She shook her head. "I can't. Janie will be home soon."

He nodded his understanding. "Babes, it's a little late for me to be asking this but…are you on any kind of birth control?"

Wincing, she admitted she wasn't. It was embarrassing that at twenty-nine, she had been so caught up in the moment she'd given no thought or regard for responsibility."

His hooded eyes seemed to darken from turquoise to deep cobalt. "Nothing would make me happier than if we made a baby."

"Given your current marital status, that's a complication I'm sure you don't need. We should have been more careful. I had no right to…"

"Shh." He brought his lips to her temple. "No regrets. I'll call you later." He pulled her close for one last lingering kiss before excusing himself and lamenting he'd be spending his Saturday crawling through a damp basement to sweat pipes. Sprinting down the stairs, he waved goodbye and bounded out the door.

Jenna watched as he jogged to his truck. As it pulled onto her street and sped away, she sunk into a familiar pit of remorse. "Jenna Welles, what the hell is wrong with you?"

Chapter Twenty-Five

There were few early risers in Cromline on Saturday Eric noticed as he drove down the main street. A man and woman, dressed straight from an athletic catalogue, jogged into the gourmet shop. *Designer coffee to go with the designer running gear.*

He turned off the avenue and crossed a small side road that led to the even smaller rural country road and Ina's. He fiddled with the radio, and after finding a static free station he tapped his fingers on the steering wheel in time with the music. Euphoria would be a word lacking in intensity if he were to describe his feelings.

Cruising slowly along, his mind was filled with nothing but thoughts of Jenna—holding her, kissing her, loving her. He took no notice of the trill of birdsong or the tall tufts of spring green on the road's shoulder. He took no notice of the train whistle in the distance or how bright and blue the sky was. He took no notice of the rusted truck hanging back but following at every turn.

On the wooded lane close to Ina's, the pickup barreled forward. It made a screeching circle and cut him off. Slamming on the brake Eric stopped just in time to avoid it. The near collision barely registered when his door opened, and a pair of hands grabbed him and threw him to the ground.

****

Willy Parks almost stabbed himself affixing his

badge to his shirt while running out the door. The radio clipped to his shoulder crackled at his ear. "Chief, your suspect's pickup truck was on Redbud Road all night."

"All night? Shit," Willy cursed. "Is it still there?"

"Negative, pulled away five minutes ago."

He hurried to his police cruiser and revved the engine, and then sped in the direction of Ina Cumming's house.

****

Tumbling into the dirt, Eric looked up into the ugliest face he had ever seen. Pock marks shone white over a red veined complexion, and teeth were gapped like broken spokes on a wheel. Before he had a chance to roll away, the man's foot caught him squarely in the ribs. He let out a grunt and tried to shake off the pain as he heard the stomping of more footsteps behind him.

"I got his wallet. He's got a pile of cash in it."

"Bonus! Now let's finish this. A couple more busted ribs will send the message."

Eric rose to his knees, but a boot to the cheek sent him back into the dirt. He drew his legs into his chest and slammed his attacker away with his feet. He didn't, however, have enough time to maneuver away from the second man who was wielding a baseball bat. As Eric attempted to stand, the bat landed hard at his side.

White hot pain spread through his body as he heard the snapping of ribs. Groaning, he braced for more, but his assailants took a beat to admire their work. While steeped in childish laughter, neither one noticed Eric rising. He punched one, and the hard crunch to the jaw made the man loosen his grip on the bat. As it rolled under his feet, he fell to the ground. Eric spun around and caught the other one with a hard elbow to the teeth. The two well-connected blows only bought him seconds of time before both men were on their feet and approaching.

Eric wheezed as breathing became an effort. At least two ribs, he figured, were broken. He gawped air and a fight or flight measure of adrenaline rushed through his blood to halt his pain. The provisional numbness allowed him to throw a few more punches and run to his truck. Just feet shy of it, the two men tackled him to the ground, and Eric could do nothing more than try to protect whatever parts of his face and body were the most damaged. He threw punches wherever he could.

"This was supposed to be an easy job," one of the men said. He huffed and panted hard. "Baldwin never said anything about this guy being such a brawler."

"Shut the fuck up, you idiot! Crap, now we're going have to kill…"

The man stomped over to the bat lying on the ground. He walked back slowly, swinging it through the air for practice. Eric, whose ears were ringing, and eyes narrow slashes, saw at least four bats coming toward him and made one last effort to get up. A siren wailed, and the men jumped into their truck and sped away. Eric folded back down onto the ground as everything went black.

The sharp tang of ammonia wafted into his sinuses. He roused quickly, the pain jolting him awake as suddenly as the pungent vapor. A face loomed close, distorted by the red light flashing rhythmically across it.

"What the hell happened here?" a cop demanded.

Eric struggled up onto his elbows and spat a mouthful of blood at the ground.

"Mugged. I don't suppose you plan on going after them."

"You got some ID?" the cop demanded more than asked.

Eric winced as he tried to stand. "They took my wallet."

The cop tipped his hat back away from a domed forehead and pivoted his face from side to side while clucking his tongue. "Let me get this straight, you have no identification and you're driving that truck?"

Sunshine, still low on the eastern hillside, cast glaring shafts of yellow against trees and brush. It enveloped everything in a white haze, all Eric could see through his slitted eyes anyway. "That's my truck, but like I said, they took my wallet."

"I'm gonna have to run you in."

The cop handcuffed Eric and lobbed him into the back seat of a police cruiser. He groaned in pain thinking lying on shards of glass would have been more comfortable than sitting with his arms drawn so tightly behind his back. "Do you mind telling me what I'm being charged with," he was still brazen enough to ask.

The cop glanced through the cruiser's rear-view mirror. "Disorderly conduct and driving without a license."

As Eric expected he was led to a cell, not read his rights, and not been allowed his one phone call. Like hearing the ogres say the name Baldwin, none of it came as a great surprise.

Chapter Twenty-Six

After drying her hair, Jenna inspected herself in the mirror for any telling signs of love making on her body. The soft swelling of her lips wasn't that noticeable, but the moony smile that touched her eyes might tip off a knowing friend. Thank goodness Randi was still home with her family.

Jenna picked up Janie from Anne's, and they had breakfast at the café. Beverages with three-inch toppings of foam seemed in order—caffeine to bolster Jenna and hot chocolate for Janie—the proverbial spoonful of sugar to make the medicine go down.

An hour later they were home. "Baby, it's time we had that talk I've been promising you."

"Is this about my father?"

"Yes. It's about *me* and your father. I've kept things from you I shouldn't have, and it's time I told you the truth."

Heavy-hearted, Jenna regarded the serious posture of her little girl. Janie was a month shy of her ninth birthday, nine years of being denied her father, a father who would have loved and cared for her.

"First I need to tell you something about myself."

Stalling, Jenna studied her daughter's face. Janie was suddenly a baby again, a cherub with a soft round face and eyes like big blue buttons. "Before you were born, I was a professional singer. I was…was pretty well known."

"Well known? Like famous?"

Jenna shrugged. There was no reason to downplay this part of the story. She'd have to sugar coat enough of it. "I was. I made two movies, and I had a big concert tour."

Wrinkling her nose, Janie began to laugh. "Yeah right, Mom."

"I'm serious." Jenna felt the blood rush from her face. She barely drew a breath.

Silence stretched forth. When Janie's giddy laughter stopped, she knew her daughter believed her. "But, but how?"

Jenna told her child the story of how she became famous without detail. She was a person on a journey not taking time to notice the surroundings, a person only intent upon arriving at a destination without delay. She watched her daughter's eyebrows rise with doubt, and her mouth skew crookedly as she absorbed what Jenna knew had yet to sink in.

"But, Mom, people don't get *un-famous*. Why aren't you still—"

"Something happened, sweetheart, something terrible." Jenna squeezed her eyes tight and took a deep breath before continuing. "It was something I was afraid might hurt you too, so I ran away when you were a baby."

Janie squinted and tipped her chin high as if bracing for a blow. Jenna's heart wrenched with a sudden pain as she realized her daughter's brave demeanor was something she had inherited from Eric. All the challenges he had faced, the hardship and suffering he'd endured during his own childhood had been met with the same resolve now standing before her. He didn't even know his daughter, yet he had given her his courage.

"Is that why we moved so much? Are we going to have to run away again, Mommy? Is that why you're telling me all this?"

"No, sweetheart, no more running." Jenna took her daughter in her arms and stroked her hair, the pale blonde waves silk against her palm. There were few euphemisms for the word rape, so Jenna told Janie very simply about Mark Chambers' "assault" and the terrible misunderstanding about her paternity.

It wasn't how she ever envisioned giving her daughter the "where babies come from" lesson, and the child's eyes began to fill. Jenna embraced her daughter tightly. "I wanted to tell you all of this when you were older, but your real father is here in Cromline, and he needs to know the truth also."

Jenna's confession ended with news about a cable program that might recount the sordid circumstance and media frenzy of Janie's birth. "We're going to have to be very careful about who we talk to and where we go from now on."

That bit of information, along with the name Eric Laine finally made Janie's small lips tremble and tears run down her cheeks in fat drops.

****

The wafer-thin mattress on the cell's cot did little to ease Eric's pain. He would have killed for an ice pack. Blood still oozed from his split and swollen lips, its metallic pungency making him gag. The reflux action was doing his ribs no good at all. From a small cage wedged back into a corner, Eric listened to the voices of the cops. The one who had arrested him seemed to be in charge as the other officers deferred to his orders and called him "chief." The lack of protocol during the arrest told Eric the police chief, and possibly one or two of the other cops, were somehow indebted to Ash Baldwin.

A galumph of rubber soles hitting the floor sounded. Eric closed his eyes. The lids were so swollen they were all but useless anyway. He listened as keys jangled and the door creaked open. He was given his ice pack. "Hold this to your face."

"Which part?" Eric asked, but he had already chosen his left eye.

"You feel dizzy? Nauseous? I might be able to get someone to come in and take a look at you."

"Here's an idea, Chief." Eric removed the ice pack to illustrate his point. "How about taking me to the fucking hospital? It's full of people who can take a look at me."

"You're in enough trouble without mouthing off." While the cop's tone was meant to convey authority, it girded the edge of anxiety.

Eric moaned as he swung his legs over the side of the bunk and struggled to sit upright. The musty quality of the cell, flaking paint, and the overall dank air in the small cube told him the cage hadn't been used in years, if not decades.

He had been arrested so often as a kid, he knew the drill. Depending upon the charge, minors were handed over to their parents, adults either ROR—released on their own recognizance—or sent to a county lockup to await arraignment. None of his current situation bode well for him.

"If you're not letting me out of here, you mind telling me exactly what I did?"

"I already told you...disorderly conduct, driving without a license. I can't let you go until I find out who you are. You could be a wanted felon for all I know."

Eric huffed. "Not lately. And I already told you who I am."

The police chief answered Eric's comment with a puzzled looking squint. Eric squinted back until the letters on the chief's nameplate stopped dancing.

"So...Officer Parks, does everyone whose wallet gets stolen rot in here, or just the people Ash Baldwin doesn't like?"

Flinched as if stung, Parks words were delivered in a reedy whine. "You're lucky I came along when I did. You'd be in a worse place than this cell if I'd let those boys finish with you. Nobody in Cromline gets in Baldwin's way. You show up out of nowhere and start stepping on his toes, what the hell did you expect?"

"I was *expecting* to get my phone call. By the way you forgot to Mirandize me."

Park's skin glistened with sweat. "I got your prints; that's all I need right now."

Eric placed a hand to his ribs, so he was able to take a meager breath. "Let me guess, it'll take a while to get them checked, and I don't get released until they are."

The chief mopped more beads of sweat from his brow with a handkerchief. "If you hadn't been rubbing your fingers raw putting shingles on Ina Cummings' roof, I might be able to match them up with a name."

"Assuming I've been fingerprinted before."

Park's scrutiny was a studied glower. "I think that's a safe assumption. Guys that show up out of nowhere, hanging around where they don't belong usually have a record."

Though he almost wanted to laugh, the sound that fell from Eric's mouth was a weary grunt. He thought again about his illustrious rap sheet. He scowled at crooked Officer Parks through eyes that were nothing more than lines above bloated cheeks. The look of malice he meant to convey was lost. "You're making a big mistake here, Chief."

The cop stuffed a crumpled handkerchief back into his pocket. "Look, pal, I have no beef with you. Just sit tight awhile, and when I let you out of here, you do us both a favor and get the hell out of this town before you're seriously hurt."

He stepped out of the cell and swung the door shut. It locked with a loud clank. He turned back to look through the bars. "This is a small town with a small police force. I can't guarantee the next time you get 'mugged' there'll be law around to stop it. Do you understand what I'm trying to tell you?"

Slowly, and taking painful strides, Eric walked over to the cell door and gripped the bars. "You listen to me, Chief. Ina Cummings' house better not get torn down while I'm in here. If it is, you tell Baldwin I'll bury him under a fucking putting green."

Chief Willy Parks gulped and puffed up his chest more. Still, his voice wavered when he spoke. "You talk pretty tough for a drifter who's beat to hell and locked in a cell."

"Don't stall trying to keep me here. If you don't believe I am who I say, then send my prints out so you know who it is you're dealing with."

****

Standing in the expansive foyer of the Baldwin mansion, Ash held his voice in check. He didn't scream at Willy Parks, and spoke, instead, in a dire whisper. "I told you if you didn't take care of the drifter, I would do it myself. Why in hell did you interfere?"

"J-Jesus, Ash. What the hell was I supposed to do, help the Simpson boys dig the guy's grave? You're not in the Mafia for Christ sakes."

Ash turned toward his mother and sister-in-law sitting in the adjoining living room. It was four o'clock and the start of the Baldwin cocktail hour. They were relaxing on chintz covered chairs, the pattern a busy onslaught of pink peonies. He clamped a hand on Willy's shoulder and spoke through clenched teeth. "Lower your voice. Cheryl has ears like a goddamned bat."

"Sorry." Willy shifted from foot to foot like a child squirming not to pee. "You got what you wanted. Your boy's out of the way. But my guys want to know why I'm not transferring him to county. That old holding cell hasn't been used in ten years."

Ash poked Willy in the chest, stabbing hard with his forefinger. "Well, you figure something out, and make sure you keep him there until the building inspector orders a wrecking crew to demolish the Cummings' house. You had better pray he didn't get too much work done on that eyesore."

Beneath Willy's belt and holster, his stomach rolled causing all of his cop apparatus to jerk. He belched and a smell like over fermented vinegar spilled from his mouth.

Ash recoiled in disgust. "Can't you control yourself?"

Willy covered his mouth with his fist and hiccupped more gas. "This is a real mess. I'm holding the guy with trumped up charges. I'm breaking more laws than I can count. My pension is going to fly right out the window. What if he's not just some drifter? He says he's—"

"Who? Eric Laine? He's yanking your chain. Cheryl's ridiculous rumor must have gotten back to him thanks to that old busybody he's been living with."

"But…" Willy was still wriggling and belching, while Ash's face tightened into a hard collection of distended muscles and bones.

"But nothing. How many movie stars do home repair as a sideline? Maybe Hollywood producers aren't paying enough these days. Brad Pitt probably has a part time job flipping burgers." Ash leaned close enough to make the police chief shrink in stature. "You locked him up, didn't you get a good look at him?"

"Only after the Simpsons worked him over. He's got two black eyes, but I have to tell you he held his own. In one of Eric Laine's movies he gets into a fight with these three guys and…"

Ash rolled his eyes. "You and that wife of yours spend too much time at the Multiplex. Do you honestly think the real Eric Laine ever got into a fight in his life? He's an actor. He can probably ballet dance better than he can box. As for your boy in the cell…he just got lucky."

Ash opened the door, and with a jut of his chin dismissed Willy. "I want you to find the Simpsons and make sure they don't come anywhere near the town line until your prisoner is long gone. And he doesn't get out until Ina's hovel is kindling. Do you think you can manage that, Will?"

Police chief Willy Parks answered with a nervous nod and another hiccup.

Chapter Twenty-Seven

Jenna brushed her fingers across her sleeping daughter's face and adjusted the covers. It was the fourth or fifth time she had checked on Janie since she went to bed. The child had been given a tremendous amount of information to absorb. She was frightened by the idea of the terrible man who thought he was her father, and resistant to accepting the idea of the man who was. Jenna smoothed the blankets and ran her hand across Janie's shoulders. She looked over at the dresser and the time on the cable box. It was after nine, and she realized the day had passed with no word from Eric.

"I need you," she whispered as she stared at the LED numbers. "Why haven't you called?"

****

Randi returned Monday and made herself useful by waiting on the intermittent flow of customers at the store. Jenna's wan complexion and red-rimmed eyes told her friend all she needed to know.

"Say it, Randi. Go ahead, just say I told you so."

She stammered. "Jen, I…I…"

Pounding on the register key made the machine whirr the total of the day's receipts. Jenna tore at the tape that spilled from the slot and shoved it along with the money into the bank deposit envelope.

"Do you want me to count that for you?" Randi offered.

Jenna handed the envelope to her friend and slowly sank onto the stool behind the counter. "You were right. He was just playing some sort of game with me. Ina Cummings said he never even went back to her house."

"Maybe something happened to him…an accident or…."

Jenna shook her head. "If Eric Laine was in an accident, it would be all over the news. He left. There's no other explanation."

Scribbling figures on a pad, Randi straightened the bills in the envelope. She gave an efficient tug on the zipper and clicked the lock. "You're tired and upset. You aren't thinking straight. It makes no sense for him to come here, spend almost a month trying to make up with you, and then disappear the day after you sleep together. It just makes no sense. Something must have come up…an emergency. I'm sure he'll call."

****

Three days after Eric went missing, Cromline's building inspector raided Ina's home. He scribbled furiously in his pad as he picked at crumbling mortar, shaking his head and scratching at the pad for every speck of dust that fell to the floor. He came equipped with vials of chemicals to test for lead, radon, asbestos, and whatever elements the EPA decided that, at seventy-eight years of age, she should no longer be exposed to.

Looking down his narrow nose, he clucked his tongue at cracks in walls long overdue for a skim-coat of plaster and paint. As he made his way to another room the floorboards creaked under his weight and again he turned to Ina, a pucker of displeasure crimping his mouth.

She faced away to let her eyes rove around the room

as if to commit each bit of trim, every doorknob, and each pane of wavy glass to memory. The image of a bulldozer driving over her house and reducing it to a mound of splintered wood spun with dizzying force through her mind. She could see the boards caving in upon themselves, hear the crack as they snapped in half. Every memory she kept cherished in her heart would be gone. Trees that were old friends and the precious herbs and perennials she had lovingly cultivated for more than half a century would be trampled by golf carts. Vines of pumpkins and berries, her livelihood, were going to be obliterated from her life to make way for Ash Baldwin's pro shop.

She watched the inspector more as he squinted, scraping away at chipped paint. She bit down on her lip to stanch her tears. The fate of her home shouldn't be left up to a man whose sole intent was to find the flaws. Why didn't the dour man see what Eric had seen—a brick hearth with a hand-carved mantel, spindles lolling crookedly on the staircase that were solid oak and salvageable. Antique brass doorknobs, blackened with age, could easily be cleaned. Eric had assured her everything was worth saving and would be restored.

Ina rubbed her veined hands together in worry now that the thought of her tenant had entered her mind. His disappearance made no sense. She didn't believe he would run off and leave without a word. As the days passed, she had become sure something must have happened to him. Jenna Black called and that only worried Ina more.

The building inspector made a last scrawl in the notepad, stabbing at the paper to endorse the finality of his decision. "You have seven days to vacate."

Squaring her shoulders, Ina raised her chin and steeled her eyes at the inspector. "Well then, for seven more days this is still my home and I'll thank you to get the hell out."

When the crunch of gravel abated, and the building inspector's car was gone from sight, Ina allowed her tears to spill from her eyes and zigzag down the wrinkles on her cheeks.

****

Eric looked down at a plate of runny eggs and fatty bacon. Four slices of toast, veiled beneath a layer of butter, shared the plate. "Ah…my morning dose of cholesterol, I was starting to run low."

"I'll bring you a muffin tomorrow." Willy Parks closed the cell door behind him and rushed away.

Eric ate the eggs and most thoroughly cooked pieces of bacon and discarded the rest of his meal. He stood and stretched to loosen knotty lumps in his neck but took care to avoid compromising his broken ribs. After six days, suffering was no longer an apt description of how he was feeling. Sharp pains had ebbed to a tolerable ache and his facial swelling had subsided. A stubble had sprouted and covered the bruises on his jaw, but bands of purple and chartreuse lingered under his eyes.

The chief returned and Eric handed him his plate. "Not that I don't think of this place as home sweet home, but I'd really like to upgrade my accommodations. Maybe have a room with a view, or better yet, one with a shower. Washing up in your rest room doesn't really cut it."

Willy ignored the comments and stepped back out of the cell, but Eric persisted. "Y'know, Chief, the first couple of days I was here, all I wanted to do was lie still and sleep off the pain. Now I'm starting to get *really* pissed off. I haven't been arraigned or formally charged with anything. I haven't seen a judge. Seems to me you've bypassed due process."

"Seems to *me* you're familiar with getting arrested."

"Could be. So when the hell do I get out of here?"

"When I say you get out of here."

Eric grabbed the bars with both hands and pressed his cheek up close, shouting as Willy Parks hurried away. "You mean when Ash Baldwin says so, don't you, you spineless son of a bitch!"

The plates rattled in the police chief's hand. "As soon as your prints—"

"Fuck you! You never sent them to the state police because if you had you would have let me go. I told you who I am a hundred times. Send my prints out."

He paced his cell for all of ten minutes before Willy returned. Without saying a word, the chief snapped a pair of extended link cuffs onto Eric's wrists, keeping his arms facing front. The chief trawled him to his desk and carefully rolled his fingers against an ink pad to blot them onto the print sheet.

"There. Satisfied?" Willy said.

Eric cleaned his fingers with an alcohol wipe and shrugged. "Lose the ones you took the day I got 'mugged' or did you just toss them in the trash?"

"Shut the hell up."

Once again, Willy Parks, corrupt chief of police, was in a lather of sweat, his uniform shirt dark at the armpits. Eric counted the number of times Parks brought a fist to his mouth and belched. The man looked to be fast approaching an ulcer, a heart attack, or both. He picked up the phone and called the trooper barracks.

"This is Police Chief William Parks of Cromline, badge number 8805. I'm sending a set of prints over for you to run through IAFIS, a John Doe I *just* picked up for vagrancy an hour ago."

"Just?" Eric raised his brows, smiled, and shook his head. "You are so screwed, Chief."

****

Vagrants weren't high on the list of a fingerprint match, and it took close to four hours before the chirping motor of the Fax machine peeled. Eric watched from his cell as the transmission came through. An endless roll of paper slid out of the machine and folded over onto itself like whipped cream on a sundae. Eric knew his resume would generate such a list.

Willy snatched the mass from the tray, straightening the length of flimsy paper to read it. Eric watched as the fat cop quickly scanned the mass.

"Anything interesting?" he called out.

"Very. Looks like you were quite the delinquent. I've never seen a rap sheet stamped with so many sealed juvie records."

Willy's waxy frown was replaced with a smile, and he blew a long whistle. "Well, well, well. Assault, resisting arrest, *and* attempted involuntary manslaughter. Ash was right about you. Movie star my ass."

Eric chuckled. "Stop scanning over the charges and read the name."

"No, no, no," Willy stammered. He gripped his middle just below his sternum as if he'd been stabbed. "Oh, Christ," he said, crumpling the papers. "I'm in a world of shit."

****

A buzz sounded and the heavy iron door swung

wide. At the discharge desk the prisoner gathered his personal effects from the manila envelope, putting keys and change back into his pocket before leaving the station house and walking into the bright spring sunshine. Outside a car was waiting.

"It's about time I got out of there," he said.

"Get in. I'm taking you to where you need to be."

"I'm coming for you, my love. I'll be there soon."

Stephen Powers released a tired sigh and shook his head as Mark Chambers reached for the car's door handle. "I'm really starting to regret taking this job. I don't know exactly what Bree Laine wants with you, but I do know Angel is not your love."

Chapter Twenty-Eight

Days passed and there had been no word from Eric. Jenna called Mrs. Cummings again, but the elderly woman hadn't heard from him and thought something must surely be wrong. Nick had given Jenna his number the night of the concert, so she called him. He said if Eric had something heavy on his mind he would take off for parts unknown. She supposed he hadn't been so sure of his feelings after all.

Janie never asked about Eric. She went about her days, quiet and contemplative, as she adjusted in her own way to the news that he was her father.

"Are you sure she's okay?" Randi asked. She had stayed to offer support, avoid her unruly children, and drink a nightly goblet of pinot noir undisturbed.

"I hope so," Jenna answered.

"The best thing you can do for her is to go on with your life and show her nothing has changed."

"Nothing has changed *yet*." Jenna's voice no longer broke into despair filled shudders, and she spoke in the flat tone of someone who'd come to terms with a loss. "But our lives are going to blow up if *True Hollywood Scandals* makes that documentary." She sank deep into the cushions of her sofa and curled her feet beneath her legs. "My poor baby is so confused. At first, she didn't want me to tell Eric about her; but now that he's gone and I can't, I'm sure she feels abandoned."

Randi reached over and squeezed Jenna's hand. "Maybe it just wasn't meant to be. Maybe he got cold feet. He still thinks Janie is Mark's. Maybe he still can't—"

"Accept her? I guess that makes two times I've misjudged his feelings."

Still holding hands, the two friends sat quietly in Jenna's living room. It was a lovely collection of soft colors and plump cushions, pale wood with wispy draperies and knitted throws, airy yet cozy. It was a haven, the home of a woman who'd almost realized security.

"Maybe I'm getting what I deserve. If I'd told him the truth when I first found out, my life wouldn't be spinning."

"The only thing you deserve is to be happy. You've made a great life for yourself here, and you don't need Eric Laine in it. You need to get over him."

Through eyes blurred by tears, Jenna looked at her friend. "How do I get over him now, when I never really got over him the first time?"

****

Eric nodded his head in the direction of the bunk opposite his own. "Have a seat, Chief. You don't look so good."

Eric was stretched out on his back with his head cradled in his arms. His bare feet were crossed at the ankles like a man languishing on a beach chair rather than someone who'd been beaten up and in the confines of a jail cell for six days. He sat up and studied the police chief. Sweat glazed Parks' forehead and damp rings showed under his armpits. He raised his head presenting Eric with a face that seemed to have aged in the last hour.

Dark puffy sacks dragged his eyes down, and his cheeks had melted into jowls.

"I told you who I was," Eric said.

The chief tugged at his tie. "How the hell do you have such a long rap sheet? And attempted manslaughter?"

"Tough childhood…bad luck…and the guy deserved it. I was acquitted for that last one."

Willy's mouth yawned wide as if he struggled to breathe. "Now what?"

"Now you can tell Ash who I am, and he'll probably tell you to shoot me and bury me in the foundation of one of his townhouses."

"J-Jesus." Willy swiped at his forehead, and his hand came away slick. "That's exactly what he'll do. I'm in a world of shit."

With his torso still a collection of bruises and fractures Eric grimaced as he stood. "Face it, Chief, a lot of people are going to wonder where the hell I am. My business partner knows I was here in Cromline, and so does Jenna Black and Ina Cummings. If you kill me, you'll just be in a bigger world of shit."

"Think what you want, but I'm no murderer."

Eric walked to the cell door. "I guess that's good news for me then."

The gleam of sweat on Willy's face turned to plump, shiny beads, and the rings under his arms spread. He sat on the bunk unmoving.

Eric looked back at the forlorn looking cop. "You, uh, want to open the cage and let me out of here?"

Willy plodded to the door and reached through the bars to get the key into the ancient lock. It clanked against it several times before he could maneuver it into the keyhole. Swinging the iron door wide Eric stepped through and wandered into a space with desks, bulletin board, file cabinets, and coffee maker. It wasn't much of a police station. *I've been locked up in better places than this.*

Willy motioned for a young officer clicking away at a computer keyboard to take his lunch break. Eric followed the young cop's departure with his eyes. "Weren't any of your guys suspicious? Didn't any of them wonder about me?"

Willy lumbered over to his desk. "They have pensions, benefits, and the most work they ever do is ticket speeders. They aren't exactly fucking F.B.I. material."

"Just fucking, lazy small-town cops."

Willy didn't argue the point. "So now what?"

"*Now* you're going to give me the keys to my truck. But first you're going to answer a few questions."

****

There were easily a dozen avenues of legal action Eric could pursue against Cromline's chief of police, but he chose not to. He didn't need the attention, and certainly didn't want to bring any Jenna's way. But the vise grip he had on Willy Parks was by far more of a squeeze than the one Baldwin had.

Willy readily gave his allegiance to Eric and supplied him with the names of his attackers and a promise to have a squad car standing guard at Ina's.

"Not one blade of grass gets cut," he ordered.

Looking like a big stupid dog who had just eaten his umpteenth slipper, the chief nodded.

Eric slowly shook his head as he summed up his jailer's life. Parks was a winning catch in high school who'd never considered straying from the parameters of his glory days. Eric knew the type. "What's Baldwin got on you anyway?"

"Enough for my wife to throw my ass out of the house. He has something on just about everybody around here."

"Well, he won't be using his clout for much longer." Eric reached for the phone on Willy's desk. His first call was to Jenna, but there was no answer.

"Probably out getting her hair done or something. Big shebang at the Lakeside Manor tonight," Willy volunteered.

A grumble juddered low in Eric's throat. "Is she going with Baldwin?"

"I…I think so. He'll wine and dine her till he gets her in bed."

Eric flashed Parks with the heat of the sun. "You really are an idiot, aren't you? Do yourself a favor and think before you speak."

He stabbed at numbers on the phone, and dialed Nick's cell. He held the receiver away, as a booming voice resounded from the earpiece.

"Are you done?" Eric asked after the noise subsided.

"Hell no! Jenna called a couple of days ago and said you were gone. I didn't want her to worry so I told her you went somewhere to think. When I couldn't find you anywhere, I flew back to New York. I'm in your fancy suite at the Plaza. Where the hell are you?"

"Some place I haven't been in a long time."

There was a beat of silence before Eric could hear a growl peppered with a dark laugh.

"Son of a bitch…You're in jail, aren't you?"

Chapter Twenty-Nine

Larry Belka parked his rental car on a side street off the main drag in Cromline. He wore a Polo shirt, khaki trousers, baseball cap, and sunglasses. He looked as generic and unremarkable as anyone walking along the avenue. In his pocket he fiddled with a small camera. He stepped slowly, his head pivoting at numbers on storefronts. Slung over his shoulder was a mail-bag type tote, the kind men preferred to old fashioned briefcases. In it was a larger and better camera.

He stopped at a corner and withdrew his phone from his pocket and pretended to make a call. As his target stepped from a nail salon he snapped away. Retreating behind a tree with a trunk wide enough to mask his presence, he retrieved a camera with a low light portrait lens from the bag and again snapped away.

He lit a cigarette and walked back to his rental.

In less than ten minutes he was at his motel, the room small, dingy, and paneled in something pretending to be wood. He booted his laptop and uploaded the pictures he'd just taken. On it there were already dozens of Jenna, a.k.a. Angel, and her daughter. He'd been instructed to follow her at a distance to get her routine down but not photograph her, or risk getting close enough to be recognized. But Larry Belka was not a patient man nor one who followed orders. Celebrity photographers had to be bold. He opened a digital image of the Angel-Mark Chambers love child. Larry clicked and clicked until the high-resolution picture filled the screen. "Hmm," he whispered. "This is interesting."

****

Jenna stepped across her foyer, black chiffon brushing her ankles. "How do I look?" she asked Randi, though she didn't really care much about the reply.

"You look like you got all dressed up to go to a formal wake. You need blush."

Jenna moved close to her mirror to adjust an earring that was twisted and not hanging in the same direction as its counterpart. "I'm only going to this hospital thing because I told Ash I'd go with him weeks ago. If I look a little pale that's just too bad."

Randi draped Jenna's velvet wrap over her shoulders. "A date with a handsome man is *just* what you need. Maybe it'll get your mind off…y'know. Try and have a good time. I'm going to take Janie out for ice cream." She folded her arms much like a matronly librarian in an old movie. "I don't want to see you any earlier than midnight."

A drone of sound signaled Ash's arrival. The car's engine gave a smooth rev then fell silent. The door shut with a thump followed by the insipid chirp of the alarm. Her date had arrived.

Jenna opened the door to greet him. *Had he always looked so arrogantly elitist, his nose so casually tipped toward the sky?* Jenna remembered the feel of his thin lips pressing against hers, and her stomach lurched at the thought of fending off another kiss at the end of the date. She desperately wanted to plead a headache and bow out, but Randi was standing in the living room, eyes raving like a guard dog tethered to a chain.

"Try and have fun," she ordered.

Once outside, Ash removed his tuxedo jacket and folded the garment, carefully placing it across the back seat of the roadster. His chest strained against his shirt, his weightlifting routine looking too dedicated to his laterals and trapezius muscles. It wasn't the natural ranginess of someone fit like…Jenna shook her head and forced Eric from her thoughts. She stared ahead as the car's motor hummed to life. She was having the worst date of her life, and they hadn't even left the driveway.

****

Ina had less than a tenth of her belongings packed and crammed into the bed of her truck. Whatever articles of furniture she wasn't able to move and store in her shed would be leveled along with the house in a few days. But that wasn't her biggest concern. She had made no other living arrangements and was going to be homeless.

"Well," she spoke aloud as if needing to hear the sound of a human voice one last time in the house. "Until tax time rolls around, I'll still own the land. I can always pitch a tent and sell my wares from there."

Of course not many customers would be inclined to shop at a place with splintered lengths of wood and a gaping hole in the yard. She stepped close to the curtainless window, the glazing putty not yet completely dry on the two replaced panes. "I was so close to saving you."

She looked out to take a last loving glimpse of her gardens. A black pickup truck pulled in, cut across the lawn, and disappeared in the back, away from the road. Ina blinked several times, stunned, relieved, and overjoyed. "Oh my God!" she shouted and burst through the back door.

****

Eric slowly climbed down out of the truck and hitched toward the house. He was met with a beaming Ina, but as he limped closer, her jubilant smile appeared to sink into her socks. "Good Lord in Heaven. What happened? You look like you've been run over by a Mac truck."

Eric managed a smile wrapped up in a wince. "Nope, a truck would have just hit me once. I got run over by the Simpsons."

Ina's eyes protruded from their wrinkled sockets. "Jake and Harley Simpson?"

"I didn't get a formal introduction."

"It was Jake and Harley all right, those two are such rotten apples even the worms steer clear."

Eric smiled. He had missed her colorful description of things. His landlady closed in on him, frowning and clucking her tongue as she examined the bruises on his face. "Well thank God your teeth are all intact." He flinched as she pulled his shirt from his waistband.

"Good sized kidney punch. Piss any blood?"

"Ina please don't make me laugh," he begged while holding his side.

"I just knew when you went missing, something awful happened to you."

He carefully lowered himself into a chair. "I wasn't officially missing. In custody is what Chief Parks called it."

Stamping one foot against pitted linoleum, Ina folded her arms across her bosom. "Willy Parks had you locked up all this time? I'm so mad I could spit."

Again Eric had to resist the urge to laugh as his ribs weren't up to joviality. "Forget Parks for now. I need a

194

favor. Could you go into town and get an ace bandage from the pharmacy. The Simpsons took my wallet and I'm a little light on cash, but I'll pay you back as soon as my friend Nick gets here. He's on his way."

"First things first." Ina scrambled to get pots and pans out of one of several boxes on the kitchen floor. "You need to eat."

"That's not necessary. I'm going to a very fancy banquet tonight."

Eric saluted his landlady and climbed the stairs. He stepped over the rim of a claw foot tub and turned the handles of the shower. Streams of hot water followed by blasts of cold rattled through the pipes and out of the old shower head. Nevertheless, it felt good to have even the frigid water pulsating against his aching body.

After returning from the pharmacy, Ina supplied him with a set of electric clippers meant to groom a dog. He removed a layer of whiskers from his face but intentionally left a five o'clock shadow to mask the chartreuse and purple that lingered on his jaw. Nick arrived with a tux, shirt, and tie.

After dressing, Eric inched carefully down the stairs to find his friend at the table, fork in hand. *Leave it to Ina to prepare a meal from nothing.*

"Mrs. Cummings, if I weren't a confirmed bachelor, I'd marry you. This is the best meal I've eaten in…I can't remember when," Nick said. "Mmm, mmm, honest to goodness food with no sprouts or fancy lettuce clogging up the plate."

Ina busied herself swiping crumbs from the massive slab of oak. "Bean sprouts are good for you. That's why all you California folks are so healthy and good looking."

Eric smiled, watching as Nick actually blushed.

"I'm originally from Brooklyn and the handsome lad over there," he said, pointing his fork at Eric, "is from Oregon."

Though Ina was speaking to Nick, her head was tipped toward Eric. "Well do me a favor and take care of him tonight. He says he's feeling okay, but he's favoring his right side and his eyes don't look good."

She took Nick's empty plate and threw it into the sink. Suds splashed the scuffed laminate counter because she'd dropped the plate with too much force. "Ash Baldwin was a spoiled little boy who grew into an arrogant and demanding man. He's a vengeful bastard when he doesn't get his way, and that doesn't happen much around here. Eric is about the only one I know to ever cross him, and Ash won't stop going after him."

"Don't worry. Eric can take care of himself, and I won't be far away if he needs me."

"Well I need you now." Eric tossed his jacket onto a chair, stripped out of the shirt and spread his arms wide. "I need you to wrap my ribs."

Ina gasped and shook her head. Irregular masses of color like a radar map of a storm still covered his ribs. "That bastard. I'd like to squeeze him by the balls until he hits the high note in *The Ave Maria.*"

A thunderous roll of laughter spilled from Nick's mouth while Eric gripped his side. "Ina, I begged you not to make me laugh."

Nick rolled the ace bandage around Eric's ribs, then helped him shrug into a shirt. "So what's the plan? You going to crash this hospital benefit?"

Ina stepped over with a tie while Eric buttoned up. "I guess if I write a big enough check, no one will mind. By the way, how'd you get the tux?"

Smiling, Nick rolled his eyes. "Are you kidding? Every designer in New York has one altered to fit you."

Hitching at the waistband, Eric declared the pants to be loose. "I didn't eat much this past week."

"Well, hopefully they won't fall down. Let's go."

Nick drove a limousine with Eric sitting quietly beside him. His patience with Baldwin had been stretched tight and he was probably going to lose his reserve and do something stupid. Nick in his typical fashion would be there to prevent it.

Chapter Thirty

Stephen Powers stepped up to what served as a reservation desk—a high counter with both a phone and television sitting on top and a disinterested looking woman sitting behind. He signed in using a fake name and gave the desk manager enough cash to pay for a week's worth of board.

He returned to Mark Chambers who was outside petulantly slumped in the car. "This place is a dump."

"Stop complaining. It's no worse than your apartment. They take cash and don't ask questions."

"Humph. Trails End. That bitch Bree put me in a dive on purpose."

Powers' lips were pursed together, his face bearing the expression of someone who had just eaten something spoiled. Every time Mark opened his mouth, a fetid smell filled the air. "That *bitch* is paying you a small fortune. Go to your room and I'll get Belka."

Powers drove to the back where a series of double unit bungalows stood lined up like army barracks. He knocked on number fifteen. There was no answer. "He's not here. Just go inside and wait for him. I'm catching the redeye back to L.A.. I've had enough of babysitting you."

Mark whined, "You can't just leave me here. I'm hungry. Take me to that diner we passed."

The motel sat amid a gnarled mass of plant life—

dense conifers, reedy grasses, and tiny saplings with more girth than Mark's physique. "From the looks of you, I doubt if you ever eat anything besides bar nuts and pretzels."

"I'm hungry," Mark insisted, but he appeared to be working on a good case of the shakes.

Powers delivered him to the diner, gave him the money Bree promised, Jenna Black's address, and a word of advice. "Order some food to go with the liquor. And make it simple because I'm only giving you a half hour to eat."

After ordering coffee, he went to use the rest room. He made the mistake of leaving his keys on the counter, and when he came out less than three minutes later, both Mark and the rental car were gone.

****

The dinner hour was over; the lights set low. Members of the wait staff wove through the milling clusters of the elite. They carried trays of pastries and flutes of champagne. The ballroom of the Lakehouse Manor was an expanse of paneled cherry-wood topped with carved moldings and a coffered ceiling. Deep-hued paintings of hounds, and horses, and men on the hunt assumed sizeable space on the walls.

Ash turned Jenna in time with the music. "I can't believe you've never been here. My family practically built this place with the Vanderbilts back when."

Jenna mustered a weak smile. Listening to Ash wax on about his ancestors was making the night painfully long. His hand was easy at her waist but hers lay like a dead tree branch on his shoulder. She'd eaten very little of her dinner. Salmon with dill sat like a lump in her stomach.

"I'm hoping to keep up the tradition with Baldwin Ridge, build a retreat for New York's society, give them somewhere they can go to escape the city."

Over Ash's shoulder Jenna rolled her eyes. From the tone of his voice he sounded like he believed he was performing some great and noble act. She couldn't hold back her tired sigh. Building a country club wasn't like constructing a homeless shelter.

As he moved to pull her closer, she shrugged out of his arms. "Excuse me. I need to step outside for some air."

Ash followed and snapped his fingers for the attention of a waiter. "Bring a glass of champagne over here."

Tired and edgy, Jenna made no attempt to disguise her frustration. "I wish you wouldn't talk to people that way."

Eyes that had been warm and disarming turned cool. "I asked for a drink. That's what the staff here get paid for. I'm sorry if that offends you."

Ash Baldwin picked the wrong moment to display his snobbishness. Jenna wheeled on him. "What offends me, *Ash*, is when someone born into fortunate circumstances lords his position over those *less* fortunate. People should be treated with respect whether they're serving the champagne or drinking it."

She gave him her back and swept away, leaving him alone on the terrace.

****

Eric handed a woman at a table in the foyer of the Lakehouse Manor a check, then strode into the ballroom and found Jenna, her pace hurried and her countenance one of exhausted frustration. Her lips were set in the same tired slash Alan Stark used to provoke. Not far behind, Baldwin hastened after her.

Taking a shallow breath, Eric tested the strength of his ribs. Broken or not, if the man had done anything to Jenna, he was getting his pompous ass kicked. Eric watched as she pushed her way into the ladies' room. Hands in his pockets, he loped over.

Baldwin's eyes snapped wide. "What in the hell are *you* doing here?" Both confusion and anger were written on his face, especially in the tightness of his boxy jaw.

"You look pissed off, Baldwin. Is it because I'm out of jail, or because I'm still alive?"

Ash answered with a low growl. "I don't know how you got *my* police chief to let you out, but you're both going to regret it."

"Don't count on it."

A few people lingering in the hallway were met with Ash's dismissive glare. They obediently retreated to the banquet hall, whispering behind their hands as they went. He bullied his way close, stopping only when his chest made contact with Eric's. "Looks like you haven't learned your lesson."

"You're not man enough to teach me one. If you were, you wouldn't have hired the Simpsons."

Clearing his throat, Ash Baldwin looked, for a moment, off balance. He quickly regained his composure and leaned closer. "I'm not about to soil my hands on you." Narrow eyed he grinned and spoke in a triumphant whisper. "I have other associates who will be more than willing to escort you to the town line." He sniggered. "And don't steal that cheap tuxedo; bring it back to the rental shop before you go."

Eric laughed and shrugged wide shoulders beneath

the expensive jacket he'd worn to The Golden Globes. "You must be mistaking me with someone who's afraid of you, like your building inspector or Parks. I'm never taking fucking orders from you."

"Classy," Baldwin spat.

Embarking in a staring contest, neither man moved nor spoke. Ash ended the confrontational silence by poking a thick finger in the center of Eric's chest. "I've had about enough of you. I want you out of *my* town. Whether or not you leave under your own power is up to you. I don't really care."

Eric answered with another lazy shrug.

A rhythmic tic pulsed beneath Baldwin's left cheek and his blond brows loomed low over icy-gray eyes. "You're messing with the wrong man, drifter. Interfering in my business was a stupid thing to do." His eyes settled at Eric's bruised jaw. "Thinking you can compete with someone like me for a woman like Jenna Black…insane."

The amiable ease of Eric's stance turned tight and sober. His careless grin became a cool slash. "Don't sweat it, Baldwin. Your date is over. Jenna is mine."

Grabbing Eric's lapels, Ash pushed him into the damask covered wall. Eric's shoulder blades met the plaster with a thump, and a chorus of gasps sounded from the patrons lingering by the lounge's entrance. Fighting off a surge of pain, Eric pushed back. More thumping and the muffled sounds of angry voices caused the women in the ladies' room to rush out, Jenna included. Guests hovered nearby, adopting disinterest, but still watching a scene of two men tethered to each other on the verge of fighting.

She blinked when she saw Eric, and her mouth

dropped open. "What the hell is going on? Where have you been? And what happened to your face?"

With the heels of his hands, Eric shoved Ash away. "Maybe you'd like to tell her, Baldwin."

"What the hell is going on?" Jenna repeated.

Spreading his arms, Ash spoke around an unconcerned grin. "Your friend got into some trouble in town and was arrested."

"You were in jail?" Her eyes were glittering, her head turning from one man to the other. A buzz of voices rode the air as a hesitant and curious parade of guests stepped past.

Ash's smile stretched wider. "Jail is where he belongs. Our good chief of police caught him in a near riot with two local boys. He'd been driving with no identification. Your *friend* is not only a public nuisance but a vagrant."

Jenna turned toward Eric and caressed the bruises along his cheekbone. It was comfort he'd welcomed from her before—a long ago night, after his father had beaten him, and years later, while he'd been in a hospital bed fighting for his life. Her hands slipped lower to cup his jaw. "Are you all right?"

He smiled, and Jenna slowly turned to face Ash. "A public nuisance? A vagrant? No, he isn't either of those things. He's Eric Laine, and he's a *fucking* movie star."

Laughing, Eric pulled her close. "Looks like you've been drinking wine."

Ash Baldwin's mouth yawned open for all of ten seconds before he regained his composure and his eyes settled back into his usual "I'm king of the castle" glower. "So my idiot sister-in-law was right all along?" He pierced Jenna with a glare so heated Eric pulled her behind his back.

"Right about you too, Miss Black. You're just some slag looking for a little side money from a rich man."

Jenna tugged Eric's hand before he had a chance to defend her. "Don't bother. He's not worth it."

A cluster of people were still idling in the hallway. Eric took one step forward, speaking low but close enough for his breath to drift into Baldwin's ear. "I'm used to being stared at, but if you don't want your neighbors to hear what I have to say, you might want to come outside where we can talk in private."

Though Ash was still glaring, he followed, striding with his head high and tugging at the cuffs of his shirt like a dapper James Bond. Outside, Eric settled comfortably against the limousine and slipped his hands into his pockets. Ash matched the relaxed stance, folding his arms across his chest, his sight a gleaming halt at Eric's bruises. "Why the pretense, the handyman bullshit?"

"I don't have to answer to you, Baldwin. You, on the other hand, have a lot to answer for."

Ash took a lazy breath, and a narrow-eyed smile stamped his face. "Is that so? I had nothing to do with you getting your ass handed to you or arrested. Good luck trying to prove otherwise. You may be a celebrity, but around here…you're nobody."

Staring at the ground, Eric laughed. The sound came out dark and without humor. He slowly raised his head. "I'm the nobody who's going to prevent you from stealing Ina Cummings' property."

"Don't count on it. That dust bowl of hers is going to be mine, and that old nuisance is going to finish out her days in a state home."

As Eric started after Ash, Jenna tugged at his sleeve. Then in his customary fashion, Nick materialized, and stepped between the two men.

"Ha!" Ash declared. "Tough talk coming from a man who needs a bodyguard."

"You have it backwards, Baldwin. He isn't here to protect me from you, he's here to protect *you* from *me*." Eric shrugged. "As much as I'd like to repay the beating, I think I'll hit you where it will hurt the most…your country club."

Luxury cars pulled into the circular drive, and valets in red jackets stepped out and held the doors. Couples in black tie apparel slowly trekked from the columned entryway and disappeared into expensive sedans.

"There's nothing you can do about my project," Ash said. "People are already lining up to buy the condos. Baldwin Ridge was designed by a top course architect, and I've got PGA pros, tech giants, and celebrities backing it. In fact…" He paused and smiled as if a drumroll played to introduce a proud declaration. "One of my partners is a Hollywood legend, a bigger name than yours will ever be…Jack Morrissey."

After crowing his victory, Ash smiled but his head jerked in Nick's direction. A resonance of laughter boomed into the clear night air. He snapped his head back toward Eric. "What the hell is your bodyguard laughing at?"

****

Eric and Jenna left Ash Baldwin standing in front of the Lakehouse Manor alone, figuratively scratching his head. They boarded the limo. "Why didn't you tell him you know Jack?" she asked.

"He'll find out soon enough."

"Will he help you? Can he get him to leave Mrs. Cummings alone?"

Eric stretched his arm as much as comfort allowed and brought it around Jenna's shoulder. "Babes, through the years, Jack and I have become very good friends. After I tell him what a scumbag Baldwin is, he'll be out."

The limousine crunched over a path of crushed shells. Moonlight made ripples on the lake shimmer. Music that drifted from the banquet hall faded as the car rolled through the stone and iron gates.

"But this is big business. What if he isn't able to convince his other partners?"

Eric laughed, then winced as his ribs rebelled. "When have you ever known Jack Morrissey to take no for an answer?"

Smiling, Jenna nodded. She leaned her head onto Eric's shoulder as he explained to her what had happened and why he had been missing for a week. "I never would have left you. You must know that."

A chill pricked her skin and she burrowed deeper into his arms. The limo cruised along, its passengers silent until they reached Jenna's street. She closed her eyes tightly and then finally spoke. "There's something I have to tell—"

Nick lowered the divider. "What's going on here?"

Jenna's eyes bloomed wide. She froze, rendered immobile by the scene stretching beyond the window. A slow steady glow of lights whirled through the darkness in front of her house. Two Cromline patrol cars sat caddie cornered in her driveway. A state police cruiser and an unmarked car were at the curb. Strobes of neon flickered from the unmarked car like lightning bolts. The house and sky above was cast into an eerie storm of blue.

Red, white, and orange flashed in a dizzying circle from patrol cars.

With a scream building deep in her throat, Jenna tore herself away from Eric and crawled across his knees to get to the car's door. She grappled frantically with the handle and shoved, then almost hit the pavement as she fell from the car.

Eric and Nick were less than a second behind her as they all raced up the driveway and bolted into the house.

Chapter Thirty-One

Jenna pushed her way into a barricade of blue and putty gray. "What's going on?" Her head twisted back and forth in a frantic sweep. "Janie!"

Willy Parks cleared a path. "This is the girl's mother."

"The girl!" The words tore from her throat. She whipped her head around, up, down, turning frantically till she spotted the police hovering around Randi. Jenna's knees jelled and it seemed an eon before she reached her friend. "Where's my baby?"

Randi's eyes were rimmed scarlet, and a crumpled tissue fell from her hands. "It happened so fast. One minute she was standing next to me eating ice cream and the next..." Randi gulped air, and a bellowing sob followed. "Some...some guy grabbed her and threw her in his car. I...I couldn't stop him."

"No!"

Eric pulled Jenna close, but she continued to flail her arms and scream. A State trooper, his gray uniform a severe collection of sharply pressed seams, approached. "Mrs. Black, about twenty minutes ago your daughter was abducted from a parking lot by an unidentified, white male. We brought your friend back here so she could give us a photograph and something your daughter recently wore. We're going to send our K9 unit out with the search party."

"Oh God." Jenna's body was dead weight in Eric's arms. She'd lost all balance and strength.

The trooper spoke evenly. "We're covering all the bases. This town is surrounded by woods and hiding there might be one of his options." Static and muffled voices crackled from police radios. Local officers conferred with the troopers, more of whom hurried into the house carrying computers and other electronics.

"We'll be monitoring your phone, and we have officers at the shopping center interviewing people to see if anyone noticed anything unusual."

The police went about an efficient business of putting a trace on the telephone and relaying information from the scene. Willy Parks gave directions to his men to organize a team of civilians to intensify the search of the woods and lake.

"Chief," a trooper called out. "We just got a description of a suspicious looking man who was loitering in front of the ice cream parlor."

While Eric held Jenna, Randi gripped her hand. Both women trembled as if icy breaths of fog hung in the room.

The trooper stepped over. "A woman saw a strange looking man staring at your friend and your daughter." Tilting his felt Stetson back on his head, he flipped a page in his pad to read his notes. "She said the man was blond, mid to late forties, possibly younger but 'burnt out like a druggie.' Those were her exact words."

The trooper then turned to Parks. "She said the guy had a lot of healed scars on his face. Anyone fitting that description live around here?"

Jenna screamed. She pushed away from Eric and pounded her head. Her cry was the desperate wail of someone begging for their life. "No, not him! Oh, God, please no!"

Her body was suddenly stripped of any substance and her legs began to fold beneath her. Eric swept her close as he whispered his own prayers. He wrapped her, sobbing and shaking, tightly in his arms. "I'll find her. I promise…Shh…I swear I'll find her."

"Mrs. Black, do you *know* who took your daughter?"

Eric answered for her. "You just described Janie's father, Mark Chambers."

Scribbling in his pad, the trooper asked, "is that Mark with a K or a C?"

"K."

"And your name?"

"Eric Laine."

The trooper's brows jutted high on his forehead, but his attention quickly went back to Jenna. "Mrs. Black, have you and your daughter's father been involved in a custody dispute?"

Tears streamed down her face. "N-no, h-he isn't her f-father."

"Mrs. Black?"

Eric coughed as if something scratched at the back of his throat. "Chambers is Janie's biological father, but he has no legal…" The words dissolved on his breath.

"Still, there's no reason to believe he'll harm her."

Jenna screamed. "He's a monster!" The icy bite of shock made her tremble more violently.

"Parents don't generally—"

"He isn't her father."

With his shoulders raised, the trooper glanced over at Eric.

"Jen?" he whispered.

"Mrs. Black?"

Shuffling feet, rattling paper, and the hum of voices all became silent.

"Jenna?" Eric's grip became steel. "What…are…you…saying?" His voice was a murmur, his wide-eyed stare one of disbelief and fear. With his fingers quarrying deep into her arms, he gave her an abrupt shake. "What are you saying!"

Still trembling, a leaf clinging to a branch in a storm, Jenna was weightless in his grip. "I'm so sorry. I should have told you."

****

Bodies stilled, then blurred in the room's bright light. To Eric, everything looked to be covered in a soft aura. He felt his throat constrict, and the buzzing of a million insects swarmed inside his head. He struggled to speak. "How long have you known?"

Jenna didn't answer. Her head hung limp toward the floor, her body flagging as if she might faint.

"How long!"

"Since your accident, your…your brother told me your blood type."

Jenna was practically folding over but Eric shook her again. "Four years? You've known all this time and you never said anything!"

Nick, who'd remained silently standing at attention, approached. "Let it go for now. We have to concentrate on finding Janie."

Randi batted at Eric. "Let her go. My goddaughter would be here, safe at home if you hadn't shown up. You led that animal to her just like you led him to Jenna ten years ago."

As Jenna slipped away to weep into her friend's arms, Eric felt his chest tighten. A dull ache radiated from his middle and out. Pain touched him everywhere. Dizziness overcame him and he had to claw at his tie to breathe. The room, fallen into silence, became a storm of activity as the trooper gave more orders to his men. "Run a check on Chambers to see if his whereabouts could be other than Cromline."

"It's him." Eric's voice was a dark utterance. "Don't waste your time trying to find out where he's been. He's here and he's got Janie."

"We don't want to chase our tails over this, Mr. Laine. If there's any possibility—"

"It's Chambers! And he's a sociopath!" With Nick following, Eric half limped, half stormed to the door.

"Mr. Laine, where are you going? Don't do anything to interfere with this investigation."

Empty eyed, he faced the trooper. "I'm not going to interfere. I'm going to find my kid."

The trooper appealed with hands outstretched, his shield glinting on his pocket. "You don't have the resources we have. The best thing you can do is sit tight."

"I have something better than resources." Eric turned and stepped though the doorway. "I know Mark Chambers. I know how the sick fuck thinks."

Chapter Thirty-Two

Larry Belka returned to his motel room with cartons of food from a local Hunan restaurant. He set his meal aside to upload more pictures to his laptop. Outside, the sound of a car's engine hummed. Stepping to the window, he pulled the dense curtain aside. An emaciated figure stepped from a cluster of trees carrying something wrapped in an overcoat. A small hand fell from under the cover of material.

"No, no, no." Larry gagged on his words, and pressed his hands to the window. "What the fuck did you do, you crazy bastard?"

****

Mark almost dropped the child as he withdrew the room key from his pocket. She was unconscious, deadweight in his arms. He'd lurked outside her house for close to an hour, and then followed after she and a woman drove away in a van.

He dumped his burden onto the bed with no more care than tossing trash in a bin. Smiling, he stared down. After grabbing her, he'd forced half a bottle of antihistamine down her narrow throat. "Like mother, like daughter," he whispered.

For all of Mark's regrets, and for all the disappointments that shaped his life, he still had the memory of the brilliant Los Angeles morning when he'd sneaked into Jenna's Malibu mansion with a handful of crumbled roofies in his pocket. He took an easy breath through his nose. He'd always have that memory. And now, he had the result borne of his pleasure—his child.

He picked up the stationary phone and dialed the next room.

****

The tinny chime of the phone made Larry jump and drop his cigarette. A garbled voice sounded in his ear. "Belka, get your ass and your camera over here."

Larry slammed the cover of his laptop and grunted curses as he raced around the musty room to collect his things. Clothing was slung over chairs, and toiletries were on the bathroom counter. He pulled everything in an unselective sweep into his suitcase. Packing his photographic equipment was more time consuming and he grappled with trembling fingers to disassemble lenses and cables to put into cases.

An urgent pounding sounded at the door. "Hey! What the hell is taking you so long?"

Larry yanked the door open and dragged Mark inside. "Shut the fuck up. Do you want the whole place to hear you?"

Swigging from a half empty bottle of tequila, Mark swallowed and let out a perfumy belch. "Say thank you. I just made it easier for you to get your shots. I got the kid in my room." Mark's words were a proud proclamation, and he did an unsteady shuffle of dance steps as he spoke. "Maybe Bree will give us a bonus."

Wheezing, Larry wheeled on Mark. "A bonus? Are you out of your fucking mind? What you're going to get is twenty-five-to-life and I'm not about to share a cell with you. I'm getting out of here. You're on your own."

Mark's face melted into sagging folds. "What about

the pictures?"

"Pictures? I'm not taking any pictures now. We were supposed to set Angel up, catch her early in the morning taking the kid to school, or in a park. You jump in and I snap away." Larry scrubbed at the thin remnants of hair on his perfectly domed skull. "Those were the pictures Bree Laine wanted me to take. She wanted pictures of you, the kid, and Angel plastered on the cover of the tabloids so she'd be scared enough to go back into hiding…forever!"

"But this is even better," Mark announced. His eyes glowed a milky blue in a sea of red. His lips sagged in an uneven grin. "We send pictures of me and the kid to the tabloids…real cozy shots of my little girl sitting on her daddy's lap. The tabloids will pay a fortune and so will Bree." Mark tapped his temple with a cigarette-stained finger as if he'd made a brilliant discovery. "Then I start making noise about custody, and I'll get whatever I want from Angel. The bitch will be sending me blank checks for the rest of her life."

Larry squinted at Mark as if another head grew out of his ear. "Are you crazy? I just told you I was supposed to get pictures of you, Angel, and the kid *together*. Now because of your stupid stunt I'm not going to get any."

Taking another swallow from the bottle, Mark shrugged. "Well…we still have the kid. The tabloids will pay *mucho dinero* for pictures of her and—"

"You sick, stupid fucker!" Belka tugged more at his stringy hair. "How fried is that brain of yours? I can't take pictures of her now, and I'll have to destroy the ones I already have."

"But they're worth big bucks."

"They're evidence!" The color of Larry's face

reddened to the shade of a Christmas rose. "You kidnapped her! I can't sell pictures of a kid whose been kidnapped to the papers. It'll look like I was in on it."

"I didn't kidnap her. She's my kid."

Larry pounded at his temples and cursed. "You have no right to her. Even if you did, you can't just take her."

Mark's head hung between his shoulders, and his features drooped as if melting from his face. "She's my baby. I can do whatever I want to her."

"What the hell *did* you do to her? No, I don't even want to know." Larry mopped the stream of sweat running down his face with his sleeve. He rushed about the room to gather the rest of his things while Mark took another lazy swig from his bottle.

The two men were an overused comparison trope— Larry, fat, sweating, and frantic—Mark, gaunt and rheumy-eyed. "Relax," he said. "I gave her enough allergy syrup to keep her out till I'm ready to take her home. She'll never be able to identify us."

"You did what? Oh shit!" Seized by more shaking, Larry began urgently throwing his equipment in their cases. "You're fucked in the head. And I have a big news flash for you. She isn't your kid."

"What the hell are you talking about?" Mark's lips hung slack and he belched again to sour the already dank air. "The whole world knows she's my kid."

The handles of Larry's bags slid against the clammy moisture on his hands. His suitcases bulged, fat as whisky casks, because items were wadded up inside instead of neatly folded. "Look, Chambers, I made my career taking pictures of Eric Laine. I can tell you how many eyelashes the guy has. Trust me, the kid is his. Do yourself a favor and get the hell out of here."

Larry hurried from the room, jumped in his rental car, and zoomed away.

****

Eric sat in the limo, quiet and tense, as he tried to form a plan. Jenna's admission pounded inside his head. He dropped his face into his hands, remembering with clarity how he felt when he'd first seen Janie. She'd been a tiny bundle in a bassinet, just an hour old. Though the moment had been glancing, he'd made the decision to love and care for her as his own. Three days later, she was gone from his life, and he had never gotten the chance. He had never gotten over the hurt or the loss. His pain now was tenfold, so acute he had no choice but to push it from his mind. He had to find his daughter, and tuning into Mark's depraved way of thinking was the only way to do so.

"Where to?" Nick asked.

"Ina's. She knows this area better than those cops do."

Nick sped to the farmhouse, screeching the limousine to a halt and spraying gravel at the clapboard. The lights were still burning and Ina came rushing out. It was clear something was wrong. Eric told her and she didn't dedicate one moment to alarm. "What can I do?"

"Coffee, caffeine will clear the cobwebs," Nick suggested.

Eric added his own appeals. "I want you to give Nick the name of every liquor store and bar in the area, and every cheap motel from here to the city. Nick, call all of them to see if anyone fitting Mark's description was there."

Ina fed Nick the names of places while he retrieved websites and numbers from his phone and called. Eric picked up his cell and tapped one of his contacts. The whirring ring on the line sang to him before Jack Morrissey answered. "Hey kid, what's up?"

Again, Eric delivered the news with no lead-in.

"Holy Mother of God. What do you need?"

"The F.B.I." Eric scratched at the back of his neck as barbs stung his skin. "You worked with a couple of consultants when you filmed *The Bureau*. Do you think you can get a hold of them?"

"Give me about ten minutes, and I'll have anything you need to know."

Eric asked Jack to find the flight Mark Chambers was on and the make and model of the car he rented.

"Consider it done."

"Bingo," Nick shouted. "No luck with the motels but there's a package store over on Route 55. Sounds like Chambers was there. I have the manager on the phone."

Eric took the receiver from Nick and said a quiet prayer that the person on the other end might supply some useful information. A man came on the line. "You're looking for someone who was in here tonight …blond fellow, scars on his face?"

"Yes, sir, I am. It's very important. Can you remember anything at all about him? What time he was there or the car he was driving?"

"Well…it was at least two hours ago, maybe more. He bought an expensive bottle of tequila and paid with a hundred. That's why I remember him…that and the yellow hair of course. The wife bought a kit one time and ended up with the same color, and boy what a sight she…"

"Sir! Please. Did he say anything?" Eric was pleading, his heart hammering while the man on the line continued to speak. The laidback blather made Eric's temples throb and his chest tighten.

"Well…I gave the hundred a good going over and that seemed to tick him off. Made a nasty crack about our wine selection, too." The man stopped speaking and sighed. "Nervy son of a bitch."

"Sir! Did you see his car?"

"Sure did. White, mid-sized, looked new."

"Thank you…"

"Hold on now. The guy did say something that might be important. He said he was meeting up with a photographer from Los Angeles. Claims I'm going to see him on the cover of all the big magazines. I laughed right in his face…seen prettier fish in *Field and Stream*."

"Did he say where the meeting was?" Eric's heart was pounding so loud it competed with the phone at his ear.

"No, he didn't, sorry."

Eric hung up and turned toward Nick. "Call all the motels again. See if Larry Belka is staying at any of them."

Chapter Thirty-Three

With a shaking hand, Mark lifted the bottle of tequila to his lips and drained the last drops. The child lying on the bed stirred. "I should just put my hands around your throat so you never wake up."

He staggered to the bathroom to pee. Above the sink, a rust-dotted mirror hung. He studied his reflection. At one time, admiring his face had been a pleasurable obsession. Now he recoiled from his image. His face was framed by a receding hairline, and scars zig zagged over his weathered complexion. He sniffed back tears. Fame, money, the life Mark desired, was all Eric's. And now the kid, the one thing Mark could claim as his own, belonged to Eric, too.

"I'm so sick of losing out to you. So sick of seeing your face everywhere." The crushing despair that caused him to snivel like a lost child lifted, and Mark swiped at his tears. Fury wiped away his sorrow.

He stepped from the bathroom and loomed above the child curled up on the bed. Baring teeth in the manner of an animal, he circled his prey.

****

Oblivious to the bedlam and chaotic sounds of phones, radios and voices, Jenna sat on the edge of her daughter's bed. She clutched a mug of tea she had yet to take a sip from. Randi was at her side staring vacantly. An officer occasionally knocked on the door to tell them no news had been reported, but everything possible was being done to find Janie.

In a voice hoarse and dry from crying, Jenna turned to Randi. "He'll know."

"Who, Jen...know what?"

"Mark. Mark will know. He'll know Janie is Eric's and he'll hurt her. As soon as he looks into her eyes he'll know."

A new stream of tears ran down Randi's face and she hugged Jenna, holding tight. Nested between them was a small, stuffed puppy that usually lay by her daughter's pillow. Rocking, she held it to her breast and a keening moan spilled from her throat. "Please, God, please don't let him hurt my baby."

Through her tears, she looked toward her daughter's dresser. Trophies, ceramic statues, and photographs cluttered the surface. On weak limbs, she stumbled forward and picked up a frame. It was a dance recital portrait with Janie's small face enveloped in pink satin, tulle, and sequins. Jenna traced the image and sank to her knees.

She was still hugging the frame when the strong arms of her brother enfolded her. "I'm here, sis. I'm here."

****

Both Nick and Eric lunged for the phone, not allowing the instrument to finish the first chords of the ring. It was Jack calling with information. "Chambers flew in today, on standby out of Chicago on Midwest Air. He landed in LaGuardia. The ticket was bought at the airport and paid for in cash. Here's the interesting part, two tickets were bought at the same time, one for Chambers and one for a Stephen Powers. There's a private investigator out of L.A. with the same name."

Eric pounded his fist against the table. "Jesus fucking Christ. That's the same detective Stark used years ago to dig up dirt on me."

"It's got to be the same Powers. Do you think he hired the guy to find Jenna?"

"No."

"Chambers then?"

Eric braced his hands on the top of a chair, holding tight for balance. "The only person I know vindictive enough to drag Mark Chambers back into our lives is Bree."

Jack gave Eric more of the information he'd garnered from the F.B.I. consultant—car rental, return flight, and Powers' cell number. "He's booked on the last flight back to L.A. on United. Hopefully, you can catch him before he gets on the plane, and he can tell you where Chambers is."

Eric scribbled the flight number. "I need you to find out one more thing for me."

"Name it, kid, anything."

"I need to know if Larry Belka is here in New York. He's that sleaze photographer who used to harass Jenna before he moved on to me. Call Nick's cell when you find out."

"You got it, buddy…Tell her to hang in there. If anyone can save her kid, it's you. I'm speaking from experience."

Eric nodded as if he could be seen through the line. He'd saved Jack's daughter Meghan from an overdose a decade ago. He swallowed what felt like a gritty stone and squeezed his eyes tight. He whispered a faint thank you and broke the connection.

Ina brought a mug of coffee over and ordered Eric to drink. His spine was rounded and his chest rose in staggered bursts as he breathed. He was fading.

A dozen calls to Stephen Powers' cell netted the same voice mail recording. The phone was either out of range or out of juice.

Nick hurried over with his own phone hidden within the bulk of his hand. "A guy fitting Belka's description has been at a place called The Trails End all week."

Eric angled his face to Ina.

"It's a dump over in Newton, about six miles away," she said. "Take 55 North and get off at the next exit. Make your first left. It's way up the hill. Go!"

Nick and Eric rushed to the limousine. Eric, bruised, tired, and weak, threw himself into the car and called Jenna's house. He gave them the license number of Powers' rental and his flight information.

An authority-filled command sang through the line. "Mr. Laine, how did you find all this out?"

"Does it matter? Just find the car and stop Powers before he gets on that flight back to Los Angeles."

"Mr. Laine, you have to let us do our job. You can't—"

Eric pressed "end call" and let his eyelids fall.

"Why didn't you tell them about Belka and the motel?" Nick asked.

"They can handle the roadblocks and find Powers." Eric's voice trailed off. He'd just taken the biggest gamble of his life, the biggest gamble of his daughter's. Gut instinct told him if Mark held Janie captive in or near the secluded woodland inn, a convoy of police cars could mean the end for her.

Chapter Thirty-Four

US Naval helicopter pilot Kyle Welles gathered his sister in the consoling embrace she so desperately needed. "Randi called and told me about Janie. I got my CO to give me the time off. I flew up from Norfolk, compliments of Uncle Sam. I told Mom and Dad to stay put. I hope you don't mind."

Jenna shook her head. "No, they could never handle this." She melted deeper into her brother's hold. "I can't live without her. I can't. I'm so afraid…and Janie, she must be so…so terrified. My baby is all alone with that monster."

"What do the police say?"

"Every twenty minutes they tell me the same thing. They're doing all they can and haven't found her."

"Let me talk to them." Kyle jogged down the stairs and through a mass of busy law enforcement to approach the trooper in charge. "Officer, I'm Lieutenant Welles, Mrs. Black's brother. Any news?"

The trooper brought Kyle to a bulletin board where a large map was pinned. "I've got units combing the woods and we have roadblocks set up here." The trooper struck at the map. "And here. We've confirmed Chambers flew to New York, but he hasn't checked into any local hotels. No one fitting his description checked in anywhere using an alias either. We received a tip to look for a man named Stephen Powers."

"Who?" Kyle asked.

"He's a private detective from Los Angeles. Our theory is Chambers hired him to find the child since he believes he's her father."

"But he isn't."

"We know that." The trooper leaned over a table where a minutia of electronics blinked and pinged like carnival rides. Two officers in headsets weeded through crank tips and the unrelenting press. The trooper stretched his arms while laying his palms flat against the wood. "As long as Chambers believes he is, the safer your niece will be. Eric Laine ran out of here, vowing to find her. I hope he doesn't try any stupid heroics."

"Does Eric know he's Janie's father?"

The trooper pushed away from the table and furrowed his brow. "Lieutenant, your sister is understandably a basket case. Her friend isn't doing much better. What we thought was custodial interference got bumped up to a kidnapping. So before agents from Child Abduction Rapid Deployment get here, I need to know the whole story."

****

A broken neon sign that intermittently flashed a handful of its original letters buzzed atop the roof of The Trails End. The limousine slowly crunched over dirt, rocks, and twigs. Stephen Powers' rental car was nowhere in the lot.

"What now?" Nick asked.

"We go to the front desk and see if Chambers or Belka are here."

Nick's head was angled away from the hut that served as the main office, to the white and black trimmed clapboard boxes. "I say we just bust into every room until we find him?"

"No." Eric pushed his hair out of his eyes. "If he's here I don't want to make any noise and spook him. Besides, I'm not in any shape to knock down doors."

Nick put a hand on his shoulder. "This isn't your fault."

Taking little comfort in his friend's statement, Eric slowly shook his head. "It won't matter whose fault this is if I never get the chance to make it up to her, will it?" He turned, his eyes burning from the glare of neon. "Mine or not, I'd be right here trying to save her. You know that don't you?"

"Of course," Nick answered. "Of course."

They opened the door and stepped inside. A woman of about fifty with fiery red hair sat at the counter, her attention glued to a portable television. She was clearly annoyed by their questions but became tolerably agreeable to helping after Nick placed a hundred-dollar bill on the counter.

"Listen, boys. This ain't the Waldorf. Couples come in, do their business, then get the hell out. I don't pay much attention to who checks in, but a guy with a face full of scars…that I'd remember."

"What room is the short stocky one in?"

The woman threw back her head and spat a laugh like the braying of a mule. "All of them."

Incensed, Eric slammed a hand on the counter hard enough to make an odd collection of items resting on it bounce. "The one who's been here all week! The one we asked about when we called. What room is he in?"

"Jeez, mister, calm down. He's in bungalow fifteen."

As Eric and Nick hastened out, she called, "take

whatever you're looking for with you, okay?"

Outside, they slowly and quietly stepped to the bungalow. Lights burned inside and Nick tapped on the door. It creaked open.

****

Janie groaned and twisted her small body against the mattress. Mark stared down at her, watching to see if she was coming to, but she just shifted and settled deeper into worn linens. He lifted the bottle of tequila and brought it to his lips. It was empty and he pounded the bottom desperate to force the last drops into his mouth. The feeling of bugs, hundreds of prickly little feet seemed to suddenly skitter against his skin. He'd fucked up and needed to get away, but cops were probably already crawling all over the place.

The child moved again. Golden hair spilled over her shoulders. The stirring memory of Angel, her velvet skin and silken hair sliding between his fingers, fleetingly replaced the panic. But the little girl, sedated and groaning on the bed, wasn't the product of that long ago morning of bliss. A cry, born deep in his chest, tore from his throat.

****

Bungalow fifteen was empty. Eric rubbed his eyes. He barely had the strength to utter curses of frustration.

Nick upended the wastebasket, and packaging for a burner phone, and two gigabyte thumb-drive fell out. "Belka was here." A bag of Chinese takeout, still stapled and closed, sat on a table. A pair of shoes was by the bed, and a bottle of antacid tablets on the nightstand. "Looks like he left in a hurry."

"Shit." Eric kicked one of the chairs and knocked it against the muddy colored wall. "He knows where Mark is. And he knows he has Janie." Eric rubbed his middle. His ribs felt like they were stabbing into his lungs. He would gladly make a deal with the devil and endure the pain forever if it meant finding his daughter safe.

"Call Jenna's place again; tell the cops to look for Belka, see if he booked a flight anywhere. Tell them what we found here."

Nick made the call quickly. "What now?"

"We're going with your first plan. We're going to start knocking down doors."

They stepped outside. Most of the bungalow windows were dark. In some there was a faint, flickering glow of a television. A coyote howled somewhere in the distance. An owl screeched, and the cry of either a baby fox or cat pierced the air. Eric whipped his head around when he heard a man yelling.

****

"Wake up!" Mark Chambers trembled with rage and panic. Janie's inert body fluttered as he shook her. "Wake the fuck up!"

He needed to see the fear in her expression, to see the overwhelming terror in Eric's eyes. But the child's head lolled heavily on her shoulder, and all Mark could see was the slow, steady pulse at her throat as she slept. It was pointless. She wasn't going to come to.

"This is all your fault!" he shouted "You and your cunt of a mother's. Eric was my friend, but she ruined everything."

Growling, guttural and low, he slipped his arm around Janie's throat and began to squeeze.

****

Jenna sat limp on the edge of Janie's bed, holding the stuffed puppy in her hands. Kyle was back at her side, his arm tight around her shoulder. She gasped and sprang to her feet panting and choking.

"What's wrong, Jen?" Kyle grabbed her, grappling to still a sudden trembling that quickly turned into turbulent shaking.

Randi jumped from her spot on the bed. "Is she having a seizure? Why is she shaking like that?"

"I don't know," he said. "Jen, can you hear me? Sis, what is it?"

"He's killing her!" Jenna clawed at her throat. "He's killing my baby!"

****

Nick barreled past Eric and slammed his shoulder into the door where the shouts came from. The lock easily gave way and the door swung wide. Under a shower of plaster, Eric rushed into his worst nightmare. He stopped to a dead halt. Mark's eyes were red and raving. His arm was tight around Janie's throat.

"Let her go," Eric pleaded. "She hasn't done anything to you. Let her go."

Mark grunted and tugged harder. Tears poured from his eyes. "Fuck you. F…fucking big hero rushing in to save the day again." Mark's lips smacked together, wet with saliva and the tears coursing over them. "You aren't going to beat me up, break me to fucking pieces this time. One snap and she's finished, come near me and she's dead."

Eric held his hands, palms out in front of his chest. "Take it easy, Mark. I'll give you whatever you want. Just let her go."

"Stay back," Mark demanded. "I swear I'll do it. I know she isn't mine. Come near me, and I snap her neck."

Helpless, Eric watched the shallow rise and fall of Janie's chest. "She's barely breathing. She isn't getting enough air and her lungs are going to collapse."

Eric kept his hands raised in supplication and forced himself to appear calm even though his insides were rocking with fear. One flinch in the wrong direction and his daughter's life would be over.

Mark flexed his wiry arm as more tears spilled from his eyes. "Looks like I'm finally going to get my chance to pay you back." His words rode on choking sobs. "I might as well do it. I have nothing to lose. After your trial, Angel's big shot Hollywood pals saw to it I couldn't get a job in a fucking taco stand."

Mark pulled Janie up an inch higher, one small increment that parted her feet from the dirty carpet. "You got it all…money…fame. All I have is a face full of scars!"

Eric fought the urge to rush to his daughter and pry her out of Mark's grasp. But his former friend was crazed, his glassy eyes hot with tears, his scars like worms crawling along his ruddy face. Eric knew Mark would break Janie's neck if either he or Nick charged. Her one and only chance was to force reason to penetrate Mark's twisted rationale.

Eric took a deep breath, a slow and calm pull of air. "You're wrong. I have nothing. Because of you I lost my family. You already got your revenge. We're even. Let her go and you can walk out of here."

"Bullshit. You'll never let me go." The capillaries in Mark's eyes were so red and broken they glowed like a horror movie apparition. Janie, unconscious and limp, hung from his arm like a rag doll in a child's grip.

"I give you my word." Eric spoke evenly, every

syllable in the same docile tone. "You know I'm not a liar. Let her go, and I'll let you walk out of this room." Eric took a solitary beat to let his heart catch up with his breath. Janie's chest was rising in ever smaller spurts and a thready whistle accompanied each attempt her body made in its struggle for air.

He spoke again, his tone almost serene. "But, if you don't, and I mean right now, then Nick and I will take you out of here." He pointed to the burly Lombardo who nodded, once, his immense body still and somber.

"We'll take you to a place where the cops will never find you." Eric forced his sight from his child spilling from the crook of Mark's folded arm to his eyes. "I'll beat you far worse than I did the day I caught you raping my wife. I'll fucking torture you. I swear it. Kill my daughter, and I'll torture you every single day for the rest of your life. You'll beg to go to prison. You'll beg for a death row needle."

Mark's eyes pitched back and forth. The smell of sweat filled the air. The room was silent except for the imaginary ticking of a time bomb. His eyes vaulted around the filthy room and ended their journey at Eric.

"You will beg me to kill you."

Mark released his grip and Janie slid to the floor. He flew past Eric and Nick who both rushed to her.

The child's lips were tinged blue. Eric pinched her nose and blew a hard breath of air into her mouth. "Please, baby, please," he crooned between breaths.

Janie coughed as air reached her lungs. Once her breathing became steady, Eric drew her into the shelter of his arms and cradled her head against his chest, against his heart. Her lids fluttered. Caught somewhere between sleep and wakefulness, she gripped the arms holding her.

"It's all right," he said. "You're safe now. Daddy's here. I won't let anyone hurt you again. Daddy's here."

She gripped the arms now holding her as if somehow knowing she was safe.

Chapter Thirty-Five

A carnival of emergency vehicles screamed into the lot of the Trails End Motel. Eric rode in the ambulance with his daughter, holding her hand. She drifted in and out of consciousness and the beginnings of bruises appeared on her throat. Paramedics slipped a tube around her head to feed oxygen into her nose. Her heart rate and blood pressure were low, but not dangerously so. Nick followed close behind in the limousine.

A barrage of reporters greeted the ambulance at the hospital, a scene all too familiar for Eric. Nick, whose area of expertise was fending off the media, stayed close to his friend's side as he walked next to the gurney. Janie was rushed to an examination cubicle and attended to. Eric shook his head sadly when asked by the nurse assisting the doctor for her medical history.

The door of the ER parted wide. The heavy swish of opening then swinging shut allowed a burst of sound from outside to spill through. The small hospital's security staff was ill prepared to handle even the small number of local reporters, and it was Nick who pulled Jenna from the crowd. She ran and gathered Janie in her arms.

Eric watched her take their daughter's face in her hands and stare as if she might never stop. Letting out a loud sob, Janie flung her arms around Jenna's neck. She cried and trembled as Jenna rocked, and soothed, and rubbed her back. "It's okay, it's okay."

Janie spoke around sobs and hiccups. "Somebody grabbed me, Mommy. I was so scared."

"Shush, it's over now, baby. It's over."

Eric, still standing quietly beside them, noticed how Janie was also comforting Jenna. Her small hand was on her mother's shoulder, and she patted in a steady rhythm. They were soothing each other. They were a team...a family. He quietly backed away through the curtain.

****

A doctor examined Janie and found no external bruises other than the ones around her throat. A more in-depth exam with a laryngoscope showed no damage to her larynx or tonsils.

"The body responds remarkably to stress," the doctor explained. "Adrenaline can temporarily halt pain, and muscles tighten to protect our organs."

A sigh of relief fell from Jenna's lips, as Janie told the doctor "nothing hurt down there."

"What about the drugs?" Jenna asked.

"She came to on her own; her heart rhythm and pulse-ox are good. She's going to be groggy and definitely sleep like the..." The doctor caught himself before concluding the inappropriate analogy. "Just keep an eye on her."

There was no need for any further interviews by the police since Eric and Nick positively identified Mark Chambers as Janie's kidnapper.

In a little over two hours, she was released from the hospital. Jenna draped her jacket around her daughter, and Kyle, who had been waiting outside the cubicle, lifted his niece into his arms to carry her from the examination area.

Jenna spotted Eric standing near the door. She knew she should weep her gratitude, but she couldn't face him. He stepped close, close enough to be heard, but not close enough to be a part of the family intimacy. "I know your friend's husband picked her up, so I thought Nick and I should stay at your house so you aren't alone."

"I'd appreciate that...Kyle has to leave early in the morning." The inside of Jenna's mouth was like parchment and her heart thudded heavy in her chest. "I can't thank you enough. If you hadn't gone—"

He held up his hand to dismiss her. "Don't. I didn't do it for you."

****

Officers of the New York City Transit Authority apprehended Stephen Powers at the gate of a midnight flight to Los Angeles. He was held for questioning in the abduction of Jane Marie Black. State Police nabbed Larry Belka trying to board a flight at a small airport close to Cromline. On route, he'd tossed a thumb-drive from a bridge. Police led him away from the terminal and confiscated his bag. In it was a laptop with dozens of pictures of Jenna and her daughter.

Mark Chambers, driving a rental car he'd hidden in the woods behind bungalow sixteen, was pulled over by the local police for driving erratically. He was less than a mile from where state police had set up roadblocks.

Chapter Thirty-Six

Reporters and photographers were stationed in spots around Jenna's front yard. They sprang to attention as a limousine and police cruiser pulled onto Redbud Lane. Early morning darkness was disturbed by lights from news vans and explosions of electronic camera flashes. The glow of otherwise dark windows also illuminated the street. Jenna's neighbors had stayed up to watch the drama.

It was Kyle, rather than Eric, who carried Janie into the safety of the house. As much as he longed to offer his daughter protection, he stepped aside while the uncle she knew and trusted carried her.

Once safely inside, Jenna rushed up the stairs to put her daughter to bed.

Kyle, Eric, and Nick shifted about the living room where few traces of the police investigation remained. As quickly as the equipment had arrived, it was whisked away. Kyle breached the silence. "Janie is sleeping with Jenna, so I'll take her room. You guys probably aren't used to sleeping on something the size of a cot." He excused himself and made his way to the stairs.

Eric let his body sink onto the couch, and he rested his elbows on his knees. His hands dangled toward his feet. For the first time in hours, he acknowledged the pain that still tore at his side and groaned.

"Go get some sleep," Nick ordered.

"I doubt if my brain will shut down any time soon. I think I'll just sit here awhile."

Nick nodded. For all of his bulk, his height, his Brooklyn born fight and attitude, he was a gentle giant. He patted Eric's shoulder in a soft swipe. "That was nice work back there at the motel. You were the only one who could have saved her. Chambers knew you meant business."

Outside, beams of light were still aimed at the house. A blending of voices created a low hum as reporters recorded their stories.

"You want me to take care of that?" Nick asked.

"Fuck it. They'll only come back in the morning." Eric leaned back in his seat and ran his fingers through his hair. "This was a hell of a way to meet my kid for the first time. It wasn't what I expected when the night began."

"The important thing is she's safe. Now you and Jenna can work things through."

Eric slipped his shoes from his feet and wearily stretched out on the sofa. He closed tired, bruised eyes and said to his friend, "no, it's over between us."

****

Morning editions across the country carried the bizarre story of the kidnapping. Once again, the names Mark Chambers, Eric Laine, and Jenna Welles, a.k.a. Angel, were splashed in bold type on the front pages of most major newspapers. A throng of reporters congregated in front of Jenna's house waiting for a statement and the answer to a long-asked question.

Who was the biological father of Angel's daughter? Was it her ex-husband or the man who had, at the time, claimed to be having a torrid affair with her?

****

Eric woke groggy and in pain. Nick was already standing sentinel at a window with a cup in hand.

"Did you get any sleep, Nick?"

"Some," came the gruff reply. "Your ex-brother-in-law was up with the birds. There's coffee in the kitchen."

Eric hunched over as he tried to stretch his spine and flatten the knotty tightness from his neck. "What's it look like out there?"

"About what you'd expect."

Carelessly shoving his hair out of his face, he unfolded his tender body in slow inches until upright. An assault, a week spent on a paper-thin mattress, and a forty-foot fall some four years earlier, were all simultaneously gripping muscle and bone. He uttered a shaky hum as he stood and limped to the front door. His shirt was creased with wrinkles, the tails hanging over equally rumpled tuxedo pants. He looked like the morning after a very good, or very bad prom.

Nick at once voiced a protest as Eric grabbed the doorknob to turn it. "What the hell do you think you're doing? You can't go out there like that."

"Watch me."

"Do you really want to be on the cover of every tabloid in America looking like something the cat dragged in?"

"I don't give a shit. I want this whole thing over, and the only way to do it is to give them their story."

Nick continued to plead his argument as Eric walked out into the morning light. "At least put your shoes on!"

Outside the clicking and whirring of cameras resounded like a nocturnal symphony of forest wildlife. It was a sound Eric Laine had become immune to over the years. He stood stock-still until the last mechanical chirp finished assaulting the air. A deep thrumming began to echo. It was a low melding of voices that quickly rose to a crescendo as reporters fought for his attention. He pressed his tongue to his teeth and pierced the air with a whistle.

"I'm only going to give you a minute, so listen up. Last night my daughter was kidnapped by Mark Chambers, the man who assaulted my wife ten years ago. You know her as Angel. Those of you who were members of the press corps back then know there was speculation about the paternity of her baby. I'll set the record straight. Her daughter is mine."

Spasms gripped his torso, and he brought one hand to his side. More cameras shuttered to capture his pain. "The details of why she and I divorced are private. The reasons she gave up her career...simple. Look around. It should be obvious to every one of you holding a camera or microphone. The other reason is behind bars where hopefully he'll spend the rest of his life."

"Eric!" one reporter shouted while waving his microphone at him. "What about your divorce? Are you getting back together with Angel after it becomes final?"

"None of your business. Now you're on private property. Get out of here, all of you. Leave us alone...please."

Eric stepped back inside and leaned against the closed door. His aches, the dull insistent pains, were as much emotional as physical. The reporter's question stung. Getting back together with Jenna, a dream so close to coming true had withered and died with one sentence. "I'm sorry, I should have told you."

Why, Jen, why? Why didn't you?

****

Gently, Jenna adjusted the blankets and pulled them up around her sleeping daughter's chin. She stroked Janie's soft cheek and placed a kiss on her forehead before going downstairs to face Eric. She found him sitting at the kitchen table sipping coffee, alone and waiting.

Beginning the long and overdue conversation was one of the hardest things she had ever faced. She owned no reserve of courage. The integrity of her secret lived only in her conscience, building overtime until it became fact. In reality it wasn't. Keeping his child from him was indefensible.

She took a seat at the table. Eric looked broken, and Jenna fought the sting of tears. It would be too cruel to beg for sympathy by crying. She could at least spare him that.

"How is she?" he asked.

"Still asleep. When she was little, she would cry if she was having a nightmare. She didn't."

He nodded behind his cup. "Good. That's good."

"Yes, it is." Jenna twined her fingers together and took a slow breath. "I can't ask you to forgive what I did. The most I can do is explain why."

Her eyelids lowered, and she stepped back to a morning when the sun had barely broken the eastern horizon. With her newborn in her arms, she'd been secreted away from a Los Angeles maternity hospital to a private airstrip. The rest of her story was a decade's long list of moving from incidental place to incidental place. "Having security and living behind a gate hadn't kept me safe. Disappearing, changing my name, and moving around did. At least it had until last night."

Eric sat mute and still, as if long resigned to her reasons for running away. When Jenna confessed to hiding because her fear of Mark had followed her across the ocean and back, Eric nobly fell on his sword. "I brought him into our lives. What he did to you was my fault."

"No. It wasn't." Jenna's words were a soft dispute. "It was never your fault." She pressed curled fingers to her cheeks, closing her eyes and taking more slow breaths. "As the years went by, I began to accept Mark manipulated *you* because of me, because I was a celebrity. The blame is on him, no one else."

Silence suspended the conversation. Eric's hands were wrapped tightly around his cup and his lips were drawn down. Mottled bruises under his eyes were a dark contrast to the pallid color of his cheeks. Jenna quailed when he shifted in his chair and winced in pain. Laying his palms flat against the table he sucked his breath through clenched teeth. She automatically slid one hand across the table to bring her fingers close to his, but he drew away from her touch. They made eye contact for the first time, and for the first time since they sat, Jenna could see the paradox of emotion struggling behind the bruises. His brows were set straight and low over eyes that looked unfocused and far away. She watched as he clutched his mug as though it were a talisman he needed to steadily grip for strength.

"When you found out…when…when I was in the hospital four years ago…why didn't you tell me?"

Gutted by the memory, Jenna brought her hands to her chest. She could still hear the radio broadcast reporting he'd been critically injured. She could still see a road blurred by tears as she sped to the hospital to say goodbye. "You were so weak. Every time you opened your eyes, I wanted to tell you, beg you to hold on, but you never stayed conscious long enough."

With her hands still pressed to her breast, she stood. Watching the man she loved, sitting exhausted and in pain, was breaking her heart. She had, on a long-ago night, vowed never to hurt him and never to leave him. She had done both.

His body sagged in his chair. He brought his hands to his face, pressing the heels into his eyes. "So, you just left? That was it?"

"No. I didn't want to leave, but I had no choice. Bree was ranting, and the doctors thought the disturbance would…" Jenna no longer had power over her emotions and tears streamed down her cheeks. "The doctors thought my presence would hurt you more."

Raising his head, he finally looked long and deeply into her eyes. His were wide, but empty and sad. "Hurt me? Seeing you was the only thing that kept me alive."

"It wasn't my place to be there. You were married. You had a new life."

"And a daughter."

His words rode on such a desolate breath Jenna felt as if her body was caving in on itself. "Your brother, Bree, even the doctors insisted I leave."

"You should have told me later, after I recovered."

"I know. But…"

"But what?"

"I didn't know you anymore. I didn't know who Eric Laine the celebrity was. I couldn't just pack my daughter up and send her to visit a father who was a stranger, and a stepmother who…well…handing my little girl over to Bree wasn't acceptable."

"And having Janie grow up without a father was?" Eric exhaled what sounded like a dying breath. "You decided not to give me the chance to be a dad to my only child. I know how badly you wanted to protect her, but you cheated both of us."

"Please try and understand. I had no idea what kind of a father you would be. Our last few months together, you'd changed. You were sullen and distant…and…and then the night Janie was born it all spilled out." Jenna sobbed remembering a broken young man, crying as he admitted he could never accept her baby. "You can't imagine how it feels to be completely shattered by someone you trust and love as much as I loved you."

The last sparks of emotion—understanding, sentiment, light, all seemed to retreat from Eric's eyes and fade into nothing. He threaded his fingers together and lowered his head. "I do now."

****

Food was warming on Ina's stove, but although Eric couldn't remember when he had last eaten, he had no appetite.

"You have to have something," Ina urged. "Have a seat. Where's your friend?"

"Sleeping in the car."

She rubbed her hands together as she wove her way through the maze of boxes to where he stood. He was ready to drop, but the exhaustion he was feeling had little to do with lack of rest.

"How did things go? Is the little girl all right?" she asked.

"*My* little girl," Eric corrected, then quickly apologized for the sharpness of his tone. "I'm sorry, it's been a long night." *It's been a long ten years.* "If you don't mind, I'm going to go up to my room and get some sleep." He moved to the stairs, but midway up he stopped and looked over the railing. Ina was standing silent among her belongings—possessions she'd packed in preparation for the demise of her home.

He called down to her. "I'm not really in any shape to finish the repairs. And I have a world of things I have to straighten out. I'm going to hire a contractor to finish up here. That'll be one less thing I have to worry about. So don't give me any shit, okay?" He winked, mustering a smile that took great effort to give.

"There goes that filthy mouth of yours again. I hope I can find a bar of soap in here." Though she was bent over a box, Eric could see her wiping her eyes.

Chapter Thirty-Seven

"Mom?"

The light touch of a hand resting on Jenna's shoulder woke her. She jerked in the chair where she'd drifted off. Early afternoon sunshine sliced into the bedroom through the slats of the drawn shutters. Jenna squinted as dust motes floated toward her. "Baby, what are you doing awake?"

Janie climbed into her lap. "It's almost two."

Jenna hugged her daughter, the pressure so firm Janie balked. "Mommy, you're crushing me."

"Sorry." Jenna eased her daughter an arm's length away to study her. There was a ring of red around her throat and the space below her eyes was clearly tinged with a darker hue than the rest of her pale skin.

"Baby, how do you feel?"

"Kind of tired considering I've been asleep all weekend. Is Uncle Kyle still here?"

"No, he left this morning."

"Oh." An unspoken inquiry hung in the air before Janie spoke again. "Anyone else?"

"Do you mean Eric?"

As Janie's blonde head lowered, she bobbed a shaky yes.

"He slept on the couch, but he left this morning, too."

"Is he coming back?"

Jenna nodded. "He wants to, but we both thought it would be best for you to get some rest first."

"I guess he knows, huh?"

"Yes."

Jenna gave her child a reassuring smile and swept strands of pale-yellow hair from her eyes. Janie was sure to have questions; but silence lay like a layer of fog, complicated and difficult to maneuver through. They sat quietly for a long while before she spoke. "How did he find me?"

"I don't really know."

Jenna's mind slipped back to a night she'd never forgotten. She could still see the mix of people laughing and drinking, music shaking the air, and a girl collapsed on a floor, her heart silent. Closing her eyes, Jenna could see Eric hurtling the bar to save her.

"He's smart, and he's very brave. I once saw him give CPR to a girl who wasn't breathing. If he hadn't helped her, she would have died."

Almost rounding into a ball, Janie settled even deeper into Jenna's arms. "Now that he knows I'm his daughter, do you think he'll want to see me…or anything?"

"Are you asking about visits…custody?"

"Both, I guess."

Jenna rested her head against the back of the chair and glanced up at the ceiling. A faint shadow of phosphorescent stars glowed. She'd glued them there when Janie was five, and she wondered how long her baby would want to continue sleeping under the fairylike constellations.

"He'll want what's best for *you*. Always. Maybe we could start small and have him come here to see you.

Would that be okay?"

"I guess." Janie tugged at her bottom lip and asked earnestly, "Mommy, what am I supposed call him?"

****

Eric drove slowly. A casserole only Ina could have thrown together so quickly was warming the passenger seat. Jenna had called and invited him over. His daughter wanted to meet him, and Ina theorized all problems could be solved over a good meal.

By the time he reached Jenna's, the food had cooled enough so he didn't have to meet his daughter wearing mitts with black and white spotted cows embroidered on them. He handed Jenna the platter but lingered in the foyer waiting for an official invitation. Little more than a week ago, he had boldly strode across the hardwood floor and followed her up the stairs to make love. The memory stung because his happiness had been so unfairly short lived.

"C'mon in." She tilted her head in the direction of the living room but veered toward the kitchen with the dish in hand. "Janie's upstairs. I'll call her down."

Eric sat on the couch and coughed into his hand. How would Jenna introduce him?

Janie, this is Eric Laine, your biological father.

Janie, this is Eric Laine, the man who said he hated you the night you were born because he believed you were someone else's child.

Janie, this is Eric Laine, the other half of your genetic makeup, technically that makes him your father.

The sound of feminine voices roused him from his pitiful rumination. He stood, straightening his bruised body in a gentlemanly fashion as the two most important people in his life entered the room. Jenna didn't make any of the bizarre introductions he'd imagined and broke the ice simply. "Sweetheart, this is Eric."

His daughter raised one hand and waved, wiggling her fingers shyly. "Hi."

"Hello," he answered.

Blinking, he tried not to stare. His little girl was beautiful. He had thought so the morning he'd seen her trotting to a car. Although he'd held her in his arms the night before, this was the first time he was really getting a good look at her. It was amazing. *She* was amazing…perfect.

Did all parents think that of their children? Eric had no way of knowing, but Janie looked incredibly like her mother and Jenna *was* beautiful, an opinion not exclusively his.

He extended his hand and a smaller one reached out to rest in it. "I'd like to make up for lost time. But…but only when you're ready. We could go to a movie, or out to dinner. Um, I hear you're a gymnast so maybe I could go to one of your games."

Janie's eyes narrowed and she scrunched her nose as if either displeased or amused. Eric had no way of discerning the expression. "They're called meets. But how did you know I was a gymnast?"

"Your mom told me. But there's still a whole lot of things I don't know about you."

His daughter shrugged her small shoulders and rocked on her heels. Her posture seemed a little uncomfortable, but mostly shy. "Me too," she said. "I mean…there are a bunch of things I don't know about you, except that you're a movie star."

Tipping his head, Eric returned the shrug. Actor, producer, and businessman were all acceptable job titles.

Movie star was his all-time least favorite even though there'd been a time "Busboy" was figuratively tattooed on his forehead.

Janie looked up for a moment and smiled crookedly. Then her line of vision returned to her feet. "I sometimes make believe I have a dad, and that he's somebody really important. I guess you are, huh?"

Sighing, a little corner of Eric's heart broke off and died. The only daddy his daughter had ever known was an image invented in her imagination. He dropped down to one knee and draped his arm across his thigh. The position put him at eye level with her. "Janie, your uncle Kyle is in the service. I have a brother who was, too. Those guys are important. Doctors, firemen, teachers…they're the important jobs. Me, I'm just a guy who acts…pretends. Sometimes it's a lot of fun, and the pay is great, but that doesn't make me any more important than the next man. You're only really important if somebody needs you."

Jenna stepped over and put her arm around Janie's shoulder. Eric could see a glossy shine in her eyes.

"See, I told you he was smart."

****

For the first time in her young life, Janie Black shared a meal with both of her parents. Jenna made a salad to go with the casserole and the trio passed the salt, and pepper, and butter like a family. They didn't talk much at first, but as the chill thawed, Eric asked scores of questions. Janie told him who her best friend was, and her teacher's name. After dinner, Jenna played one of her gymnastics tapes, and Eric cheered and slapped his knee and told her how great he thought she was. "That kind of stuff blows me away, you're terrific."

Janie offered a sideways smile, one pale brow lifting. "Terrific? I face planted on one of my tumbling passes and fell off the beam."

"But you got a medal." It was clear Eric wasn't being denied his proud parent moment.

"We all get a medal," she admitted with a shake of her head.

When Jenna announced it was bedtime, Janie asked him to accompany them upstairs. "I want to show him my room."

But what the child really wanted was to know what it felt like to have both Mommy *and* Daddy tuck her in.

****

Eric slowly perused statues, trophies, and the collection of books that lined shelves. He nodded his approval. "This is a real nice room."

He took inventory so he could replicate everything for his house in North Carolina. His most fervent wish would be to one day soon have his daughter visit. The large corner space with the window seat would be the first room in the old house remodeled.

As he continued scanning the room, he noticed a threadbare toy dog lying on the pillow on Janie's bed. He picked up the worn creature, holding it gently as he had done so long ago. After his unforgiveable behavior the night of her birth, he'd gone to a Rodeo Drive store to buy a layette. He'd bought the little stuffed puppy to give to her.

"That's Pup-pup," Janie said. "I know I'm getting kind of old, but I still sleep with her. I guess that's lame, huh?"

The tattered animal shook a bit in Eric's hand as he studied it. It was no longer a shade of snowy white, and its head lolled to one side because the stuffing in its neck, he supposed, had been flattened by Janie's fingers. Pup-pup no longer had a nose and its glass eyes were scuffed.

"I don't think it's silly at all. Looks to me like she's been keeping you company for a long time."

Eric handed the dog to Janie and she hugged it. "I've had her since I was a baby."

Coughing, he bit back the rare threat of tears. "Hey, Jen," he said after clearing his throat. "I could use that second cup of coffee if you don't mind."

"Sure. I'll go downstairs and make a new pot."

Eric winked and smiled at Janie. "I just wanted to get rid of your mom." He paused, his eyes again settling on items—wall hangings, the pink striped window coverings, a shoe with no apparent counterpart. He spoke quietly. "I know you don't know me, but I'm going to ask you for a big favor if that's okay."

She nodded.

"I don't want you to blame your mother for anything, none of it, not what happened last night, or for the secret she kept. Can you do that?"

"But she said she was wrong. And…and you're mad at her…aren't you?"

He sighed. "I'm not mad. I'm just sort of getting used to things, like you are. And I'm going to work really hard until I have everything figured out."

He brought his finger to his temple, tapped it, and smiled again. Janie looked at him. Her eyes locked with his for a few precious moments, and she smiled back.

****

Jenna returned to tuck Janie in. With Pup-pup clutched in her arms, the child said goodnight and rolled to her stomach. Eric and Jenna went down to the kitchen for coffee.

"How is she...really?" he asked. "I would have thought she'd be more upset. And she never mentioned Mark. Don't you think that's strange?"

"The average kid *would* be traumatized by what happened. But Janie's life has never been average."

"Tell me about it. I really need to know."

Jenna nodded and began slowly. Her words sounded like a confession filled with guilt and regret. "We've lived a life of isolation; and I think she always sensed there was something unusual about it. We were always moving, switching it up between big cities and really small towns. I never talked about my past, and the older Janie got, the more she suspected I was keeping something from her. There's a part of her that might be relieved for everything to finally be out in the open."

Eric pushed his mug away. "It's probably too soon for me to be offering an opinion, but don't you think she should see someone?"

"Of course I do." Jenna expelled a pained and weary sigh. She picked up their empty coffee cups and placed them in the sink. "Being kidnapped isn't exactly like having a scraped knee. I'll ask her pediatrician to recommend a child psychologist."

Eric stared at his clasped hands. "I'd like to come and hear what they have to say. I also want to pay. I should be the one to pay."

"I have insurance for—"

"I don't want you to have to take her to some doctor just because he or she's on your plan. Let me at least do this, do what a father is supposed to do."

"Okay."

She and Eric talked more about what lie ahead. He

desperately wanted to believe he and Janie could form a bond and become a family. "I want to get to know her, but I won't force her into a relationship."

"You won't have to." Although Jenna scooped away his cup, she waved the half empty carafe to offer him more of the brew. He declined a third cup.

"So, what now?" she asked.

Eric rubbed the back of his neck. His to-do list was infinitely long. "After I get Ina squared away, I have to get back to Los Angeles. My divorce hearing starts in two weeks. Then there's still Baldwin and Mark. I may be spending the next year going back and forth to court." Eric snorted and lifted his lips into a sardonic half-smile. "At least this time around, I'm not the one in the defendant's chair."

Jenna's sober expression told him she didn't find his comment amusing.

He eased his hands into his pockets. "Not funny, huh?"

"No, not at all."

"Yeah, well I have something else to tell you that you might not find amusing."

Jenna groaned. "What now?"

Eric grinned. "I'm gay."

Chapter Thirty-Eight

Laughter boomed in Eric's ears—a loud guffaw coming through the telephone and a howl from Nick who sat next to him at Ina's kitchen table. Eric cursed into the phone, turned, and repeated the anatomically impossible suggestion to his sniggering friend. Ina studied the newspaper and alternated her glance between Eric and the tabloid.

He narrowed his eyes. "Oh, come on. Don't tell me you're actually reading the article."

"Well…no. I was just ah…looking for…um…"

"What? Stock quotes in *The Inquisitor.*"

Ina joined Nick in a rupture of laughter.

"Okay, kiddies, get it out of your system…You too!" he spat into the phone.

"Sorry, kid." Jack Morrissey snickered on the other end of the line. "I had no idea. But if there was ever a broad on the planet who could make a man switch teams, it would be Bree."

Eric gnashed his teeth. "I'm not laughing, you old fart. She fed this story to the tabloids as a smokescreen. She doesn't want their leads to be anything about me and Jenna."

"Well, don't worry, kid. Nobody believes this shit. Although the guy in the picture with you is, what do the girls all say, a hottie?"

"Go to hell, Morrissey. I called to discuss something

important. Can you put me back in the closet for the time being?"

"Okay, okay."

Nick and Ina discarded the newspaper and sat at attention as Eric explained to Jack what Ash Baldwin had done.

"The son of a bitch tried to kill you!" A bellow came through the phone loud enough for Nick, Eric, and Ina to all jerk in their seats.

"I'm more concerned with what he tried to do to my friend. He strong-armed the town building inspector into condemning her house so he could steal her land."

"Listen, kid. I'm only in on this deal because Meghan's husband is the great grandson of the guy who designed Pebble Beach. The family is golf course royalty and they aren't going to let that image be tarnished by a guy who tried to steal land from a little old lady."

Jack promised the status of Ash Baldwin as a partner in the country club consortium would be amended.

****

The wheels of justice turned at a slow and steady pace. Jake and Harley Simpson were caught in Daytona after trying to use one of Eric credit cards. Both brothers admitted to being hired by Ash Baldwin to attack Eric. Legal troubles, both criminal and civil, would keep Baldwin busy for an indeterminate length of time and deplete a good portion of his wealth. Eric opted not to sue so Baldwin would have enough money left to compensate Ina for her emotional pain and suffering. Ina Cummings would never have to worry about losing her home again.

Janie Black was spared the pain of having to testify against Mark Chambers. On the advice of his court appointed attorney, he took a plea bargain of twenty-five-years in prison. Wearing a bright orange jump suit and manacles, he was led to the county sheriff's van.

Chains connecting his ankles and wrists jingled a nervous melody as he sat shaking from the effects of drug and alcohol withdrawal. Thin and faint-hearted, he had never in his life been able to defend himself—not in a school yard as a boy, and not in a bar-fight as a grown man. He would certainly not be able to defend himself from the advances of barbaric, prison inmates. During the short drive back to the county lockup to await his transfer to prison, he cried like a baby.

****

Ina handed Eric his work boots. "These are practically brand new. Are you sure you don't want to take them with you?"

"Keep them here. I'll need them when I come back. I'll have to check the house to make sure the contractors did everything right."

"Well at least let me pack you some sandwiches for your flight."

Eric was about to explain that outside food wouldn't make it past TSA, but instead accepted her offer. The braised beef tenderloins served in first-class didn't hold the appeal of one of her club sandwiches. "Sure, that would be great." He'd eat her BLT in the limo.

A lump formed in his throat as he watched her hurry away. He was truly going to miss the sweet old lady. Morning coffee and guessing at the answers on *Jeopardy* every evening was a routine he enjoyed and one that would be hard to replace. He had no real permanent home or family to return to. After he finished packing, he slowly made his way down the stairs to say goodbye.

"Here's the rent I owe you."

Scrunching her gray brows, Ina eyed the thick package he'd pressed into her hand. "Do I need to count it?"

He winked and flashed his movie star gleam. "It's all there. Of course my addition may be a bit off."

"Now, young man, I told you when I met you, I wasn't a charity case."

"Ina," he began softly, "I just want to make sure you're taken care of, not because you need charity, but because I love you."

She grabbed for a tissue stuffed up her sleeve and dabbed at her eyes. "You're going to have to bend down so I can kiss that handsome face of yours. I can't very well reach it way up there."

He bent over and gave her a tight hug. "I'll be back soon."

Grabbing his bag and his lunch he walked out the door. Through the car's window he saw her on her front porch, waving the tissue. He leaned out and waved back until the limousine turned onto the road and the cloud of dust it kicked up settled.

****

Jenna's glance wavered back to the hall clock. Eric was coming by on his way to the airport to say goodbye to Janie. He'd spent the last two weeks trying to cram as much quality time with his daughter as he could. The time was up, and he needed to return to Los Angeles. He promised Janie he would be back in Cromline as soon as possible, and Jenna didn't doubt his vow. He didn't break promises.

Janie seemed subdued, and it worried Jenna. In a very small amount of time, her daughter had gotten very attached to him. Jenna understood more than anyone how easy it was to love Eric Laine.

He and Janie shared dinners and saw every age-appropriate movie in theaters or on home video. He even made his first judgment call as a parent and took her to the ice cream parlor. It was an apprehensive moment for both father and child, he confessed. He described to Jenna how he felt Janie's small hand tighten in his own as they walked through the parking lot. It was a hurdle they jumped together and the first time, not counting the kidnapping, he helped their daughter through a traumatic event.

He had missed all the skinned knees and sniffles. He'd never dried any of her tears or shared any of her triumphs. Jenna had stolen it all from him.

She wished now, as she had then, that he'd been at her side when Janie won the second grade spelling bee, or first place on the balance beam. Jenna wished she could turn back the clock and give him all the happy smiles he'd missed. Two short weeks wasn't nearly enough time to make up for everything. Now he was leaving—too soon for Janie, too soon for all of them.

A car with Nick behind the wheel pulled into the driveway. The Town Car was a sight Jenna's neighbors had grown accustomed to. He'd stuck around to protect her and Janie. By now everyone in Cromline knew the true story of the elusive single mom. Thankfully her neighbors respected her privacy. Then again, the media had reported enough to satisfy their curiosity.

****

Eric rapped his knuckles against the door, and Janie answered. Her mouth was drawn into a pout and her eyes downcast. "Hey, what's this? Where's my smile?"

She shuffled her feet against the mat at the entryway. "I wish you didn't have to go."

"Aw, kid, I wish I didn't have to either, but—" He pushed back the sleeve of his jacket and glanced at his wristwatch. "I have an appointment at court…oh…in just about eighteen hours. But I'll be back here as soon as I can."

"How long?"

"I can't honestly say, but tell you what, I'll call every day. You can count on it."

The child seemed to struggle to find a smile. She fell short of her mark by yards. Grabbing her, Eric threw one arm around her shoulder and swayed playfully. He rubbed the top of her head with his knuckles and earned a genuine smile. "I promise to bring you something back from California, something great. How'd you like a T-shirt?"

She scrunched her nose and shook her head.

"Oranges?"

"Uh, uh."

"Water from the Pacific Ocean?"

"Nope."

"Well then, what should I bring?"

Janie looked up, her eyes wide and earnest. "I just want *you* to come back."

He clasped his hands to his chest and sighed. "What color Ferrari do you want?"

Giggling, Janie bounced in place, her pale-yellow hair sweeping across her shoulders. "Do they come in hot pink?"

"I'll have it covered in pink rhinestones, if you want."

Eric bent down to give his daughter a hug. It felt

natural, comfortable. He and Janie clicked, and for that he was grateful. As he knelt down to say goodbye, he wished with all of his heart he could get past the feeling of betrayal and hurt he still harbored toward his child's mother.

Jenna stood by, silent, her face frozen into a forced looking smile. When the trio walked outside, Janie trotted off to the limousine to say goodbye to Nick, but Eric held out his hand to stop Jenna from following. "Got a sec?"

"Sure."

He stared at the ground, speaking more to his shoes than to her. "My lawyers have worked out a settlement that Bree has accepted. I have to meet with my manager and then a real estate agent to put my Pacific Palisades house on the market. I should be back in a few weeks."

"Janie will be glad."

Lifting his head he met Jenna's eyes. They shone golden in the spring sunshine, her dark lashes framing the faceted gleam. They were luminous, or maybe shining with the beginning of tears.

"I'll miss her," he said. "Maybe we can come to some sort of schedule for the summer. I'd like to take her to North Carolina for a visit if that's okay with you."

Though her face appeared to pale, Jenna nodded her agreement.

"I...I wish things were different," he said. The admission was genuine. Eric had been struggling with his feelings since learning the truth, torn by what he wanted and what weighed against his heart.

Lifting her shoulders, Jenna met his look with a blank yet considerate gaze. "You can't help the way you feel."

"I'm sorry." He took her face in his hands and softly kissed her. "I still love you. That hasn't changed. That will never change. But I just can't think about you and me right now. I wish I could."

A cloud passed overhead and masked the buttercup brilliance of the sun. For a moment all the colors of spring—grass, garden blooms, and sky washed gray. "I asked you to forgive me, and you can't. I understand. Have a safe flight. I'm going to say goodbye to Nick."

Jenna jogged down the driveway and away from him.

Chapter Thirty-Nine

Eric Laine's life as a movie star resumed the moment his plane touched down at Burbank Airport. There was something about being in Los Angeles that brought a certain brilliance to his life. In Cromline he could pretend to be a nonentity, just a regular guy banging a hammer. But in L.A. he could be nothing less than a celebrity of the highest magnitude. He wanted no part of it. For the first time in his career as an actor, he snubbed the fans that followed him. He refused to acknowledge the crowd chaperoning him to his limousine.

One of Nick's cars whisked him to Jack's estate where the staff gave him the usual five-star treatment.

"Welcome back, Mr. Laine."

"What can I do for you, Mr. Laine?"

Just leave me alone, was what he wanted to say.

Later that day, he sat through a meeting with his attorneys, met with his agent, and reluctantly signed on to present an award for something that escaped his memory the moment he agreed to do it. None of it was what he wanted. What he *wanted* was another slice of Ina's pie. He *wanted* to eat it while he watched the sun set over hills ripe with waves of spring grass yet to be cut. He *wanted* to know his daughter was scrambling to do her homework because she was expecting his visit. He *wanted* to fall into an exhausted, peaceful sleep because he was spent from a day of hard work, a belly full of good food, and a night of love making in the arms of the woman he adored. He *wanted* to get beyond the disappointment and beat back the feeling of betrayal that stubbornly refused to surrender, but he couldn't. And until he did, he was never going to have what he *wanted.*

****

After another restless night, he readied himself for his divorce hearing. He straightened his tie, almost adding a gold tie clip with a mother-of-pearl inlay, until he remembered it was a gift from the woman he was on his way to disentangle himself from. He should have been feeling relieved to be finally gaining his freedom, but divorce number two was a reminder of another failure.

A light rap sounded at the door. "Knock, knock." It was Jack. "My people treating you okay here?"

"Better than the staff at a five-star hotel."

"You don't look like a man happy to be living in the lap of luxury."

Eric crooked his head around at a space filled with furniture covered in gem hued velvets arranged atop luxe Persian carpets. Yards of silk flanked the windows. The Morrissey guest cottage looked like a harem's tent. "Luxury is overrated."

"Tell that to the poor shmuck who gets his water from the faucet," Jack chided.

Eric studied the pair of three-thousand-dollar sunglasses in his hand. He'd come a long way to nowhere.

Jack gripped his shoulder and squeezed. "I'm just fucking with you, kid. We both know what it's like to be flush, and what it's like to do without. Remember, you can do a lot more good in this world with money. You couldn't have saved your little old lady from losing her home if you were poor. Don't ever apologize for being rich."

Eric nodded. "I suppose. I'm adding senior citizens to my list of charities."

"Well, you can count on contributions from me," Jack volunteered.

"That's because you are a fucking senior citizen."

The comment earned a laugh from Jack, but he quickly sobered. "Speaking of charity, I really hope you aren't planning on turning over half of everything you own to that she-witch."

"I'll give her whatever it takes to get her out of my life."

Jack shoved his hands into the pockets of his cashmere trousers. "You shouldn't give her one red cent."

Eric spat a sound that was half laugh and half lament. "C'mon, Morrissey. You've been through this enough times. California is the community property capitol of the universe. The 'she-witch' is entitled to half of everything."

"But, but after what she did…couldn't you leverage that into a better deal?"

Eric swiped a set of keys from the table and ambled to the door. "I'd gladly have her ass thrown in jail, but I don't have anything concrete to use against her."

"But… But," Jack continued to argue.

"But nothing. I got her to agree to end the marriage."

Jack followed through a towering stucco archway. "So you're letting her walk?"

Taking an easy breath, Eric walked out into the

bright Bel Air sunshine. He slipped his sunglasses onto his nose and gave his friend a two fingered salute. "Don't worry, Jack. Today I get my freedom, and my wife gets everything she deserves."

****

Flanked by her attorneys, Bree Davis Laine swept into the conference room with a smile of confidence lighting her face. Eric imagined she was more than happy that the multi-million-dollar portfolio of assets in the Laine-Davis coffers was to be split evenly. All real estate, including Eric's farm, was to be sold and the profits divided.

Sounds from throats being cleared and briefcases clicking open started the official process. The head of Bree's team, the most cocksure looking member of the firm, read documents in an efficient manner. His smile equaled, if not exceeded Bree's.

"Well then, all we need are some signatures," Eric's lawyer added.

Eric grinned, his eyes sparking confidence and fastened on his opponent. "Just a sec."

A young man stepped up to the table and addressed Bree. "Bree Davis-Laine. You've been served."

Her head snapped, whip-like, in Eric's direction. "What the hell is this?"

Her attorney grabbed at the envelope and tore it open to read the contents. "He's suing you."

"Suing me! For what?" Bree's eyes grew wide. "How can he sue me?"

Her lawyers huddled together at the table to read the subpoena as Eric nodded for his own lawyer to produce another packet. In it was a collection of papers as thin as a college rejection letter. "I'm suing you for pain and suffering on behalf of my daughter."

Bree sprang to her feet and spoke around a laugh. "You can't prove I did anything, and she isn't *your* daughter in case you forgot."

"Wrong on both counts," Eric said. "DNA proves Jane Marie Laine is my child. And by the way, Mark gave you up."

Other than the quick blink that made her eyes pop wider, she looked cool and unruffled. She brought her hands together prayerlike, her glossy fingernails glowing under high-hat lights. "Mark Chambers is an unhinged drug addict. If the police believed anything he said, I would have been arrested. As for your *child,* are you really willing to make her relive everything for money?"

One of Bree's lawyers tugged at her arm, urging her to sit. "Mr. Laine, my client had nothing to do with the unfortunate incident back in New York. You're grandstanding to get a better settlement. Judges frown on extortion."

Eric's steady stare went far beyond anger. It was outrage, fury, the wrath of a father confronting the person who hurt his child. He leaned across the table, close to Bree, his voice fixed and low. "You led a man…no, not a man…an animal to a little girl. You knew Mark was a rapist, an *unhinged,* fucking sociopath, yet you still delivered him right to my daughter's doorstep. What the hell is wrong with you?"

Eric's lawyer faced Bree's team. "Your client was smart enough to deal in cash, so we have no paper trail linking her to Chambers. What we do have is the photographer, Belka's, corroboration that he and Chambers were both hired by Mrs. Laine to frighten Jenna Black and her daughter. Powers, the detective, refuses to talk right now, but we have a flight manifest that puts him on the same plane with Chambers. The police seized a rental car with both Powers and Chambers' prints. We have a waitress in a diner who saw them together, and a motel clerk who remembers both Powers and Belka. We also pinged calls from a burner phone we confiscated from Belka to the Laines' New York apartment building. Security cameras place Mrs. Laine there." The lawyer turned toward Bree. "We can connect a hundred dots of circumstantial evidence against you. My client's daughter will never have to testify."

"Circumstantial," Bree repeated. "Good luck."

Eric removed papers from the second envelope and slid them across the table to her. He immediately drew his arm back so his hand wouldn't graze hers. He'd never in his life touch Bree Davis again.

"This is a very different offer. In it is enough cash for you to live pretty well for a few years and the deed to a nice two-bedroom co-op in Brentwood. You can keep all your jewelry."

Bree turned to her attorneys. "Tell my husband he and his circumstantial dots can go to hell."

Eric took out a solid gold pen from his pocket and signed both divorce agreements. He made his way to the door. "I'll be back in ten minutes. That's all the time I'm giving you to decide which papers to sign."

With a tap of his finger, he flicked the glossy Mont Bleu pen so it rolled toward her. "One agreement will make you comfortable…the other, undeniably wealthy but with a giant lawsuit that will wipe you out hanging over your head."

Eric opened the door, turned, and smiled. "Millions

of dollars in damages are awarded every day because of circumstantial evidence. There's no reasonable doubt in a civil trial. Ask your lawyers."

Bree turned, and her mouth hung slack. The unflappable head of her legal team was suddenly pale and sweating.

Eric's smile stretched even wider. "You can keep the fucking pen."

Chapter Forty

Spring cleared a path for summer. Untethered and financially unscathed by his divorce, Eric returned to Cromline to celebrate his daughter's ninth birthday. Janie had a simple sleepover with friends from school and her gymnastics' teammates. Anne came to help dole out cake and ice cream and to keep the noise down to a dull roar. With Eric in attendance, most of the moms lingered a bit, gushing, blushing, and acting more like adolescents than their daughters.

Cheryl Baldwin, Jenna's newest "best friend" brought Janie a gift in a large box that housed God only knew what. Tiffany and the three Britneys had suddenly developed a new-found fondness for both Janie and Riley. The girls, though neither cared, were finally on Cromline Elementary's A-List.

For Jenna life continued as usual. She ran the store and stayed active at Janie's school to help with all the year's end functions like field day events and class trips. She had regular luncheon dates with Anne and talked endlessly on the telephone with her parents and Randi to assure them she and Janie were fine. A security detail hovered nearby if needed.

Reporters who had clamored for stories about Eric Laine and Jenna Welles seemed to be satisfied for the moment. New scandals from the entertainment world replaced the saga of Angel and the "Busboy." It was at long last a story with finality.

Alan Stark tried to lure Jenna back into his fold of clients, but she declined. She had no interest in acting or singing professionally, at least not for any time soon. After all that had happened, life was peacefully and thankfully returning to normal with one small exception.

She was pregnant.

****

Randi's voice was a firm decree coming through the phone line. "You have to tell him."

"I know, I know," Jenna answered. "I just have to find the right way."

"Well don't wait five years this time."

Jenna took a long breath. She was almost two months along and in the full throes of midday sickness. "I need to lie down."

"You need to tell him!"

Slumped on her couch, the phone was at her ear. "Randi, if I tell him he'll—"

"He'll what? Marry you? The rich, gorgeous, famous father of your children will marry you? I'll think of you when you're sipping champagne by your infinity pool, and I'm grabbing a wine cooler from the ice bucket on my pressure treated deck."

The memory of two teenage girls fresh from a small-town graduation and arguing about red-carpet galas versus frat house beer pong flashed in Jenna's head. She smiled at how grateful she was to have Randi for a best friend.

"Listen to me, Jen. You tell him, and when you get married this time, stay that way. I can't go through another ten years of this shit."

Exhausted and fully settled in the down filled

cushions, Jenna put her phone on speaker. "I thought you didn't even like him."

"I *didn't* like him when he was married to that bitchy vampire-woman. I like him just fine now."

Jenna sighed into the receiver. "If I tell him and we get remarried, I'll never know. I'll never know if he came back out of love or responsibility."

Through the phone line, she heard a loud crash followed by an even louder wail. "Oh crap. What did you guys break now?" Randi shouted. "Jen, I gotta go. Tell him!" she barked, and then hung up.

Hugging a pillow, Jenna burrowed deeper into her sofa. It was two o'clock, and she decided on a quick nap before picking Janie up from school. Just as she started to drift off, she heard the sound of a car pulling into her driveway. Through the sidelight, she could see a shining black Lincoln. A woman, slender, wearing rhinestone studded sunglasses and what looked like an explosion of editorial designs, climbed out. She was holding a very wiggly baby. She shifted the child to her hip while she fished through a huge pastel-colored bag stamped with designer initials. Retrieving a pacifier, she popped it into the baby's mouth, and rang the bell.

Jenna opened the door, and her bottom lip fell. It was Meghan Morrisey, Jack's daughter, the girl Jenna last saw being carted into an ambulance after Eric saved her from a drug overdose.

"Here, take this," Meghan said. She handed off a cherub dressed in layers of baby couture. "Jesus, you live far from the city." She spoke as though she had seen Jenna yesterday rather than almost ten years ago. "It took my driver forever to get here. Damned kid slept all the way. I think my tits are going to pop." She put her hands over large breasts to illustrate her point, then unbuttoned her blouse. She took the baby back and strode over to Jenna's couch to nurse him.

"So how the hell have you been?"

Jenna was too stunned to speak.

"Get me a glass of water," Meghan ordered. "Nursing makes me so thirsty."

She explained she had gotten Jenna's address from her father. She also explained that she was "deliriously" and "happily" married. Her husband was "disgustingly" rich, and she lived in a lavish penthouse in Manhattan. "Gave up all my bad habits. Not my sense of style though." She crossed one paisley-stockinged leg over the other.

As she fed her son, whose name she proudly announced as Ocean Amadeus Morrisey Millwood, she got down to the business of why she was visiting. "My husband and I live on the Upper East Side, a block away from Eric and Bree's place. Whenever they were in New York, we would get together."

"You and Bree are friends?" Jenna was surprisingly hurt by the admission.

"Friends? With that demon bitch? I wouldn't have looked at her on the street if it wasn't for Eric. I could have killed him when he married her." Meghan popped her other nipple into her son's mouth, took a sip of water, and continued her rant. "Bree Davis was the second biggest mistake of Eric's life…losing you the first. Now he has a chance to be happy and instead of fixing things, he's just moping around and crying the blues to my dad, and Nick, and whoever else will listen to him cry about how he can't get past the fact that you lied to him." Meghan looked lovingly down at her nursing baby.

"Men," she spat. "I hope this one doesn't grow up to be an asshole."

Wide eyed, Jenna looked and listened as Meghan delivered her oration while efficiently feeding, burping, and changing her son. There was no arguing, nor was there any segue into the one-sided conversation. Each time Jenna opened her mouth to speak, Meghan held up a hand. "That beautiful man spent nine years being miserable without you, and now he's just wasting more time. Daddy and I think someone needs to light a fire under his stubborn ass. There's a gala at the Frick on Friday, and you're going. I've fixed you up with someone who will make Eric so jealous he'll put the fucking Hope Diamond on your finger." Meghan stood, propped her son on one hip and blew out the door. "Frick-n-Friday." She laughed as she stepped to her waiting limo. "See you then."

****

When Meghan called to finalize their plans, Jenna argued and gave myriad excuses for not being able to attend the gala. "I already have plans—There's too much traffic on Friday—I have nothing to wear."

"A. You're lying. B. I will send a car. C. I've already arranged to have a dozen couture gowns delivered to your house. Pick one!" Meghan harangued, whined, and threatened to drag Jenna to the Frick by her hair if she didn't agree to go. Her last appeal was a sensitive and heartfelt entreaty. "If it wasn't for you and Eric, I wouldn't even be alive. No two people deserve happiness more. Please let me help."

A day later, a selection of eveningwear arrived by courier, and later that afternoon, a stylist, seamstress, and dresser were also knocking on Jenna's door. But when

Friday dawned, the day clear and the sky as blue as a morning glory, Jenna came down with a skin prickling attack of nerves. She called Meghan and itemized more excuses for needing to bow out, being camera shy at the top of the list.

"Camera shy? You've been on the red-carpet enough times to wear a rut in it."

"It's not only that," Jenna admitted. "I just don't think going on a date to some bougie affair is going to help make things better between me and Eric."

Meghan's long sigh hissed through the phone's speaker. "So what's *your* plan then? Are you going to sit around and hope he's done brooding in a year?"

Jenna brought her hand to what was still an indiscernible mound below her navel. Her breasts were already spilling from the cups of all her brassieres. In another month, there would be no hiding her condition.

"All right, I'll go." Jenna hung up and, for the first time since agreeing, she realized she had no idea who her date even was.

****

Janie opened the door, wide-eyed and breathless as she greeted Eric. "Did you see the limo? Did you?" She was bouncing in place, a firm but gangly collection of limbs that blurred his vision. "Mommy says she's been in limos lots of time and they're no big deal, but I think they're cool!"

"Your mom's right. They're just long cars."

His comment put an end to Janie's animated gamboling and she offered innocently wide eyes to him. "Don't you want to know why it's here?"

Eric lifted his shoulders in a shrug, but his jaw constricted as he spoke. "I imagine your mom has plans."

"A date!" Janie shrieked like an audience member of an early Elvis performance.

Eric was bringing his daughter with him to Ina's and grabbed her bag from the floor.

"Don't you want to know who she's going out with?" Janie asked.

"No, Jane, it's not really my business."

"Did you just call me Jane?" She appeared to suppress a building spill of giggles and pressed her face into her pillow. "Mom only calls me Jane when she's mad at something...like the time I used magic markers as lipstick...or the time I tried to flush my dirty sneakers down the toilet...or the time I—"

"I get the idea."

A tap on the stair treads caught his attention and he turned. He stared, rapt, unmoving, his heart's rhythm quickening into an escalated patter. Jenna was floating from one riser down to the next. She lifted her gown's hem, and her shoes sparkled like fairytale glass slippers. He tried to draw his eyes away, but it was as if his head was pinioned in place.

Her gown was a pale gold spill of silk with a draped neckline. A pattern of crystal beads sewn like twining vines made her shimmer as she stepped. Her hair was set in waves, one side tucked behind her ear, the other glancing her face, throat, and bare shoulder. Eric followed her journey till she reached the bottom of the stairs, and even then, he found tearing his eyes away an unattainable labor.

"Eric!" Janie shouted and snapped him out of his trance. "I'm ready to go."

He swallowed hard, still staring at Jenna. "Have fun tonight." After grabbing his daughter's pillow, he opened the door and stomped past the waiting limousine. Janie turned toward her mother and smiled.

****

In the morning, Jenna awoke mildly nauseous, her eyes heavy and her breasts throbbing. She was exhausted but more sad than tired. Eric's words *"have fun tonight"* stayed with her the whole evening. He didn't care about her having a date.

The event at the Frick had been a gathering of New York City's beau monde and had something to do with libraries, or museums, or Discovery Times Square. As she attempted to mingle, *"have fun tonight,"* was all she heard.

She tried being gracious as Meghan trawled her from one end of the museum to the other. Jenna tried being sociable, approachable, and even attentive to her date, Brett Masters, the twenty-six-year-old, gorgeous and strapping baseball star who'd come to the Frick straight from Citi Field where he'd hit two home runs. He was engaging and charming, but *"have fun tonight"* was all she'd heard.

After brushing her teeth, she gave a cursory swipe with a cloth to the mascara smeared under her eyes. She'd been too tired when she'd gotten home at one a.m. to wash her face. A light tap sounded at the side door.

She glanced at the clock. It was barely eight. "What the hell?"

"Coming," she yelled as she pattered down the stairs. Through a window she could see Eric leaning against the railing. She opened the door. "Is Janie okay?"

"Fine." Without invitation he stepped inside. "Are *you* okay? You look a little beat."

"Oh, it was a late night, and I'm just out of practice."

Jenna reached far and wide for light and airy but her eyes felt unevenly squinty. "Um, why are you here so early?"

"We're doing some gardening today, and our daughter needs crappier clothes. I don't want her to ruin what you packed."

"Oh."

Jenna and Eric stood, staring and waiting for the other to move, or speak, or just break from the gaze that had taken hold. "I'll run up and get her overalls and an old T-shirt," she eventually said.

Upstairs, she changed into shorts and a tank top. Back down in the kitchen, she handed him a bundle of clothes and a pair of tatty sneakers. "Here you go."

"I made some coffee. I hope you don't mind."

"No, not at all, but I've switched to tea."

Jenna filled the kettle and dropped a decaf bag into a cup as Eric made himself comfortable at her table. Though he braced his hands around his mug, he never took a sip. He stared as if sizing her up to form an opinion. "Did you have fun last night?"

"It was okay. A lot of names. It felt strange being back in that world."

"I know the feeling. I don't much care for it."

Jenna fought the urge to roll her eyes, or cluck her tongue, or make any gestures that showed displeasure. While she didn't miss the cultlike idolatry of her short-lived celebrity, it chafed that Eric lived in its exclusive circle. "I'm sure you've been to enough red-carpet events over the years to be used to them."

He finally took a sip of his coffee, placed the cup down, and folded his arms in a tight press of "leave me alone" body language. "I'm *used* to tolerating them."

"Mmm." Her attention flitted away, and she stared

past him. She would always view Hollywood as a litter filled alleyway. Adultery, addiction, suicide, and sexual depravity lived behind every door. There was almost no one in the business of make believe who hadn't paid the price of fame.

"At some point, tolerating attention doesn't cut it," she said.

Eric's eyes narrowed into two blue slashes. "Yet you went to a celebrity studded event last night. You're on Page Six."

Acid churned in a sudden and uneasy circle in her stomach. "I had no idea."

"No idea? No idea that the rediscovered princess of pop on the arm of the biggest player in the major leagues would make it to the papers? C'mon."

The shrill whistle of the kettle was a startling peal that made her almost jump. She hurried to the stove to turn the burner off. "The thing at the Frick was for charity, and Meghan Morrisey pestered me into going. You know I have a hard time saying no to anything."

Eric bolted from his seat so quickly he almost upended his chair. "Did you have a hard time saying no to Brett Masters, too? When I said he was a player I wasn't just talking about baseball."

"Are you serious?" Jenna rushed over, tipping her face up so she and Eric were nose to nose. "It was a blind date. He was a perfect gentleman."

"Humph," Eric scoffed. "Masters is in the tabloids with a different woman every week. Gentleman isn't how any of them describe him."

Jenna's cheeks grew hot. "You of all people should know the tabloids never print the truth. Brett is very sweet. In fact, he invited me to tonight's game as his guest and for a quiet dinner afterward. I was going to pass, but now you've made me curious. I think I'll go and see what *all* the fuss is about."

A flush of red that matched the heat in her face tinted Eric's skin. He looked down and into her eyes. His glinted ire. "Don't you dare."

Jenna shoved and brushed past him. "You told me there was no future for us, so you don't get to tell me what to do." She turned and fired her words at him. "You don't get to tell me what to do anyway!"

Following on her heels he shouted, "I never said there was no future for us. I said I needed some time."

"Oldest line in the book."

Eric flung his arms wide. "Book? What book?"

"It's a metaphor." Jenna marched to her door and pulled the heavy oak panel wide. "Don't you have some gardening to do?"

He grabbed Janie's clothing and stormed through. "Have fun tonight," he spat as he jumped into his truck and roared away.

****

Architects had modified the original plans for the town houses and shops of Baldwin Ridge Country Club. They added scrollwork, gingerbread details, and reversed gable ends. The result would be a quaint yet elegant Victorian village named The Glade at Cromline. Ina Cummings' house, almost restored and perched at the end of the grounds, fit right in.

Ina and Janie carried flats of impatiens to the fence that ran along the shady side of the house. "Do you want to tell me what's got your daddy so worked up? He's found a hundred things wrong with my house he didn't notice a couple of weeks ago."

On cue, Eric shouted from across the yard. "Would you look at this!"

The girls pivoted around to see what he was complaining about. He had been doing it all day. He was on his knees scrutinizing the clapboard by the back door. "The painters didn't give this section two coats of primer before adding the topcoat. I can practically see the old paint coming through."

Ina threw down her hand rake and marched to where he was examining the siding. "There is no old paint showing through. You replaced those boards yourself. It's all new." She shook her head and stomped back off to her annuals. She and Janie shared more head shaking and eye rolling as Eric continued to study obscure corners of the property.

"My mom had a date last night," Janie confessed laughing.

"Did she now?" Ina poured planting soil into a shallow hole she'd dug, and Janie deposited a plant that would grow into a collection of bright pink blooms.

"Aunt Ina, if he's this mad over my mom having a date, do you think that means he still loves her?"

Tilting her huge sunbonnet back away from her face, Ina leaned on the shovel she'd been tilling the bed with. "Oh, honey, I don't think there was ever any doubt that your daddy loves your mother." She winked and a web of wrinkles framed her eye. "But sometimes men just need a little reminder of how much they do."

"That sounds kind of sneaky."

Ina tipped her face at the sky, a sunbathed blue dotted with fleecy clouds. "I prefer to think of it as gentle prodding. Men seem to always need it." She dropped a plant into a hole and tamped dirt around it. "As for your daddy…let's let him stew until his mind catches up with his heart."

****

"Hey! I'm going inside to get my caulking gun. Those windows aren't sealed tight. You'll have a draft like a tornado next winter if I don't fix them." Eric looked out toward the fence, but Ina and Janie had moved out of earshot and ignored him. *Good thing,* he reflected the thought back to himself. He sounded like a two-year-old blustering over a missing toy.

He huffed off through the back door and marched directly to the kitchen counter where he had tossed his cell phone. He picked it up and pounded Jack Morrissey's number on the keypad.

"Talk to me, kid. I was waiting for you to call and bitch."

"I didn't call to bitch. I called to find out what Meghan was thinking by fixing Jenna up with somebody like Brett Masters." He drummed his fingers on the counter waiting for his answer, but Jack's laugh crackled though the receiver.

"Well!" Eric shouted.

Jack's laugh became heartier. "My little girl is a romantic fool and just wants everyone to be happy."

Eric's jaw tightened. "She's a spoiled brat. The next time I see her I'm putting her over my knee. You tell her I know what she's up to and it won't work."

"That's my baby you're threatening, slick." Jack's warning sounded wrapped in humor and Eric fumed more, his fist a steady beat against his thigh.

Jack's tone sobered. "By the way, it already *is* working or you wouldn't have called. It's bugging the hell out of you that Jenna went out on a date."

281

"Brett Masters doesn't date. He seduces. He's a rich, famous, good-looking jerk who dumps a different woman every week. Don't you ever read the paper?"

Jack's voice, the gravelly baritone familiar to millions, was steady and stern. "You listen to me, kid. I love you like a son. Stop being such an asshole. You're the only goddamned rich and famous, good-looking jerk who dumped Jenna. Don't blow it again. Get over all that nonsense you have going on inside that thick head of yours and ask her to marry you."

The line went dead.

Eric shoved the screen door open and strode over to Ina and Janie. "Am I being an asshole?"

"Yes," they answered together, with Ina adding a reproach for the language. Eric squatted down and clasped his daughter's waist in his hands. "Could you give us a couple of minutes, honey? Go inside and have a snack or something, okay."

"Sure, Eric."

He shook his head and called to her as she ran off. "Are you ever planning on calling me Dad?"

Janie angled her blonde head to one side and curled her lips into a smile. "Yep. As soon as you marry my mom."

"How do you like that," Eric said as he and Ina watched the child gallop away. "She's a nine-year-old extortionist."

"She has a point. Maybe she can't accept that you'll always be around until you become a family."

"Having your parents living together doesn't guarantee you'll be a family. No one knows that better than me and my brother and sisters." He kicked at a clod of dirt, and it exploded into a spray of dust. "Besides,

Jenna's the one who left. She was the one who wanted a divorce."

Ina fiddled with the empty flower cartons and condensed the flats one on top of the other. After placing them down, she pressed her fists into her hips. "Look, you both made mistakes...whoppers from what I understand. Seems like Jenna's gotten past it. If you don't forgive her, you're going to lose her again. Is that what you want?"

Eric looked into the deep wisdom and sincerity of Ina's eyes. "It wouldn't be fair to any of us if I make a commitment until I've come to terms with everything one hundred percent...until my feelings are clear."

"Oh you dear, sweet boy." Ina's voice skirted the edge of both comfort and sarcasm. She stabbed the center of his chest with her forefinger. "That's horse shit and you know it. You finally have a shot at true love, and you're too afraid to take it." She poked him harder, and her gnarled finger left a dot of dirt on his chambray shirt. "Happiness is never guaranteed, so I won't tell you what to do. What I will tell you is what not to do. Don't come over here every time she has a date and re-fix my damned house." She spun on her heels.

"But...but."

"But nothing," Ina shouted as she walked away. "If you've gotten yourself this bent out of shape because Jenna went out with another man, it seems to me your feelings *are* pretty clear!"

Smiling, he caught up with his landlady and kissed her weathered cheek. "Janie has a gymnastics practice at three. Take my truck. Mine has seatbelts that actually work, and her bag is already in it." He sprinted across the lawn and climbed into Ina's rusted pickup. He turned the key that always dangled from the ignition and rumbled out of her driveway.

****

Jenna yawned and popped another dry saltine into her mouth. She wasn't bothered by morning sickness but after a lingering midday episode, she felt exhausted. Depression wove its way into the network of emotions that were spiraling through her system and hitching a ride on her hormones. She was about to have a cleansing mother-to-be cry when she heard the backfiring engine of a truck sputter to a halt in her driveway. Eric. From her window she could see him heading toward the kitchen door on the side of the house. At first glance, she thought with concern something must be wrong for him to be back in his torn jeans and dirt-streaked shirt, but his slow loping stride convinced her otherwise. She stepped away and scrambled to the stove to boil water for another cup of tea as if she hadn't a care in the world.

"Hi," he said, leaning in the doorway. He shuffled his work boots on her mat and Jenna was stabbed with an acute reminder of the twenty-year-old man she had fallen in love with so easily and so completely.

"Oh, does Janie need more clothes?" *Not a care in the world.*

They played a staring game for a while before he asked for permission to come inside. Jenna stepped away from the stove, and as he entered, he unintentionally brushed against her. Even the slight, almost inconsiderable feather of bodily contact caused a thrill to pass between them. It always did. She sucked in a gulp of air, feeling the restive energy in the room.

He offered his hand. "Come here."

Jenna timidly accepted and they stood, silent for a

time. He eventually brought her hand to his lips and softly kissed her fingers. As she opened her mouth to speak, he cut her words off with a kiss, one lighter than the one he conferred upon her hand.

"Why did you do that?" Her words were a shy breath.

"Because I love you. And because I've been an ass. At least that's what everyone keeps telling me."

"Huh? Who?"

"Oh let's see. There's Nick for one, and Ina, of course Jack and Meghan, and most importantly our daughter." Eric grazed his knuckles across Jenna's cheek and brushed strands of hair from her eyes. He gazed into them, as if he never wanted to look away.

Sunshine streamed through a window and a buttery glow was soft against cream-colored cabinets. A curtain gently fluttered and a breeze brought the scent of roses inside.

"I hope I haven't come to my senses too late."

"Meghan set me up to make you jealous. My date was a fake."

"I know. I don't care. Even a fake date made me crazy. I can't stand the thought of you being with someone else."

Jenna's eyes started to well up and she dabbed at them. "There's never *been* anyone else for me, not in all these years. It's always been you."

"Then don't ever leave me again, not ever. I'm no good without you. Everything I have is meaningless without you in my life. I knew the moment I first saw you that we belonged together. That you were mine."

Collapsing into his arms, Jenna clutched at his shoulders, clinging to him, and wondering how she had managed to live for nine years without that strength beneath her fingertips. "Then don't ever let me go."

"I won't."

She stiffened, suddenly seized by a sour agitation that roiled in her stomach. "Never mind. Let me go!"

"What?"

"Let me go!" Jenna pushed away, gagging her words as she ran to the sink to throw up.

Eric stepped over to her and stroked her back. "You overdo it last night?"

Jenna shook her head.

"Shit, I hope my declaration of love didn't do that to you," Eric said.

"No." She was half laughing, half groaning. Gulping water to rinse her mouth, she spit a very unladylike mouthful into the sink and patted her lips with a tea towel. "This wasn't how I pictured telling you."

"Telling me?" Eric suffered a short blip of confusion before he spotted the box of saltines and bottle of pre-natal vitamins sitting on her center island. A pendant light shone down on them as if they were an extraordinary showcase prize. They were he quickly realized. They were.

His heartbeat quickened and his skin flushed. Never in his life had he felt such joy. He pulled Jenna into his arms. She wrapped her own around his neck and clung to him as a feeling of bliss filled her. They didn't speak, but stayed locked in each other's embrace for a very, very long time.

Chapter Forty-One

A farm in North Carolina, One year later:

Jenna stood at the kitchen's center island wrapping something in aluminum foil. The room was airy with banks of gray Shaker cabinets, retro appliances, and hand-hewn ceiling beams. An open sitting area was warmed by a reclaimed brick hearth.

Nick lumbered over. "He did a nice job in here."

"It's great having a husband who knows how to use his hands."

"I'm sure it is." Nick winked, and Jenna flushed scarlet.

She went back to the chore of clearing away the remains of a very large breakfast. The meal was the last in a weekend of festivities to mark the baptism of Ethan Samuel Laine. It was an intimate gathering of friends and family in perfect keeping with the low-key lifestyle of Eric and Jenna Laine.

"You threw a nice shindig."

Jenna waved her hand in the air and fluttered her eyelashes. "Thanks. It wasn't the grand *soiree* my predecessor might have thrown, but it was fun."

The screen door opened, and without looking up Jenna ordered, "Take those dirty boots off before setting one foot in here."

"Yes, ma'am," Eric drawled. He kicked off beat up

work boots and discarded them in the mud room. He ambled over to his wife and kissed her. "We'd better get packing."

"Already done."

"You are the best."

"I know."

Eric walked over to the wriggling bundle cooing and reclining in what he'd dubbed the "bouncy thing." After lifting his son in his arms, he pressed his cheek to the baby's feathery tufts of hair. He took a long and easy breath. "I'll never get tired of this smell. We should have six more."

Jenna coughed but the grating sound was edged with humor. "I'll consider two."

Eric buried his face in the folds of the baby's chubby neck. "But we make such beautiful little people."

With her arms folded and one brow raised, Jenna shook her head. "The last time I checked, your contribution to the 'making' part was a lot easier than mine."

Nick stood away from the table and reached into his jacket pocket. He handed Eric an envelope. "While you two decide on how many kids to add to your brood, put this in the bank for the latest…my godson."

"You didn't have to—"

"I'm from Brooklyn. I take my *padrino* duty seriously."

Smiling, Eric slipped the envelope into the back pocket of his jeans. "Okay, but no pinky rings till he's at least three."

"Deal."

Janie bounded through the door with a dog of questionable lineage at her heels. She scratched the little wire-haired pup's ears. "Daddy, are you sure the guys will take care of Dusty?"

"Positive, they'll take him out to the corral when they exercise the horses. And if it will make you feel better, he can sleep in the bunk house with them."

The Laine farm had expanded to a ranch of sorts. A new stable, bright red with a shining copper cupola, was the jewel in the crown of the property. There was an indoor riding arena and yards of paddock fenced enclosures for the horses. With the exception of a new, two-year-old chestnut and mini-Palomino, the high-end stable was still home to Eric's senior, swayback animals.

"Get in the shower," Jenna ordered. "And wear something comfortable. It's a five-hour flight to Los Angeles."

Janie snapped her fingers. "Darn, I bet Riley that I would be in California before she got back to New York."

Eric raised an eyebrow as he questioned his daughter. "How did you think that would be possible? Don't they teach you geography at school?"

"Sure, but it's three hours earlier in California." The comment earned another provisional look from her father as she hurried off toward the stairs.

Eric appealed to Jenna. "Please tell me she was kidding."

"She was. She's smart…but she's also a smart-ass."

"Well, when Anne and Riley come back to visit this summer, I may hire a tutor as well as a riding instructor just to be on the safe side."

Nick laughed and shrugged out of his chair. "I guess I should go pack, too. I'll call ahead and remind my guys to have a car waiting for us at the airport."

The Laine family was going on a trip to California. Jenna still owned a mammoth of a house in Malibu and was anxious to walk its halls, exorcise its demons, and put it on the market. Eric, as always, was besieged with pleas from his manager and agent to commit to a new film and thought the least he could do was return to L.A. and turn the offers down in person.

Options to do movies, tour, and record an album had been presented to Jenna as well, but the comeback trail didn't call to her as much as raising a family did, so she also declined. But the door was open if either of them changed their minds.

****

As their plane sped through the sky, Jenna sat, her hand casually resting on Eric's thigh. The baby was sleeping peacefully on his chest. Across the aisle Nick softly snored in his seat while Janie, next to him, gobbled an ice cream sundae. "I love sitting up here in first-class. I'm never flying steerage again."

Eric narrowed his eyes. "It's called coach, and don't think you'll never fly back there. Life won't always be a big red bow. If you're lucky enough to go places; it won't matter how you get to them."

"So do I finally *get* to ride the bus to school?"

"Smart-ass," Jenna whispered to her husband. "Maybe we shouldn't let her know you have a private jet just yet."

Stroking his infant son's back, Eric smiled his agreement. "We won't be using it until I have it made child friendly…and burn some sage."

Janie went back to her sundae, and Jenna laughed. Eric tipped his head close to hers. "Do you think we're being ungrateful to turn down so many offers? There are a lot of people who would sell their souls to be in our position."

Shrugging, she took her sleeping baby from her husband. Jenna reveled in the warmth and heady scent. "Everything we turn down just gives some new kid a chance to have a dressing room with a star on it."

He amended her statement. "You mean a luxury trailer with their *name* on it, don't you?"

She shrugged again. "I never wanted that trailer. I always wanted a dressing room, old and messy with costumes hanging on a coatrack…greasepaint littering a vanity table."

"Do you want to go into theater?"

Jenna hugged her son tightly. "It was my first love. But I wouldn't even consider it while the baby is so little."

The jet cruised smoothly through the air as a flight attendant walked the aisle with a bottle of champagne. Eric and Jenna thanked him but waved away the offer.

"Inspired Artists would kill to have you back," Eric said. "They have a New York office."

"I know," she admitted, wrinkling her nose as if embarrassed. "They've already asked if I would be interested in a revival of *South Pacific*. It wouldn't go into rehearsals till next year and it would be a limited run."

"Sounds perfect."

"Mmm." A frown tugged at her mouth. "Revivals don't always open cold. There may be out of town dates. I wouldn't go without you and the kids; and I remember how—"

"How I flat out refused to go with you on your tour when we were married the first time?"

"Yes."

Eric sighed a shame filled breath of regret. "I should have gone with you, but I was a kid and a sullen idiot. I thought I was being noble when all I was really being was unsupportive." He looked at his love with tenderness and adoration in his eyes. "I'd follow you to the ends of the earth and back."

Eric leaned close and rested his cheek against Jenna's temple. He *would* follow her. Go wherever life took them. And if Broadway was where his beautiful and talented wife wanted to be, he would be right there, first row center, applauding and jumping from his seat to lead the standing ovation as she took the final bow.

A word about the author...

Laura Liller scaled the steps of the elevated train trestle in her Bronx neighborhood at an early age. Her destination was New York City's High School of Art & Design—four short years later, The Fashion Institute of Technology. Laura hopes her art background and love of period clothing and architecture help her to "illustrate" her books as well as write them.

Laura currently lives in Upstate NY with her husband Mike and two cats. She has two daughters she lovingly refers to as "the girls who abandoned her." Laura is a typical romance fan and loves sipping wine outside by her fire pit with her husband.

Thank you for purchasing
this publication of The Wild Rose Press, Inc.

For questions or more information
contact us at
info@thewildrosepress.com.

The Wild Rose Press, Inc.
www.thewildrosepress.com